DEDICATION

To Nana,
who always told me to follow my dreams and find a good man.

I think I made you proud on both fronts. ♥

Forever to Fall

Book Five in the Buckeye Falls Series

Libby Kay

Forever to Fall
Copyright © 2024 Libby Kay
All rights reserved.

ISBN: (ebook) 978-1-964636-05-4
(print) 978-1-964636-06-1

Inkspell Publishing
207 Moonglow Circle #101
Murrells Inlet, SC 29576

Edited By Audrey Bobek
Cover Art By Emily's World of Design

PROLOGUE

15 Years Ago

Mallory Lawson always wondered what her wedding day would look like. She had no idea it would be as rustic and lovely as where she stood now, hands linked with her best friend, the dimple on his cheeks popping as he gazed adoringly back at her. The old oak tree swayed in the breeze, the wind swirling her chocolate hair around her face. The feeling of cool grass tickled her toes and a few insects flitted around her bare legs—but none of that mattered. She was marrying Beckett Fox, and the world could swallow her whole and she wouldn't notice.

"I do," Beckett said, sliding a ring onto her left hand. The metal was solid and cool against her flushed skin, and Mallory imprinted the moment to memory. She wanted to remember every detail, every facet of how the sun reflected off the ruby stone, how the diamonds twinkled like daytime stars.

"Kids! It's time for dinner!" A familiar voice echoed from the farm house down the hill. "I made French bread pizzas."

"Oh dang," her brother, Evan, exclaimed as he tucked the Bible he was using for the ceremony under his arm and charged toward dinner, dust skittering off his sneakered heels.

Mallory tried not to let it bother her that she hadn't gotten to kiss her husband yet, but she tried not to dwell. She was on the cusp of becoming a teenager, there would be time for those logistics later.

Beckett didn't follow his friend, instead staying close to Mallory. "Um…" he said, voice trailing off. His eyes darted all around them, from their clasped hands to the house in the distance and the leaves rustling overhead. "I guess we should like…" His words faltered, hand lifting to scratch the back of his neck.

Finally, his gaze snagged hers and he smiled. Mallory was familiar with Beckett's smiles. He had one for Evan, when they were playing baseball and running around in the dirt. He had one for his grandparents, when Gramps would tussle his red hair and tease him; another for his Gram when she made his favorite apple cupcakes. Then there was the smile he flashed her now—slightly crooked and showing the gap in his teeth. Mallory's own grin reflected from Beckett's glasses, the frames never sitting quite right on his nose.

"We should?" she asked, her tiny heart hammering in her ribcage. In her dozen years on the planet, she'd never felt so nervous—so alive.

Beckett licked his lips, scuffing his sneakers on the ground. While Mallory didn't want the confines of shoes on her big day, he'd settled on the new sneakers he got for the upcoming school year.

"Kiss," he blurted out, his cheeks and ears immediately turning crimson. Even his smudged glasses couldn't hide his hopeful, yet embarrassed, expression.

Mallory's eyebrows shot up, hitting her bangs. "You *want* to kiss me?" She was incredulous and giddy at the same time.

"I dunno," he countered, now staring at a patch of crab

2

grass like it held the secrets to the universe. "To, you know, make it official?" He kicked the spot on the lawn, careful not to get his shoes dirty.

Mallory glanced down to the ring on her hand, her favorite trinket in all the world. It sparkled like an oasis in the desert. "Yes," she said with more confidence than what she felt. "We should."

Beckett flashed her that special smile, inching closer until their toes touched. Mallory took a deep breath and leaned in, smacking her lips against his before they sprang apart. Before she could say anything, he grinned and shrugged. "Time for pizza?" He turned tail and bounded toward the house, following the path made by her brother. His red hair gleamed in the afternoon sunlight, turning him into a honing beacon.

Mallory stood frozen, her lips tingling from the contact and the confusion and excitement of the moment. Reaching her hand up to her mouth, she sighed. Despite her young age, she knew that was likely the most romantic moment of her whole life.

But she was also a kid who was ready for food, so she grabbed the hem of her dress and started running. "Hey, save me a slice!"

CHAPTER 1

"I'm going to ask CeCe to marry me." Her brother's declaration should not have come as a surprise, but that didn't stop Mallory Lawson from choking on her hamburger, a blob of ketchup sliding down her chin.

Dabbing her face with a napkin, Mallory collected herself before asking her brother for the dirt. "Um, when?"

Evan leaned back in his seat, his own burger completely forgotten. He crossed his arms over his chest and stared down his sister. "Um, when? Geez, Mal. I was expecting a little more enthusiasm." He flapped his hands between them. "Really? When? Hopefully CeCe will be a little more excited." His lips dipped in a frown, and Mallory hated that she was the cause. Her little brother was her best friend, and while they loved to tease each other, Mallory would take a bullet for the man sitting in front of her. She had no doubt he would do the same.

Holding her hands up she said, "In my defense, I thought you brought me out to talk about our plans for Mom's birthday. Telling me you're going to pop the question is a big freaking deal." After lowering her hands, she balled up her napkin and tossed it onto her plate. Despite her excitement, she felt a tug in her gut she wasn't ready to decipher.

Could it be indigestion or jealousy? It was anyone's guess.

"I'm aware, but come on. This can't be a surprise." Evan picked up his soda and drained its contents in one gulp. She'd kill to have his metabolism.

Mallory studied her burger, now cooling and half-eaten. It wasn't that she was surprised, or even upset, by her brother's announcement. He and CeCe had been dating for well over a year, and they'd been friends for longer than that. They clicked together, like the last two pieces in a puzzle, and she couldn't think of a better couple to walk down the aisle. The trouble wasn't the person Evan wanted to legally bind himself to, but the fact that it was her brother. Her *little* brother, who was a year younger and already settled down. She would never begrudge him his happiness, but it certainly made her feel like an old maid. And Mallory hated how surly she must look.

Squaring her shoulders, she met Evan's gaze and started over. "It's not a surprise, and I think it's a great idea."

Finally relaxing, Evan grinned and leaned closer. "You do?"

Mallory waved off Evan's question. "Of course I do. CeCe is one of my favorite people, and you two are clearly made for each other." Evan's smile only grew at her words, and she started to feel better. The world didn't make sense if her brother wasn't smiling. He had this joyful, easy-going manner about him that was so contagious the CDC had him ranked as an infectious disease.

The waiter came by with their check, which Evan promptly swiped off the table. "I've got this," he told a protesting Mallory. "I just signed that contract for the website for the law firm off Main Street."

Reaching out, Mallory yanked the slip from his grasp and stuck out her tongue. "I just got a raise at the hospital. Save the money for the ring."

Evan snatched the slip back and tucked it into his jacket

2

pocket. "I'm using Nana Lawson's ring, so I don't need to save."

His statement brought Mallory up short, her dinner doing somersaults in her stomach. Bile rose, and she had to clear her throat twice before words formed. "You're taking Nana's ring?" The question escaped on a whimper. Eyes burning, she forced herself to blink back the tears. Maybe she could pass them off as happy tears?

Not sensing her concern, Evan shrugged. "Yeah, why not? Sophie and Emily didn't want it, and I think it would suit CeCe." There was no doubt the ring would match CeCe's low-maintenance lifestyle. The white gold band was simple, yet studded with a ruby and diamonds. She could see her future sister-in-law cooking up a storm with the ring, her nimble fingers making short work on a ball of bread dough.

Yet there was something hanging in the air between them—words left unsaid that made Mallory flinch. What Evan wasn't saying, what no one wanted to admit, was that Mallory didn't have any prospects of her own. Usually undeterred by her single status, she now felt like expired milk left to curdle in the refrigerator. Their nana had left the ring to her grandchildren to use as they saw fit. She knew her elder sisters wouldn't want the ring, as they both had different tastes and didn't respect the tradition of wearing a family heirloom.

On the other hand—literally—Mallory had often borrowed the ring as a girl and performed fake wedding ceremonies. One time she married her teddy bear, Mr. Beany, while another time had her Barbie wear the ring as a necklace for her wedding to Ken. One of the few benefits of Evan trashing her doll collection was that Barbie's head now came off with ease for wardrobe changes and accessorizing.

In the further reaches of her memory, Mallory had another time she'd played fantasy wedding. A summer's afternoon on a farm, the breeze filled with the hint of fall

3

and the aroma of apples and spice. That had been a fun day, a day that she should not remember with such vivid clarity—or such longing. But Mallory wasn't ready to think about that memory, or the boy attached to it. Now wasn't the time. But then again, it rarely was.

Evan snapped his fingers in front of her face. "Earth to Mal." He chuckled as she came back to the moment. "You're a million miles away. What's up with you today?"

Mallory sighed. She was exhausted from working another double shift in the ER. She loved her job as a nurse, but there were times she felt like a wrung-out sponge; dried up, misshapen, and generally ignored. Even this impromptu meal with her brother came after a twelve-hour shift. She hadn't even bothered to go home and change, opting to keep her scrubs and messy ponytail. If she went home to freshen up, she'd likely fall asleep in the bathtub and drown. For all the ways she imagined herself dying, drowning alone at twenty-eight in her bathroom wasn't at the top of the list.

"Sorry, I guess I'm just tired." Her breath escaped in a long puff, her shoulders slumping. Mallory blindly hoped her brother would leave it, but that wasn't Evan's style. He was a dog with a bone—worse, a golden retriever with a favorite toy. His eyes shone with hope and concern.

"What have you been up to?" he asked, reaching over to steal a few of her forgotten French fries.

Mallory swatted his hand away and huffed out a humorless laugh. "Saving lives? I don't know, Ev. It seems like lately all I do is work."

"That's not true. You came by and helped with the food truck at the county fair last month."

With a snort, she nodded. "Yeah. Somehow I feel like working at my brother's food truck isn't exactly a relaxing vacation, or even much of a social life." Saying it out loud stung, but Mallory rallied.

Evan was offended. "We had a blast."

Mallory couldn't argue with him, because she did have fun. The trouble was, she didn't have the same type of fun

4

as everyone else. The truck was owned by Max, who was Evan's boss and friend. Max and his wife Ginny were there, as were Evan and CeCe. The four of them included her, but it didn't stop the fifth wheel sensation from creeping in. She was used to tagging along to other couple's events, but it didn't mean she always liked it. She wanted her own other half, someone just for her.

More often than not recently, Mallory craved more from life. Her sisters were both married with kids and careers, and they didn't live as close as they used to. Evan and Mallory had always been close, but he was busy expanding his freelance web design career, working at the diner, and seeing CeCe. She didn't fault her brother his success, or his relationship, but she still felt like the odd woman out.

And the ring. She hated how much she resented the loss of something that wasn't even hers. A tiny voice in her head shouted at her to stand up for what she wanted, but she didn't want to make it an issue. Evan seemed set on the ring, and she needed to respect it and move on. Granted she'd mourn the loss of something that was never really hers, but that didn't mean she couldn't be an adult about the whole thing. He was getting married first, and that was that.

Desperate to change the subject, she went back to the reason they got together in the first place. "So how are you going to pop the question?"

Evan's eyes lit up as he explained his grand plan. "I have a few ideas," he started, licking his lips as he rattled off his thoughts. "My first option is something simple, intimate. We're always staying late at the diner, and since it's where we met, I thought it might be nice to do something there."

Mallory didn't hate the idea, as it was clearly a special place to Evan and CeCe. "I think there's potential there. What else are you thinking?"

"You know how we're going to Chicago in a few weeks?" Mallory nodded and Evan continued. "Well, I was thinking it might be nice to do something there. It used to be CeCe's home, and she's going to show me around all her favorite spots. Maybe I could do it from the deck of the Hancock Building? Or down by the lake? I don't know, that's still just a thought." He shook his empty glass, the ice rattling in time with her heart.

"Whatever you decide, don't make it a spectacle. You know CeCe would hate to be the center of attention." Her future sister-in-law was a lot of fun and clearly in love with her brother, but she was also no-nonsense and hated public displays of affection.

Evan rolled his eyes, easily slipping back into bratty brother mode. "Oh wow, really Mal? You don't think I know what my fiancée would like?"

At the mention of the word *fiancée*, both Lawson siblings beamed and giggled. "Oh my God, Ev. You're going to get married." Mallory covered her chest with her hand as tears prickle her eyes.

"She has to say yes first," Evan said, humor tinging his voice.

"She will." Mallory had no doubt. These two people were made for each other, and she looked forward to watching their new life unfold. Evan doted on CeCe, and she kept him on his toes. It'll be a fabulous life for two of her favorite people.

Evan reached out to pat his sister's arm. "Thanks. I hope you know I want you standing up there with me on the big day."

"Aww, Ev. Are you asking me to be your best man?"

Blanching, Evan pulled his hand back and rubbed at the back of his neck. "Well, uh. I was thinking of asking Foxy to be my best man. We've been friends forever, and I thought it made sense to have him up there." Watching his sister's face fall, he hastened to add, "But you're right. Gender stereotypes are BS, and I should be able to have a woman up there with me. Besides, CeCe hardly knows Foxy."

Every mention of Foxy, or Beckett Fox as he was known by everyone else on the planet, felt like taking a punch right

6

to the solar plexus. "You're asking Beckett?" Saying his name brought a flush to Mallory's cheeks and a sense of dreaded anticipation coursed through her. She covered her nerves by chugging her water. God, she wished it was something stronger.

"Yeah? I mean, of course. Foxy would kill it, that is if you don't mind. I assumed you, Em, and Sophie would be busy with girly things with CeCe. Foxy can handle the bachelor party and all the crap I don't even know to think about." It all made sense, naturally it did, but that didn't stop Mallory from gasping for air. Every second spent thinking and talking about Beckett took months off her life.

The reasons didn't matter, but they were justified. Because since they were kids, playing around his family farm, Mallory had been utterly in love with Beckett Fox. From his lopsided smile and crooked glasses to how funny and sweet he was, Mallory had fallen for Beckett years ago and learned how to hide her feelings. You didn't date your brother's best friend, and you certainly didn't fantasize about what would've happened if you ever saw each other again. *Nope—definitely not.*

After clearing her throat past the growing lump, Mallory asked, "And where does Beckett live now?"

She prayed it was somewhere remote and far away, like Arizona or Siberia. But Evan quickly burst that bubble. "He's actually just got a place in Buckeye Falls."

Mallory didn't hear a word after that. Her ears rang like she was in a church bell tower. Beckett was back in central Ohio, and suddenly her girlhood crush didn't seem so simple. How would she function knowing he was around? They would breathe the same air, walk the same streets. Buckeye Falls wasn't that big, so they were bound to run into each other.

Beckett was coming home, which meant Mallory had to put her heart into Witness Protection.

*

7

Beckett Fox dropped the last of the boxes onto the floor, his back aching and his face covered in a sheen of sweat. His glasses slid down his nose for the fifth time in as many minutes and he cursed himself for not wearing contacts. To save a few bucks on moving, he'd opted to skip the moving crew in favor of free labor that only lifelong friends could provide. As he came up behind him, Beckett heard Evan drop a box and huff out a sigh.

"Man, if we're this exhausted now, imagine when we're in our thirties." Lifting his shirt up, Evan dabbed at the perspiration on his brow.

Once he'd plodded toward the kitchen, Beckett snagged two beers from the fridge and handed one to Evan. They clinked bottles before falling back onto the couch, which was still covered in plastic wrap. The couch made a squeaky sound as Evan got comfortable. "Thanks for coming out and helping, Lawless."

Evan smirked at his old nickname and took a long pull from his beer. "Anytime, Foxy." Surveying the mess around them, Evan quickly amended, "Well, maybe not anytime soon." He grimaced as he shifted again on the couch. "I think I pulled a muscle I didn't know I had."

Beckett chuckled as he sipped from his beer. It had been a long few months, and he was relieved to finally be in his own space again. "Hopefully this is my last move for a while." He thought of the big empty house he used to share with his grandfather and bit back a grimace. It was time to put it on the market, but he wasn't ready yet. Some places were too important. Some memories were too important...

Over the last months, Beckett had watched his role model and only living relative wither away before his eyes. Cancer had taken every ounce of strength Gramps had, but it never dulled his spirit or sense of humor. During one of his last lucid nights, he'd called Beckett into his room. This wasn't unusual, but his request was.

"I want you to do me a favor, son," Gramps had said

between coughing fits punctuated with bloody handkerchiefs. He'd covered his mouth and heaved again, and when Beckett saw the red spots, he felt weak and powerless against the disease eating his Gramps from the inside. The man before him was a mere shadow to the vibrant, joyful man of his memory.

Beckett squeezed his hands into fists and fought a surge of tears. He wanted to stay strong, even up until the end. He could fall apart later; he *would* fall apart later. "Anything, Gramps."

Patting his grandson's balled fists, the older man pulled himself upright and met his gaze. Lately his green eyes had been glassy, fogged over from months of chemo and medications. But at that moment, they were crystal clear and laser-focused on Beckett. "I want you to find your other half and settle down. When I'm gone, there's no reason for you to stay in this old house alone. Go out, find your girl, and make a life for yourself."

Shaking his head, Beckett feared the old man had lost it. "I don't have a girl, Gramps." Beckett hadn't even had a date in over two years. From Gramps's diagnosis and treatments to working overtime to pay all the bills, he barely had time to catch up with friends let alone find a girlfriend. Well, and there was the other reason, but he wasn't dwelling on that now.

"Don't play coy with your old grandfather," he'd chided. "We all know you do."

Forcing out a laugh, Beckett tried to lighten the mood. "I want to know what new meds Nurse Flannery is giving you, because I want some. It doesn't seem fair that you get all the fun." He winked, feeling anything but playful.

"I'm talking about the Lawson girl," Gramps said with more force than Beckett had heard in months.

Color drained from Beckett's face at the mention of Mallory. To say he hadn't thought about her in a while was a lie; a lie so big it threatened to consume him. But he wouldn't stew on that now. Barely able to speak, he asked,

"What do you mean?"

Emerald eyes staring into his soul, his grandfather confirmed Beckett's suspicions. "Mallory, of course. I want you to find her and figure it out."

"Figure it out?"

Gramps nodded vehemently.

"Gramps, Mallory is a friend, not the *New York Times* Sunday crosswords." The term friend did not fit Mallory. For starters, they hadn't seen or spoken to each other in ages, not since his grandmother's funeral when he'd mucked it all up.

When college was done, both went in search of their own futures. The biggest reason they hadn't seen each other was because of who Mallory was—his best friend's sister. He would never do anything to jeopardize his friendship with Evan, even if it did break his heart. But that didn't mean Beckett didn't screw things up when he had the chance, a reality he was still trying to avoid.

What didn't make sense now was Gramps's insistence that he find Mallory. To his knowledge, he'd never shared his true feelings about her to anyone, least of all his grandfather. Pulling himself to standing, Beckett stepped back toward the door. "I'm going to find your afternoon pills, okay?"

"You can find all you want, but you must listen to me. I don't have a lot of time left, but I need to know you're taken care of."

Misunderstanding, Beckett gestured over his shoulder to his grandfather's desk. Stacked neatly in the center of the desktop were stacks of legal documents. Everything from his will to his bank statements were morbidly stacked and filed, ready for the old man's demise. "I have everything sorted out with your attorney. Remember, Gramps?"

Raising his hand and slapping the top of his mattress, his grandfather grew agitated. "I'm dying, I'm not senile. I know all the legal stuff is sorted. What I'm talking about, son, is love. You need to follow your heart and get your girl."

"Gramps, I—" Beckett's voice faltered. He had no idea how long his grandfather had known his feelings for Mallory. Worse yet, he didn't know if that meant everyone knew.

"Your grandmother saw it first, back when you were children." Resting his head back on his pillows, Gramps stared up at the ceiling as if watching a movie, his eyes darting all over the exposed beams. "I remember she found you two playing out back, holding hands and singing a little song. She told me you'd met your soulmate, and I wasn't going to argue."

His grandfather's story shook Beckett, who stumbled back to his perch on the edge of the bed. "Soulmate?"

Cutting his hand through the air, the older man continued. "Your Gram, bless that woman, was a romantic. When we met after the war, she said she knew we were meant to be." He stopped his story long enough to shake his head and smile. "That woman knew more about me in five minutes of meeting than I did about myself in the first twenty years of my life. Here I was, back from Vietnam and ready to live again. I didn't want a wife and kids, but bless her, she knew we were meant to be."

"You and Gram were amazing together," Beckett said, trying to keep the subject on track. But it was no use. Gramps was on a mission.

"So as I was saying, you need to ask your friend Evan for Mallory's number. Cut the crap and get your girl. Life is short, son. I want to die knowing you are taken care of, and she is the one who will do the best job."

"This isn't an interview, it's real life. And I'm not even sure she wants to see me." That statement made Beckett's skin crawl; worse than the time he'd walked through a massive spider's web in the barn. Mindlessly, he'd pawed at his skin to shake the sensation.

As Gramps closed his eyes and drifted off to sleep, he muttered, "Life is only sweet because you share it with your person."

11

Those words rang through Beckett's head on a loop for a month until Gramps finally passed. They clanged around his skull now, too, as he sat with Evan in his new apartment. Lost in his musings, Beckett had missed something Evan had said.

"I'm sorry, man. What did you say?"

Evan drained his beer then placed the bottle on a stack of boxes. "I said, I want to ask a favor."

Beckett snorted. "Considering you just spent your day off helping me unload a moving truck, I can't really say no."

Evan grinned, one of Beckett's favorite sights. His buddy was like a golden retriever in human form, always happy and always willing to help. If he had a tail, it would doubtlessly wag every minute of every day. He loved the guy like a brother, like family. "I'm going to ask CeCe to marry me, and I'd like you to be my best man."

His beer forgotten, Beckett leaned over to clap his friend on the back. "Oh, wow, congratulations. Of course, I'll be your best man. When are you popping the question?"

Evan slumped with relief at his friend's eager agreement. "Not sure, but soon. I've been talking to Mal about it, but I haven't decided on the perfect proposal yet."

The mention of Mallory spiked Beckett's blood pressure, and he had to look away. His cheeks flushed so hot, the wall paper threatened to melt off the walls. Damn his pasty Irish ancestors for blessing him with fiery red hair and skin as white as Wonder Bread. Surely Evan could see what mentions of Mallory did to him. He might as well wear a neon sign professing his love for his best friend's sister. *Nothing to see here, folks. I'm just drowning in my love for Mallory Lawson.*

After pulling himself to his feet, Beckett stalked back to the fridge for more liquid courage. The topic of Mallory rarely relaxed him. "So, um, how is Mallory?" He was fairly certain she was local and still single, but he'd never pushed the issue with Evan. His grandfather's words rang through his head as he waited for an answer. *Please be good news…*

Clearly not picking up on his friend's inner turmoil, Evan kicked his feet out and propped them up on a box of books. "She's good. Still an ER nurse over in Columbus, but she lives pretty close to here. Neither of us wanted to be in the same town as our parents, and Buckeye Falls is too perfect."

He wouldn't get an argument out of Beckett, who always loved visiting the little hamlet. The people were friendly, the food scene was inspired, and the cost of living couldn't be beat. When the time came to start planning his future, it only seemed natural to come here. And it had nothing to do with a certain brunette nurse with a heart of gold. *Nope, not one bit.*

Evan checked his smart watch and groaned. "I hate to move and run, but I promised CeCe I'd be home for dinner."

Beckett strode to the door and cupped his friend's shoulder. "Look at you, Lawless, all domestic."

"Pfft, it's pretty great, Foxy. Don't knock it 'til you try it." He bounded toward his car, spinning on his heel before getting behind the wheel. "Hey. How do you feel about a little housewarming in a week or two? You could meet some of the other Buckeyes. It could be fun."

Since he was currently speaking to his only local friend, Beckett could not disagree with Evan's logic. "Sure, sounds fun."

"Great! I'll get Mal on it. You know she loves to plan a party." With a final wave, Evan got in his car and drove away.

Beckett went back inside and flopped back on the couch. After yanking off his glasses, he rubbed his face and pondered his decision to move here. Did he make a mistake by coming here? Could he live in the same town as Mallory and not be a lovesick fool? He didn't think so, but he also knew he couldn't stay away forever.

Gramps's words rang through as he drifted off to sleep on the couch, surrounded by dozens of boxes and forgotten beer bottles. *Life is only sweet if you share it with your person.* There wasn't a doubt in Beckett's mind; Mallory was most definitely his person. Now he needed to figure out what to do about it.

CHAPTER 2

"You're telling me I can buy your book in bookstores and everything?" Mallory asked her friend as she drizzled syrup all over a short stack.

Alice Snyder beamed at her, nodding so fiercely her head could have popped off. "Yes!" She squealed, digging an overstuffed envelope from her tote bag. "When James and I were in New York we got everything sorted."

Mallory snatched the papers from her friend and hurried to scan through them. "Holy crap," she said on an exhale. "Alice, they want at least two books? That's amazing." She reached across the table and hugged her as firmly as she could without crumpling the papers or getting syrup on their clothes. "I'm so excited for you."

Once they broke apart, Alice dabbed at her eyes with a napkin and grinned. "I can't believe it's all happening. I've been talking about doing this for years, and it's finally happening."

"You've earned it," Mallory insisted, understanding all the hard work her friend had put into her writing passion. While only friends for the last year, the two had grown close. Alice was the sister of Buckeye Falls' mayor, Anthony, and was currently dating one of the hottest artists in the country,

James Gibson. When the pair got together months before, it was clear that Alice was head over heels. Mallory savored every moment of their courtship and loved living vicariously through Alice. Plus, it didn't hurt that James was a minor celebrity and fueled her passion for pop culture gossip.

Alice sliced into her omelet and took a greedy bite. "Well, I think James gets an honorable mention here. His friend is the reason I got an invite to meet the publisher in the first place."

"No argument there, but your writing is why you have that fat contract." She gestured to it with her fork and took a bite from her pancakes. Evan had added extra chocolate chips, and she felt a cavity form as she chewed. *Totally worth it!*

For a few minutes, the pair ate in companionable silence, both too distracted by their breakfasts to talk beyond their obsession with the diner's food. "I always love the food here," Alice said between bites, "but I can tell when CeCe is cooking. This sourdough toast is ridiculous. How can bread be this amazing?"

"Because she's the freaking best," Evan chimed in, leaning in to refill their coffee cups. "I take it everything is delicious." He winked at his sister.

Alice and Mallory nodded, both with matching satisfied smiles. "Please marry that woman," Alice said sarcastically. "If she was my type, I'd jump on that train." Evan shot Mallory a warning look that confused Alice. "And I think I just said the wrong thing." It was a statement, not a question.

Evan's voice was low. "Mal, I thought you weren't going to say anything."

Mallory balled up her napkin and tossed it at Evan's head. It bounced off his blond curls before falling to his feet. "I didn't, dumbass, but you certainly did." She raised an eyebrow at her brother who had the manners to look embarrassed. He rubbed the back of his neck and scanned around them to see if anyone was listening. Fortunately, everyone else was too invested in their pancakes and waffles to pay them any attention.

"Oh, my God," Alice stage whispered. "Did you pop the question?" She clapped her hands in front of her, fanning herself from the impending news. Both Lawson siblings shushed her, Mallory adding a kick under the table for good measure. Alice rubbed the sore spot but didn't complain.

"No," Evan said, waving his hands for her to keep the volume down.

"But it's on the menu," Mallory added, seemingly pleased with her food analogy.

Evan rolled his eyes but continued, "I'm working on it. Now both of you keep quiet, or I'm not giving you any to-go muffins."

Alice's eyes grew ten sizes as she fell back in her seat. "Blackmail."

"That's harsh, Ev," Mallory agreed. It was a poorly kept secret that CeCe had been trying new muffin recipes for an online contest, and everyone in town was eager to try them. Those muffins were half the reason Alice got out of bed that early, as she tended to operate at a snail's pace on weekends.

"I'm serious, Mal." Evan pointed at his sister before turning his wrath to Alice. "And I love you, Alice, but you are sisters-in-law with CeCe's best friend and the biggest gossip in Buckeye Falls. Zip it." No one could argue with that assessment of Natalie, Buckeye Fall's First Lady and all-around gossip hound. She might as well wear a megaphone around her neck.

Mallory raised her hand, pulling an invisible zipper closed over her mouth. "I'm a vault, and Alice is too."

Alice crossed her heart and picked up a piece of toast, eating half of it in one bite. "Me too. Please don't take away my carbs."

Evan relaxed and picked up his coffee pot. "I'll be back with your muffins, but I'm watching you." He gestured between them before backing away.

As soon as he was in the kitchen, Alice looked over her

17

shoulder to ensure they were alone. "Holy crap! Why didn't you say anything?"

Mallory kicked her again and laughed. "Because I knew you'd get like this. At least don't geek out in public, Alice."

"Pfft, whatever." Alice shimmied in her seat and ate the last slice of toast.

Evan returned with their checks and two paper bags. He slid the goodies in front of them, pointing to each bag as he explained CeCe's latest creations. "This one is a caramel pecan banana muffin, and this one is a double chocolate zucchini muffin with peanut butter chips."

Alice snagged the chocolate one and stuck out her tongue.

"Real mature." Mallory laughed as she scooped up her muffin and tucked it in her purse. No one needed to know she wanted the banana muffin all along.

"Those are for your silence," Evan cautioned Alice as she slid from the booth.

"If I promise to never say anything ever again, will you give me some cheesy bites?" A devilish grin cracked her face. Mallory was impressed with Alice's strategy; Evan didn't know who he was messing with.

Crossing his arms over his chest he said, "There are four in there already."

Alice giggled and clapped her hands. A lottery winner would appear less enthusiastic. "I love you Lawsons!"

"Do I get the goods too?"

Evan gave his sister his full attention. "If you say yes to this favor, I promise to have CeCe make a whole batch just for you."

Mallory was skeptical. "I thought this was for my silence. Now you want favors too?"

"I think you'll like this one, promise."

Raising an eyebrow, she waited for Evan to continue.

"I need your help planning a housewarming party for Foxy."

Mallory's pulse spiked and she felt her mouth go as dry

as cotton wool. "What?" she asked, striving to keep her tone light. She had to swallow three times before she relaxed.

Evan shoved his hands in his pockets and leaned back on his heels. "He's basically moved in, but he doesn't really know anyone in town. I know you are great at party planning, so I hoped you could help me get something together."

Picking up her coffee cup, Mallory tried to hide her sour expression. Her attempts of hiding were interrupted by Alice's question. "Who, or what, is Foxy?"

"My oldest friend, Beckett Fox. He just moved to Buckeye Falls." He hitched a thumb toward Mallory, completely unaware of her internal meltdown. Warning alarms sounded in her head, blaring louder than the weather sirens of a tornado drill. Couldn't he see the steam shooting from her ears?

Alice inched closer. "Old friend, huh?"

Evan, completely oblivious, kept on talking. "Oh yeah, since we were in elementary school. Mal's friends with him, too. Isn't that right? We all grew up together."

"Mmhmm." Was the only sound she could muster without looking completely deranged.

Helen, one of the other waitstaff, called Evan's name from the kitchen and he excused himself. "Text me later and we'll gameplan." He waved over his shoulder as he strode back to work, his sneakers slapping on the tiled floor.

After draining the last of her coffee, Mallory hurriedly packed up her things. Snatching the check in her hands, she tried to stand up, but Alice was too quick. "Yeah, I don't think so. You're going to spill the beans on whatever this is." She mirrored Mallory's pinched expression and twirled her finger around her face. "You were asked to plan a housewarming, not an execution."

"Same thing," Mallory muttered as she eased back into the booth.

Alice checked her watch and grimaced. "I have ten minutes until I need to get to the library, and you need to start talking." The look she gave her friend left no room for argument.

"*Cliff Notes* version?" Mallory asked hopefully.

With a nod, Alice tapped her watch. "Get talking. I want the abridged version now, and the full story over drinks and that promised box of cheesy bites."

"Beckett is Evan's best friend."

Alice blinked, waiting for more. "And he's a total asshole?"

The notion of Beckett being anything but perfect brought a belly laugh from Mallory. "Hardly, he's a sweetheart."

"A sweetheart who's mean to you?"

"No!" She practically shouted her denial. "Beckett is like Evan, kind of. He's super sweet, patient, smart, kind, funny, and—" Her voice hitched as she flushed, images of all the reasons she loved Beckett flittering through her skull. Given the time, she could recite all the qualities she adored about him. Her head suddenly felt crowded, like when that last person squeezed onto an already crowded elevator.

Alice smirked. "You like him." It was a statement, not a question.

Mallory's rebuttal came out as a squeak. "I do not. He's Evan's friend, I've known him forever." She flapped her hands in the air, as if able to send the truth away on the wind.

"How much of forever have you been pining after the guy?" Alice leaned over the table and poked Mallory's arm. "Something is definitely up."

"Nothing is up. I just haven't seen him in a while." Knowing that wasn't enough of an excuse, she added, "Work has been crazy and I guess I'm tired. The idea of planning a party seems daunting."

"If you think it will be a problem, we can ask Natalie or Ginny to help. It's kind of their job." Alice snorted, referring to the very successful event planning business her sister-in-law and friend ran. They could plan a large

20

corporate event or a small wedding without breaking a sweat.

Mallory waved off the suggestion, although she appreciated Alice's willingness to help. It wasn't her fault that Mallory hadn't been honest. "I'll figure it out."

Alice glanced at the time again and groaned. "You get a pass for now, but I know you're holding out on me." She gathered her treats and sniffed the bag. "Ugh, and this is the only reason I'm keeping my mouth shut about the other thing. I'd sooner eat a box of hair than lose access to these delights."

Joining her friend, Mallory handed her credit card to the hostess and checked her phone. "You still free for happy hour next week?"

Alice shot her a thumbs-up. "You know it. James is out of town for a meeting with his agent, so the timing is perfect." She kissed Mallory on the cheek before stepping outside. "Text me!"

Mallory paid and walked to her car, her mind going at a thousand miles an hour with no destination. She needed to help Evan with the party, otherwise she would have to come clean on why she didn't want to. It was annoying to have yet another reason to be involved with Beckett beyond the wedding festivities, but she wouldn't wallow—much.

Once she was behind the wheel, Mallory realized she couldn't pinpoint why planning the party threw her. It was more than just seeing Beckett again. What she told Alice wasn't a lie, as she felt overwhelmed with her workload at the hospital. But being in Beckett's space, celebrating his return to her life, it felt too private to share with others, even with Evan. "Just rip the Band-Aid off," she chastised herself the whole drive to the market.

Whenever she was ready, she would text Evan for Beckett's address. There was no use hiding from the man. Not only was Buckeye Falls too small, but she also wouldn't live in fear. Maybe the time had come to face her past head-on—consequences be damned.

21

*

Beckett woke up on the floor of his new apartment, a candy bar wrapper stuck to his cheek. The night before had been a lonely one, filled with boxes to unpack and papers from his grandfather's estate to go through. Feeling tired and overwhelmed, Beckett opted to order a pizza and have a few beers to relax with his favorite video game. The only problem was he hadn't accomplished anything, including putting linens on the bed. He'd been in town for two whole days, and he still couldn't relax, couldn't shake the feeling that something was off.

Easing himself to stand, he pulled the wrapper from his face and let it flutter to the floor. He needed to watch his eating habits, but junk food was a comfort. And comfort felt in short supply these days. God, he missed his grandfather. He missed his laugh, missed his wit, missed how they could sit in silence and enjoy each other's company. Now that he was truly gone, Beckett didn't know where he fit in the world.

After plodding to the fridge, he yanked the door open and remembered he hadn't bothered going to the grocery store. The convenience store provided the candy bars and beer, but Beckett needed to get actual food. He covered his rumbling stomach with his hand and sighed. It was time to go to the diner and learn what all the fuss was about. Plus, he needed to see his friend again to thank him for the help with moving.

Twenty minutes later, Beckett stepped out of his car and headed toward the diner's entrance. On his way to the door, he spotted a woman in blue hospital scrubs getting into a car at the far side of the lot. His heart stuttered in his chest—was that Mallory? Doing a quick inventory of his current state, Beckett exhaled with relief that he'd remembered a clean T-shirt and deodorant. Granted, his glasses were a little smudged, but that was usually the case.

Picking up the pace, he strode toward the car and hoped it was Mallory. Then his feet faltered, causing him to stumble against the hood of a pickup truck. This was no way to have a reunion with Mallory, chasing her down in a random parking lot. She deserved a real greeting; she deserved the world. Beckett ducked low behind the truck and waited for the car to turn and leave, heading west on Main Street. After pulling himself upright, he turned and walked right into a wall.

That wall was nearly six feet tall and covered in a cotton apron. "Foxy? What the heck are you doing hiding in the parking lot?"

Beckett felt his cheeks flush. *Busted!*

"Um, I thought I lost..." His hands helplessly padded around his pockets. "My keys?" It came out as a question, and Evan raised an eyebrow. Shoving his hands in his pockets, he pulled his keys out and held them in the air. "Found them," Beckett declared with a little too much gusto.

Evan looked around the parking lot and frowned. "It's a shame you weren't a little quicker. Mal just left on her way home from work." His friend slung an arm over his shoulder and turned Beckett toward the diner. "But your timing is perfect for breakfast. The rush died down and CeCe is dying to see you again."

So that had been Mallory. Learning the truth made his skin prickle, but Beckett strained to keep his composure. With a quick glance over his shoulder, he confirmed Mallory was nowhere in sight. The realization should have relaxed him, but it had the opposite effect. He was both eager to see her again and terrified of her reaction. Would she remember the last time they saw each other? Would she even want to speak to him?

Beckett's internal monologue ended when they stepped inside the diner. His nostrils were greeted to the sweet smells of cinnamon, chocolate, and berries as Evan slapped his hand on the counter. "Have a seat. I'll bring out a menu and snag a coffee."

"Thanks, Lawless." Beckett slid onto a stool. He rested his forearms on the counter and savored the coolness. Outside, summer was taking over, and he wasn't quite ready for the dog days of crushing heat. Then again, he didn't know what he was ready for.

Evan was back in record time with a mug of coffee, a menu, and his lovely girlfriend in tow. "Hi Beckett," CeCe greeted him with a wave, her other hand clutching Evan's. Even though he'd only met CeCe a few times, it was clear that she loved his best friend. They looked at each other like his grandparents used to, with love and admiration. Their eyes sparkled with secrets and tidbits that only they knew. Man, he was jealous.

Beckett wanted that type of tenderness in his life, and he knew who he wanted to share it with. Hell, he'd had that and he'd made a foolish mistake and lost her. *Don't go there now, man.*

"CeCe, looking lovely as ever. You sure you're not tired of putting up with Lawless yet?"

With a playful eyeroll, Evan shoved a menu at his friend. "Real nice, man."

CeCe elbowed Evan and a look flashed between them that could melt butter. Beckett cleared his throat before taking a swig of his coffee. The bitterness was exactly what he needed to wake up and get his head on straight. "What's the special today?" he asked, hoping it was something sinfully sweet.

"Chocolate chip pancakes with strawberry glaze, but I also have a bunch of muffins if you'd rather something like that." CeCe held up her hand and counted off several decadent flavor combinations until Beckett felt himself drool. It was a wonder that Evan hadn't gained fifty pounds already.

"Let's do the pancakes, and I'll take a banana muffin to go?"

Evan chuckled. "Exact same order as Mal. I'm telling

you, it's crazy how in sync you two are." He rapped his knuckles on the counter and headed back to the kitchen, CeCe hot on his heels.

"Great seeing you again, Beckett. We'll stop by for dinner soon." She ducked into the kitchen and left Beckett alone with his thoughts.

Thoughts of Mallory.

Of course, they still liked the same things. Back when they were kids, his grandmother would get gallons of ice cream for the neighborhood children, and he and Mallory were the only ones who liked butter pecan. When Halloween rolled around, they were the only two kids willing to swap a Snickers for a Three Musketeer. And when everyone at the winter formal dance in high school got food poisoning from the plastic chicken, he and Mallory were saved because they had snuck in their own bag of Taco Bell.

That night had been a favorite of Beckett's for a lot of reasons, and ninety-nine percent had to do with Mallory. Agreeing to go as friends to the dance, they tagged along with Evan and his girlfriend at the time. They danced, laughed, gossiped about their classmates, and genuinely enjoyed each other's company. Being with Mallory was effortless, and he missed that feeling. The feeling of sharing your time and space with someone who saw you, someone who didn't try to make you into someone you're not. Beckett always appreciated that about Mallory, and it was a measuring stick he'd use when dating other women. So far, no one had come close to measuring up.

His musings ended abruptly when Evan returned with his breakfast. The pancakes were massive, with chocolatey decadence covering every square inch. "How are you not as big as a house, man?" Beckett asked as he cut into the first pancake. He took a massive bite, feeling a trail of syrup run down his chin.

Evan laughed and handed him a stack of napkins, which Beckett immediately swiped over his face. Thank God Mallory wasn't here to see his table manners.

"How's the unpacking going?" Evan asked as he tidied up the space around them. He carefully placed empty plates and coffee cups in a bus bin before wiping down the counter. Beckett took a moment to savor his breakfast and watch his friend's routine.

Evan had a carefree demeanor that Beckett envied. No matter the situation, he knew that Evan would be calm, collected, and more importantly smiling. That was one of the reasons he liked Mallory so much, she was like Evan, but with a twist. Like her brother, Mallory was fiercely loyal to her friends and family, but she had a sense of humor that kept him in stitches. There was also a nurturing air about her. She genuinely cared about people. For a time, she cared for him.

Glancing back down to his breakfast, Beckett struggled to stay in the moment. He wanted to engage with Evan, but his thoughts kept going back to Mallory. Even the chocolate in the pancakes reminded him of her sweet tooth, and how her chocolatey hair always curled in the summer humidity. He used to keep a stash of hair bands in his car for when they'd hang out. Within ten minutes of leaving the house, she'd begin fumbling for something to keep her hair off her neck. In a matter of moments, she'd braid her hair or twist it into an intricate pattern. He didn't know if she never noticed he had them at the ready, but he hoped she did.

"So how was breakfast?" Evan asked, finally drawing him back to the moment. He dropped a paper bag on the table, the smell made Beckett drool.

Beckett wiped at his face again, fruitlessly trying to get at the chocolate clinging to his stubbled cheek. "Delicious. You've got yourself a keeper, Lawless."

Evan's smile lit up the whole diner. "Don't I know it." Ah, the look of a man in love. Beckett hoped to someday have a smile like that on his face, but he wasn't going there now. "Take these muffins with you. CeCe is experimenting again."

"Twist my arm." Beckett snickered, knowing those

muffins would be gone in no time. "Where's a good place to grab some groceries? As much as I love living off muffins and pancakes, I need real food too."

"You'll want to swing by the corner market," Evan offered. He gestured toward the exit and added, "Turn right out of the lot and follow Main Street for about a half mile. You can't miss it."

After pulling out his wallet, Beckett tossed a few bills on the table and snatched his to-go bag. "Thank CeCe for a wonderful breakfast and these muffins."

Evan came out from behind the counter and they shared a one-armed hug before Beckett stepped back outside. Seeing his friend had shaken him from his stupor, and he was glad to have him so close again. After Gramps, Evan was one of his favorite people.

As he pulled his car into the market's parking lot, he tried not to think about his other favorite person. But it was no use, Mallory was never far from his thoughts. In fact, she was so entrenched in his head that he thought he saw her walking out of the market, but that couldn't be. Was Buckeye Falls really that small? What were the odds they'd see each other now?

Apparently pretty good, he surmised as she headed toward the same car from the diner's parking lot. She stalked forward with purpose, steering a small shopping cart. Beckett had a choice to make. He could duck behind another car and hide like a coward, or he could man up and walk over to her. Taking a deep breath, Beckett took one small step toward his future.

CHAPTER 3

If Mallory had a great guilty pleasure in her life, it would probably be celebrity gossip magazines. She could not get enough of them, and yet she hated herself for loving them. If her time binge reading Prince Harry's memoir was any indication, people like her were definitely a problem. But as she stood in the market's checkout line, she couldn't help but smile at all the fanciful headlines in front of her.

Reaching out, she snagged her favorite titles and tossed them onto the belt. While she was at it, she added a Three Musketeers bar for good measure. No reason to deprive herself when she was feeling a little lost. Mallory wouldn't say she was depressed, but she was certainly listless. Evan's pending engagement was simultaneously exciting and devastating. She wanted nothing but a happily ever after for Evan and CeCe, but she flinched when she thought of never getting Nana's ring.

Flexing her hand, she missed the weight of something that had truly never been hers. Why was she moping around about that when there were real problems in the world? Like the fact that Billboard's top performer just got divorced from her bodybuilding husband? Surely that warranted more sympathy than Mallory's circumstances?

29

After thanking the clerk, Mallory pushed her cart into the parking lot, keeping her gaze down. Running errands after work wasn't ideal, especially when she was this tired. But the notion of going home to change and then having to leave the comfort of her place felt just as draining. So when she finished with her Alice time, she'd decided to forgo vanity in the name of grocery shopping. It wasn't like she would see anyone else she knew. Even Buckeye Falls wasn't that small.

Yet as she opened her trunk and started putting her bags inside, the hairs on the back of her neck stood up. She was being watched. Standing up too quickly, her head hit the back of the trunk and she let out a muffled profanity. "Geez," she muttered as she rubbed the tender spot. A tiny welt had already formed, and she chastised her carelessness.

Before she turned around, a hand patted her shoulder and time stood still. That was a familiar touch, a touch weighed down with memories, a touch she thought she'd never feel again.

Beckett.

"Mallory! Are you okay?" His fingers gingerly dug into her skin, keeping her steady—and slightly swoony. Suddenly, she understood all the historical romance heroines who fainted at the sight of the hero. She was one batch of smelling salts away from needing a fainting sofa.

Unable to stop her feet, Mallory turned to his voice like it was a siren's song. She kept her hand on the back of her head, the other balled at her side. She would not touch this man, she wouldn't. It would be tantamount to touching the center of the sun. She'd get burned; she'd be destroyed. *Again.*

"Beckett?" She said his name in question, although there was no denying it was him in the flesh. Finally, she dragged her gaze up to meet his, and her stomach plummeted. It had been two years since they'd seen each other, but Beckett looked perfect. His tortoise-shell glasses were still crooked and a little smudged, an endearing quality that never ceased to make her heart flutter. His red hair was mussed, like he hadn't bothered to run a comb through it. His warm hands still clutched her shoulders, anchoring her in place.

When he smiled at her, Mallory nearly combusted right there in the parking lot. The market would have to erect a memorial for her, complete with copies of gossip magazines and cheap candy bars. She could practically hear her brother's eulogy, documenting her teenage-like obsessions. *Yes, Mallory saved countless lives in the hospital, but what we'll all remember is how she took a day off school when Brangelina announced their divorce.*

"Mallory?" Beckett gave her a gentle shake. "Are you okay?"

Letting out a deep exhale, Mallory grounded herself. She stepped back until her legs hit the tailgate, breaking free of his touch. "Yeah, I'm fine." She shrugged and turned back to the shopping cart and the rest of her bags. "I guess I'm distracted."

Beckett hoisted a bag onto his hip, ready to help. "You want all this in the back?"

Helpless to stop him, she got out of the way and watched him load her car. His forearms flexed with the movements, cords of muscle making quick work of the task. When her cheeks burned crimson, she forced herself to look away. *Real mature, Mal, drooling over a friend in a grocery store parking lot.*

As Beckett placed the last bag inside, it toppled over and the magazines slid out. One of the headlines read, *Exclusive Interview with Alien Baby of Taylor Swift.* She couldn't have been more mortified if an enema kit had fallen out.

Without saying a word, he scooped up her magazines and candy and tucked them back in the bag. When he straightened and faced her, she didn't miss the smirk on his face. She crossed her arms and jutted out a hip. "You might as well just say it."

His lips quivered before the dam broke and he doubled over. "I thought they determined Taylor's alien baby was in fact a zombie baby?" His deep voice hitched with his

31

laughter.

Mallory shoved his shoulder before joining in with the laughter. "Make fun all you want, but when these alien celebrity babies take over, you'll be glad I know what's going on."

"You're right," he said, shoulders shaking. "When all the little old lady readers pass on, we'll need a full report of the state of Elvis and the Elephant Man." Beckett pushed his glasses up his nose with his pointer finger and smiled, one of his real smiles that she liked to catalog and save for later. They'd shared a million smiles like that over the years, and she treasured them all. A Beckett Fox smile was rare and meant to be savored, like the last Girl Scout cookie in the box.

"It's good to see you," he said, letting his hand drop to his side.

They stood awkwardly for a moment before she finally added, "Likewise. Evan said you live here now?"

Beckett nodded, his gaze over her shoulder. His eyes seemed unfocused, like he was looking for someone far away. "Yeah, but I still have some work to do on Gramps's house."

Mallory's voice was low when she said, "I'm so sorry to hear about his passing. I would have gone to the funeral had I known." She was dying to know why he had not told her or Evan about it, but that was not a conversation for now. They were in public, and everything felt too raw, too much on display.

"I should have called, but I wasn't sure if you…" He let his words trail off, and Mallory was a little disappointed. They hadn't spoken in a while, not since a misunderstanding broke her heart. Remembering that feeling of humiliation brought her up short, and more importantly, back to reality.

Her palms slicked with sweat when she realized how disheveled she must look with rumpled scrubs, a lopsided ponytail, and makeup that had melted down her face from hours in a hot hospital. "I should go," she said, turning quickly on her heel and attempting to slam her trunk.

Beckett hurriedly stepped to the side to avoid getting his hands clamped. "Do you want to—" But he didn't get to finish his question as she stomped around the other side of her car and slid behind the wheel. He had the grace to move aside so he didn't get run over.

Mallory's eyes burned as she fumbled to turn the car on. "Come on," she pleaded as she drove away, nearly leaving skid marks in the market's parking lot. From her rearview mirror, she saw Beckett standing in place, arms helplessly at his sides. She couldn't read his expression, but that was for the best. He was a nice guy and probably didn't even remember the last time they saw each other. She needed to do the same; push it down until she couldn't remember having feelings for Beckett Fox in the first place.

Because Beckett lived here now, in the same small town she loved so much. They were bound to bump into each other again—and sooner than she'd probably like. Mallory needed to learn how to coexist with him, otherwise, her brother's wedding and her day-to-day existence would be impossible to survive.

But then Mallory had another thought. What if she and Beckett could go back to normal? What if they could be friends? What if they acted like they did throughout their childhood? Those were some of her favorite memories, and Mallory hated the thought of losing them, of not having Beckett in her life.

She'd lost him for far too long already, and even after five minutes with him, her body burned to see him again. She wanted to know what he'd been up to, what had happened to his beloved grandfather. Mallory had too many unanswered questions, and she decided she was adult enough to get some answers. She knew where to find Beckett, and she would play nice.

*

Stumbling through the market, Beckett tossed a few bags of lettuce, a random apple, and four boxes of cereal into his cart before he could think straight. Seeing Mallory again had been—a lot. There was no other way to describe it.

Somehow, she seemed both happy and annoyed to see him, which given their last meeting, he could totally understand. He had a million thoughts running through him, from potential apologies to asking what she'd been up to. Her sky-blue scrubs confirmed what Evan said about her job, but he wanted to know what Mallory the woman was doing. Was she seeing anyone? Was she happy? Did she ever get that kitten she always wanted? Was she seeing anyone? Did she still like to binge kung fu movies in her pajamas? *Was she seeing anyone?*

Beckett didn't want to invade her privacy with her groceries, but the sight of the magazines and candy warmed his heart. That was the Mallory he knew. He'd bet his whole paycheck she was going home after a long day to read magazines in the bathtub while scarfing down a candy bar or two. When they were kids, Evan would lament her habit when he needed to get ready for baseball practice or needed a shower after a game.

Not having siblings, Beckett could not fathom not having free rein over his house, but he was jealous that Evan had so many sisters to keep him company. Growing up with his grandparents had been great, basically the American dream. After his parents' divorce, neither parent wanted to stay in Ohio. His mom followed her new fiancé to his home in Boston, while his father decided he wanted a fresh start out west.

Beckett remembered sitting with his parents and grandparents in the farm house, everyone wearing matching expressions of trepidation. He was young, but he wasn't blind. It was clear his parents were headed to Splitsville, but Beckett didn't know where that would take *him*.

"Beckett, honey," his mom started, licking her lips and keeping her tone light. "Roger and I are going to move up to Boston. You know Boston, right?"

At seven years old, all Beckett knew about Boston was the Red Sox, baked beans, and lobster rolls. "Yeah?" he asked, although his mother likely wasn't looking for more questions.

His mother's cool hands reached out, pulling him closer until she met his gaze through his crooked glasses. "How would you feel about moving up north with us?"

Not even allowing Beckett ten seconds to absorb the invitation, his father soldiered on. "Now come on, son. Wouldn't it be more fun to go out to California with me? We can ride horses and swim in the ocean."

Beckett had horrible allergies and didn't know how to swim, so the notion of doing either of those things caused him to grimace. "I don't like to swim," he said quietly, too afraid to disappoint or upset his father. It was easy to fail his old man, and Beckett loathed being the source of his father's disappointment.

For a moment, no one spoke. The old clock on his grandparents' mantle kept time of their racing hearts; counting down the last moments as a familial unit. Not realizing it at the time, Beckett's childhood was evaporating into the ether. Carefree days with his whole family would soon be a distant memory; a source of heartbreak for years to come.

Finally, Gram spoke up. "Richard and I had a thought," she offered, her eyes meeting Beckett's. Her expression was warm, caring. The delicate skin around her mouth stretched into a smile. "Why doesn't Beckett stay here with us? We can keep him in school for the rest of the year and decide over summer break."

The suggestion was the right one, as everyone let out an exhale and fell back into their seats. "That sounds good to me, Mom."

Beckett's dad shifted on his seat before awkwardly patting his son on the shoulder. "Gives Beckett time to take swimming lessons." His joke fell flat and the room shifted back to uncomfortable silence.

Summer break arrived and no one came back for Beckett. His mother and Roger had married, announcing they were pregnant before Beckett turned eight. While out in California, his father reconnected with a college friend and moved to a ranch on the central coast. Whether because of his son's allergies or not, an invitation was never extended beyond the occasional holiday break.

Beckett didn't really mind, as his grandparents were always enough. They were there when he needed help with his homework, they took him to the sporting supply store when he needed a new baseball glove, Gram taught him how to bake with the apples from their farm, and they always made time for his doctor's appointments. He couldn't have been more cared for, and he appreciated all their sacrifices.

The Lawsons were kind to him, too. Their family always inviting him to dinner and summer picnics. Evan welcomed the break from all the girliness his sisters brought into the home, and Mr. Lawson liked having someone else to talk sports with over the dinner table. He never was alone, except for now.

The only thing more uncomfortable than that memory was his stilted interaction with Mallory in the parking lot, and it didn't sit right with him. He and Mallory were thick as thieves, or at least they used to be. He couldn't understand how they'd gotten to where they were now, but he knew he was to blame. A few careless words said in jest, and everything he shared with Mallory shriveled up faster than a discarded apple core.

His parents leaving shaped Beckett in ways he only now was coming to understand, thanks to copious amounts of therapy. When he thought about the important people in his life, it was always his grandparents, Evan, and Mallory. It was one of the reasons he always kept Mallory at arm's length, even though he wanted her *in* his arms. If things went south, not only would he lose Mallory, but he'd lose

Evan. He couldn't stand the notion. The Lawsons were the only people he had left.

Back at his apartment, Beckett decided he needed to do something or he'd crawl out of his skin. After kicking the same box over for the third time that day, he went to work. Three hours, ten boxes, and a million dust motes later, Beckett had the living room almost unpacked.

His collection of sci-fi paperbacks filled the shelves, and his PS5 was plugged in and connected to the router. If he finally washed the sheets and made the bed, he'd practically be ready for a housewarming party. Which, if he were honest, he wasn't in the mood for. Chuckling at Evan's suggestion, Beckett went in search of dinner. Even through his musings at the market, he'd managed to pick up the fixings for one of his childhood comfort foods—French bread pizza.

As Beckett retrieved the bread knife from the block, he heard footsteps outside his apartment. He lived on the first floor of a low-rise outside Buckeye Falls' downtown. It wasn't where he wanted to stay permanently, but he couldn't handle living at the farm house on his own. There were too many memories that weren't ready to be unpacked.

Tiptoeing to the peep hole, Beckett saw a figure in shadow. It was clearly a woman judging from the puff of hair visible in the fading sunlight—or perhaps a hipster barista who made house calls?

"Hello?" he said through the door.

He heard a squeak before "Um, hi."

Mallory.

Beckett flung the door open and found her standing there, a box in her hand and an anxious expression marring her lovely face. "Mal, what are you doing here?"

Mallory held up the box and shook it, the sounds of metal and plastic scraping together. "I'm bringing a few odds and ends to help you move in. Ev said you might not have a tool box yet."

Rubbing the back of his neck, Beckett felt his muscles

37

relax at her presence. Mallory had this amazing ability to calm him down while simultaneously causing him to burn with lust. "Oh yeah, he's right. All the tools are still at the farm."

For a moment, neither of them spoke. The sound of cicadas in the night air surrounded them, their nightly song echoing through Buckeye Falls. Mallory finally cleared her throat and gestured with the box toward the door. "Can I come in?"

"Erm, yeah." Beckett stepped back and held the door open for her, catching a whiff of her perfume as she slunk inside. Mallory always smelled like summertime: sweet and tangy like a handful of blackberries.

Mallory took a few paces inside and looked around. Beckett said a silent prayer of thanks that he had the forethought to start unpacking. It was a mess, but at least it looked like his mess. "Cute." She said the word with a small smile, plopping the box on top of the coffee table.

She turned like she was going to leave, her presence not required beyond the delivery. Instinctively, Beckett blocked the way, letting the door close behind him on a soft click. "Where are you going?" he asked, his pulse kicking up at the idea that he wouldn't see her for more than another moment.

Shrugging, Mallory pointed to the door. "Home?"

Before he could think better of it, Beckett blurted out the first thing that came to mind. "Stay. Have dinner with me."

Mallory didn't respond at first, but he didn't miss the flush that crept up her neck. "You want to have dinner with me?"

"Yes?" he replied, although it was far from a question. Beckett wanted Mallory to stay as long as she liked—for dinner or the rest of her life. He wasn't picky.

Holding his breath, he watched her face shift from confusion to acceptance. Her shoulders were tense, but the popping of her jaw subsided. He knew he'd won this round.

"Sure, that sounds nice."

"Cool."

For what felt like an eternity, neither of them moved. Beckett took in Mallory, from her change of clothes to the new color of her hair. It had always been waves of chocolate, and now there were tinges of red, catching the light and reminding him of old copper pennies. He was still in love with this woman, and he needed to make the situation right. Mallory had clearly moved on, judging from her pinched expression and how she barely tolerated his dinner invitation.

But Gramps's words echoed in Beckett's head, and he couldn't stop thinking about them. *Go find your girl...*

The trouble was, he'd found her. Beckett needed to figure out how to *keep* her.

CHAPTER 4

Mallory had fallen into a black hole; she was certain of it. Nothing around her made sense and there was a faint ringing in her ears. Yep, she was tumbling through space and time without a tether. It was surreal, standing in Beckett Fox's apartment, mere miles from her own. For more times than she'd ever admit, she'd fantasized about seeing him again. Her daydreams ranged from anger-fueled thoughts of decking him to lust filled fantasies of kissing him until she couldn't feel her lips.

While his back was turned to the stove, she pinched her arm to make sure she wasn't dreaming. Letting out a tiny yelp, she clapped her hand over her mouth and groaned. *Real smooth, Mallory.*

"Did you say something?" Beckett asked over his shoulder.

"Nothing," she squeaked out in reply. "Can I help with anything?"

He shook his head, his attention back to the cutting board in front of him. "Help yourself to a drink and have a seat. This won't take long."

She did as she was told, grabbing a pair of beers and popping the tops. After sliding one across the counter to

Beckett, she took her drink to the couch and curled up on the far cushion. Perhaps having a yard of fabric and padding between them would make it less awkward?

Beckett chopped for a few minutes and then slid a sheet tray into the oven. He tidied up before joining her on the couch. "Food will be ready in less than fifteen minutes."

"Cool," she said, taking a long pull from her beer. What the hell was she supposed to do for fifteen minutes? Discuss the current state of American politics? Go over her recent training on the best way to draw blood? She assumed she would eat and run; not sit in awkward silence for an eternity.

"Cool," Beckett replied like a robot, swigging from his own beer.

Mallory opened her mouth to repeat the blasted word for the third time, but she clamped her mouth shut. She would not be the weird one—more than she already was. She was visiting a friend, helping with the tools. This visit didn't mean anything, so why did she feel so uncomfortable?

"God, this is awkward," Beckett muttered before draining his beer and jumping to his feet. "Let's try this again."

"Huh?" Mallory scurried to her feet as Beckett threw the door open. "What are you doing?"

Gently taking her elbow, he steered her outside and shut the door in her face. She stood slack-jawed until the door flew open again, Beckett standing there grinning from ear to ear. "Wow, Mallory. What a pleasant surprise. Won't you come in?"

Mallory stood frozen in place, her feet feeling as heavy as a pair of cement boots. She raised an eyebrow but didn't interrupt him.

"I've got dinner in the oven, and I'd love for you to join me."

This was a game they used to play as kids. If one of them, Evan included, did something stupid or silly, the others would start over again and pretend it didn't happen. Clearly

42

Beckett was repeating history, and she wouldn't fight the pull to step back inside. "Why thank you, Beckett. That would be delightful."

He theatrically waved his arm in the direction of the couch once she crossed the threshold. "Have a seat, I'll bring over dinner."

A minute later, Mallory was presented with the most delicious-looking meal she'd had in ages. "Is this…" Her throat closed as she attempted to form the words. She hadn't eaten French bread pizza in far too long, mostly because it reminded her of the man sitting next to her.

Using his wrist, Beckett shoved his glasses back in place as he eased onto the cushion beside her. "French bread pizza? Yeah, please don't judge that at twenty-seven-years-old I'm barely able to cook without bread and cheese."

"No judgments here." She breathed, staring down at the piece of pizza like it held the answers to her broken heart. She was dying to know if he ever thought about that day. If he ever wondered if the vows they spoke as tweens held any merit now. It was a fool's errand, so instead, she took a bite and shot him a thumbs-up. "This is perfect." Her cheeks were full of food, and she must have resembled a chipmunk before winter.

Beckett beamed, diving into his own meal with enthusiasm. "Thanks, and thanks for coming over. I'll admit, it's been a little lonely since I came back." That should not have made her relax, but it did. No one should be lonely, but lonely meant there weren't other women visiting his new apartment.

Mallory had a lot of gaps when it came to Beckett's life. Whether he sensed the topic caused her stress or not, Evan was light on the details beyond the passing of Beckett's grandfather. "I'm so sorry to hear about Gramps." The words sounded lame to her own ears, but she didn't know what else to say.

He offered her a sad smile before taking another bite. She watched the muscles of his throat intently as he chewed.

She was familiar with every angle on this man, from the slope of his nose to the curve of his neck. Once he'd fallen asleep in her college dorm room on a visit, and she took a pen and connected the freckles on his forearm. The shapes created looked like anime cartoons, and they'd laughed for hours at her handiwork.

Despite looking like Beckett, he still didn't feel like *her* Beckett. The dark smudges under his eyes spoke to sleepless nights, the paleness of his skin proved he wasn't out in the orchards helping with the harvest, and the curling hair at the nape of his neck meant he wasn't getting regular haircuts. Although perhaps this was just Beckett in his late twenties? It could be as simple as they were strangers. *Maybe he would never be her Beckett again...*

"Thanks. I won't lie." His expression was pinched as he squeezed his eyes closed, lost in memory. "It sucks that he's gone, but I'm relieved he's not in pain anymore."

Wiping her hands on her napkin, she frowned. "I'm sorry I didn't know. I would have come over to visit if I had, it's just—" She didn't know how to answer that question. *It's just that your careless words broke my heart, and I pretended you didn't exist. I chose self-preservation over your needs.*

"You have your own life, Mal. I don't fault you for that." He toyed with the burnt edge of his pizza, flaking away crumbs with this thumb.

Mallory shook her head so forcefully, her bun bobbed against her neck in frustration. "No, that's not an excuse. Your grandparents were always so good to Ev and me. I'm sorry we lost touch." They were like family, was what she wanted to say. Yet the words wouldn't come, because she couldn't admit they were gone...couldn't admit she'd lost another part of her past.

"I'm sorry we lost touch too, but not just because of Gramps."

She would have been less shocked if Beckett jumped onto the couch and did a jig a la Tom Cruise on *Oprah*.

Averting her gaze, she studied her plate and picked off a

piece of pepperoni. She shoved it in her mouth and tried to focus on the spicy morsel and not Beckett staring a hole through her skull. "Stuff happens."

"No, I happened," Beckett said, placing his empty plate on the coffee table next to the tool box. "Look, I've been meaning to—" His words were cut short when there was a loud knock at the door.

"Yo! Foxy!" Evan's voice boomed through the closed door.

Mallory leapt to her feet, collecting their dishes and carrying them to the sink with the speed of Superman on a mission. "I'll head out," she said, her eyes focused on the task of cleaning up. If she kept distracted with something as mundane as loading the dishwasher, she wouldn't scream at her brother for interrupting the moment. For interrupting the explanation she'd been waiting ages for.

"You don't have to." Beckett urged, not answering the door despite Evan's persistent knocking. "Please, stay. I'm sure Evan is just making sure I'm not bored."

Mallory's shoulders slumped, and she tried to keep the emotion from her voice. "You two have a lot to catch up on. The wedding and everything. I'll just be a third wheel."

The statement rang false, and they both knew it. Never had Mallory been the third wheel, not even close. Their little trio always made sense—until it didn't.

"Thanks for the pizza." She gestured to the empty sheet tray and smiled. "It reminded me of—" She stopped herself before she could show her hand. Beckett Fox made it abundantly clear he wasn't interested in her, so she wouldn't make a fool of herself any longer. She'd learned her lesson, or at least she was trying to.

"Fooooxxxyyyy!" Evan's voice echoed around them. "Are you alive?"

Mallory hiked her purse strap up her shoulder and tried to step past Beckett. He stopped her progression with a gentle hand to the shoulder. Her skin burned where his fingers carefully held her in place. "It reminded you of

45

what?"

It could have been wishful thinking, but Mallory thought he looked hopeful. No, it was probably a trick of the light. She opened her mouth to respond, but Evan knocked again. "Oh, for heaven's sake." She sighed as she side-stepped Beckett and flung the door open. "Christ, Ev."

Evan's blue eyes bugged out at the sight of his sister. "Mal? What are you doing here?"

"Dropping off tools," she said over her shoulder. Without another glance, she strode to her car and slid behind the wheel. She wasn't certain, but she thought she heard Beckett calling her name.

Mallory drove home in silence, the concept of the radio or a podcast too much company for her muddled brain. She'd survived seeing Beckett twice in one day. She'd done a nice thing by helping him with the tools, and now she didn't have a reason to see him again. Well, except for her brother's wedding. But thinking about the wedding brought on a fresh surge of frustration over the ring.

As she stepped into her tiny apartment and greeted her cat, Fernando, Mallory made herself a promise. She wouldn't get swept up with Beckett again. Fawning over the man for over fifteen years was long enough. She was done waiting for a miracle, done waiting for the man to realize what was standing in front of him. No, Mallory would find a new man. She'd made it this long without Beckett, and she knew she could keep going.

*

"So Mal brought over the tools?" Evan asked as he flopped onto the couch. He sniffed the air and grinned. "Is that dinner I smell?"

Beckett chuckled, endlessly charmed by his friend's bottomless appetite. He answered his question with another. "Aren't you engaged to a chef?"

Evan winked. "Not yet, but soon. Besides, CeCe has

46

girls' night with Natalie and Ginny. I thought I'd come over here and make sure you're not bored." He nestled back into the couch and asked again, "So is there any dinner?"

"You missed dinner, but I can offer dessert." Beckett found a box of Oreos and tossed them to Evan. With lightning-fast reflexes, his friend caught the cookies in one deft motion.

"Did Mal bring you dinner?" Evan asked, his expression still playful.

"Nah, just tools. She caught me midway through cooking, so I invited her to join me." And he was damned glad he did, and even happier that she accepted the invitation. Beckett pulled another pair of beers from the fridge before joining his friend. He studied Evan for any sign of discomfort, any indication that he could read his mind and see his feelings for Mallory. Yet all Beckett saw in Evan's eyes was his signature carefree smile. The man was clueless, and that was probably for the best.

After eating half a sleeve of Oreos, Evan dusted crumbs from his hands and flung over the tool box. "What can I help with?"

"Not too much, actually. There's a new end table I bought from IKEA, and I know I'll need more than that goofy wrench thingy they toss in the box." In truth, Beckett had everything he needed in the farm house, but he wasn't ready to go back yet. Frankly, he didn't know when he'd be ready.

That was his safe space, a place filled with memories of the people who loved him. Yes, his grandparents were chief among them, but he couldn't forget about his time with the Lawsons. He and Evan got into so much mischief back then, from setting off fireworks in the middle of February from the hen house roof to hiding mud pies all over the property for Mallory or Gram to step in.

He and Mallory had their own memories too, mainly their wedding day and first kiss. Beckett revisited that afternoon more often than he would admit, and he was

47

curious if Mallory did as well. Her question before Evan interrupted played on a loop in his brain. Did she remember eating French bread pizza with him that day? Did she think of it as frequently as he did?

"Why didn't you just bring more furniture from the farm house?" Evan's question brought Beckett back to the moment, and he shrugged. Truthfully, it was a loaded question with too many emotions to unpack. Much like his current apartment, certain things were meant to be boxed up and tossed away in a dark corner. That house deserved to be filled with love and smiling faces, not a grumpy loner who didn't know how to move forward with his life.

Picking up on his buddy's mood, Evan nudged his knee as he stood. "I'm grabbing a couple of wrenches, and you're going to tell me why you look like you drank battery acid."

"I do not," Beckett replied weakly, a smile tugging at his lips. All it took was five minutes in Evan's company for his mood to shift.

Evan carefully took the planks and screws out of the box, lining everything up in size order. "This reminds me of when we'd build model airplanes and cars with Gramps," Evan said, keeping his blue gaze focused on the instructions sheet.

Beckett loved this about his friend, that he could bring up happy memories during a painful time and not have them sting. As boys, they would create, and sometimes destroy, all sorts of toys, buildings, and vehicles. For a time, Beckett assumed they'd get into some type of mechanics business, but when they went to college, things shifted. Evan found a love for computers and tech, while Beckett gravitated toward economics and numbers. He was grateful for his job in finance, especially since it was remote and allowed him extra time to help with Gramps. The work-from-home lifestyle also afforded him the luxury of hitting the road after he passed, since Beckett couldn't handle the Buckeye state another moment. Needing an escape from reality, and a certain brunette, he'd taken some time to travel the country.

As long as he had an internet connection, he could pay the bills. Yet things were different now. He didn't want to be away from home, from the people who mattered.

"Remember that time we built a house for Mal's Barbies?" Evan chuckled at the memory, already knowing where Beckett was going with this.

"Yeah, she loved that house."

"Until the stink bombs went off," Evan cackled his reply. "I don't think I'll ever forget the look on her face when she pelted me with her dolls."

"Smelling like rotten eggs was far from anyone's dream house." Beckett agreed, reveling in the memory of Mallory and her spitfire reaction. When they were young, he had adored getting a rise out of her. Then as they got older, right around a certain faux wedding ceremony, Beckett started to pay more attention to her reactions. That was when he decided he wanted to be the reason she smiled, not the reason she frowned—or threw dolls.

For a few minutes, the two worked in tandem to get the end table together. Just as Evan screwed in the last table leg, he sighed. "I wish I could figure out Mal's dream now." The admission caused Beckett to drop the last two nails, which toppled across the floor in opposite directions.

Using it as an excuse to avoid eye contact, Beckett scurried after the rogue pieces. "What's wrong with Mallory?" He hoped his voice was lighter than it felt, because nausea crept up his throat at the thought that she was troubled.

Evan adjusted the leg and took one of the screws from Beckett's outstretched hand. "Dunno, but something is definitely up."

Beckett didn't know a lot about Mallory's life over the last couple of years, and it was entirely his fault. He wasn't on social media, so he had no idea if she was sharing her life with the world. But he felt like she wouldn't, it didn't seem like Mallory. For all her love of celebrity gossip and tabloid magazines, she was a fairly private person.

After clearing his throat, Beckett asked the one question he needed an answer for. "Do you think it's boyfriend trouble?" Beckett couldn't be certain, but he felt his heart stop beating while Evan answered his question.

With a scoff, he said, "Mal doesn't have a boyfriend. I haven't seen her with a guy since that last online dating disaster."

White-hot rage surged through Beckett as his heart pounded. Granted he didn't want Mallory to date anyone, but experiencing a toxic relationship was far worse. "What did he do?" His tone was so stern, Evan looked up and blinked at his stormy expression.

"Calm down, Foxy. He was just a tool she met online. They went on like two dates until she found out he was married."

Beckett ran a hand down his face, bumping his glasses from his nose. Quickly adjusting them, he asked, "And did you rip the guy limb from limb?"

Evan snorted. "I did my part, but so did her bestie Alice. When Mal told Alice, I'm pretty sure the guy needed to leave Ohio and change his name. If that guy is still married, his wife took at least one of his balls. Mal and Alice got the other."

Shoulders slumping, Beckett relaxed. "Good, I'm glad she's got friends like that." He meant it, but he also wished that was still his job—running the bad guys out of her life. The trouble was, Beckett *was* the bad guy. He'd been careless and lied about his feelings for Mallory. It was an error he'd been beating himself over for two years now, and he needed to figure out a way to move past it.

Sitting here with Evan, laughing and messing around like old times, felt one step closer to his old self. Beckett didn't have anyone left, and he couldn't lose his friendship with Evan any more than he could lose his relationship with Mallory. Beckett had to figure out this emotional house of cards before it all fell apart.

CHAPTER 5

There was no point denying it. Beckett had turned into a romcom cliché. He could not sleep, not one wink. He wanted to blame the pizza, Oreos, and his slowing metabolism, but they were not the culprit. The issue was the 500-pound elephant threatening to crush him. He needed to clear the air with Mallory about the last time they saw each other. If Evan hadn't interrupted their impromptu dinner, he would have spilled his guts and given Mallory the apology of all apologies.

The trouble was, words wouldn't be enough. Beckett toyed with the notion of Googling *how to fix a mess you made two years ago that included ghosting your dearest friend*. He was ninety-nine percent certain there wouldn't be results, but that didn't mean he wasn't tempted to try. He couldn't be the only idiot man out there, right?

Two years ago, Beckett was in the midst of grieving the passing of Gram. She'd suffered a heart attack on the farm while picking apples. Despite getting her to the hospital in time, she never fully recovered from the incident. Her heart had been weakened, and there was nothing anyone could do. For a month, Beckett watched Gramps mourn the impending loss of his other half. It gutted Beckett more than he would admit to anyone.

Everyone shared platitudes of their sympathy.

She lived a full life.

No one was more loved than Gram.

At least she's in a better place.

Beckett wanted to riot against everyone. He couldn't believe that no one understood how she still had a full life to live; still had people who loved her and needed her. Extended family and neighbors didn't realize that Beckett's world, his short list of loved ones, was down twenty-five percent. Well, no one except Evan and Mallory. The Lawson siblings were there for the entire ordeal. They understood what he lost.

Gram was more than a grandparent. She was basically Beckett's mother. When the divorce was final, his mom retreated more and more from his life. He was never invited to New England, never saw her at the holidays. The monthly phone calls turned to annual birthday cards, then dwindled to sporadic texts wishing him a happy birthday a month too late. The half siblings that rambled around the Boston area were strangers to him, yet Beckett couldn't bring himself to miss people he'd never met.

At the time, it didn't bother him too much because Gram always spoiled him. Nothing from his parents? Don't worry, there was a three-tier birthday cake covered in marzipan baseballs waiting in the kitchen. Parents forgot his high school graduation? That was fine, because he was off to a resort in the Smoky Mountains with his grandparents. Beckett could fill a book with the times his grandparents stepped up, and he was eternally grateful.

The day of Gram's service was one of the lowest of Beckett's life. To add insult to injury, Beckett's father had appeared long enough to sniff around for his inheritance and stir up trouble. "Hey, Beckett," his father had said from the porch, hand clenched on the banister.

"Hi" was all Beckett could muster. He pulled at his tie, eager to loosen the damn thing before it threatened to choke

52

him. "What are you doing here?"

His father scoffed, rolling his eyes. "Well, my mother died. Seemed only fitting to come back and check in."

"Check in? On who? Me? Gramps?"

His father had the decency to look embarrassed, his gaze falling to a loose board on the porch. He toed at the plank and muttered something about the house falling apart. Beckett ground his teeth. He would not be baited by his dad. That man didn't care about the house or the people who lived in it. Never had, never will.

Beckett stood straight. "You didn't answer my question." After pausing for a moment, his dad huffed out a sigh, but still didn't answer the question. "Ah, I see. You're not here for a *who*, but a *what*."

That statement brought his father's head up, and Beckett braced himself for an altercation. Granted it wouldn't be physical, but Mike Fox had an uncanny ability to say the absolute worst thing at the absolute worst time. "If you must know," he started, letting out a long sigh like Beckett was putting him out. "I'm curious if Mom left me anything."

"Are you freaking kidding me?" Beckett stepped forward, coming toe-to-toe with his old man. He hadn't seen him in over five years, and he'd grown at least another six inches. Mike inched back until he hit the railing. "I'm not here to cause trouble."

"As far as I'm concerned, you're not here at all." Beckett shoved past his father and stormed off toward the orchards. It was late fall; the harvest was done and the trees were bare. The barren scene was fitting for his current mood. He stalked ahead, nearly tripping on exposed roots in his dress shoes. A sensible man would have changed before hiking through groves of trees, but Beckett never considered himself that smart.

Beckett managed to hide away from everyone until Mallory found him an hour later. She was clad in her black mourning dress, her brown hair pulled back in an artful braid. While nothing fancy, the dress hugged her curves in all the right places, giving her skin a creamy hue. She was a vision, his Mallory. And right now, he wanted nothing more than to find comfort in her gaze, in her arms.

"Thought I'd find you up here," she said, easing down on the ground and tucking her legs beneath her. "Ev saw your dad leave, in case you're wondering."

Beckett snorted. "Did he speed off with a big bag of cash? That's all he came for." Bitterness oozed from his tone, but he didn't care. In all his life, Beckett had never hated his father more than he did at that moment.

Mallory reached out and took one of his trembling hands in hers, giving it a firm squeeze. "Your dad is a first-class asshole. I'm not denying that. I saw him speaking to Gramps, but I don't know what they said. I tried to keep my distance, out of respect to Gramps, of course."

"You're one of the good ones, Mal." Beckett sighed, leaning down so his head rested on her shoulders. Even after an afternoon of helping with guests and tidying up the house, she smelled as fresh as a basket of raspberries.

"I'm here for you, you know. Whatever you need." Mallory didn't say anything else for a while. They stayed seated, watching the sun dip below the horizon. Even though his heart was shattered at losing Gram, and seeing his worthless father, Beckett felt a tiny moment of peace. Mallory was his rock, and he was incredibly grateful to be there with her, watching the sun set for the millionth time. It was reassuring, the sun going through its familiar routine. The ritual gave Beckett a little optimism that things would eventually feel right again.

After a little while, he heard footsteps stomping up the orchard row. Evan's blond head was visible in the fading light, and he raised a hand in silent greeting. "He's definitely gone. I watched him leave before I came up." He shoved his hands in his pockets and rolled back on his heels.

Beckett knew he meant his father, and he was grateful for the notice. With everything going on, he knew if he saw his father again, he'd sock him right in the teeth, consequences be damned.

"Thanks, Lawless," Beckett said. He made no move to pull away from Mallory. The need to be next to her was overwhelming. Every cell in his body screamed to be closer to her, to feel her warmth and absorb any ounce of happiness.

It took a moment, but he realized Evan was looking at him and Mallory like they were picking their noses. His brow furrowed, he frowned and shuffled his feet. "Yeah, man. No problem."

Whether sensing Evan's tone, or wanting to give the guys privacy, Mallory pulled herself up and dusted off her dress. "I'm going to go help Gramps with cleaning up." She held out a hand as Beckett stood. He made no attempt to let go, keeping barely two inches between them. This was an intimate pose, not how friends would stand. For a second, no one moved. It was as if time had stood still. Could Evan tell they were into each other? Beckett felt like it was obvious on a regular day, but today, he was practically a part of Mal's person, clinging to her like a literal lifeline.

Finally, Evan cleared his throat, jolting them back to the present. Mallory plodded past and disappeared into the trees like a ghost. Beckett missed her immediately.

"How are you holding up?" Evan asked, gesturing to the spot Mallory vacated.

Beckett nodded and sat back down, waiting for his buddy to settle before opening a vein and pouring out all the pain. That was one of the things he loved about Evan; he was no nonsense with feelings. A lot of his buddies would shy away from personal topics, but Evan's heart was always open, always ready to take on someone else's pain.

"Honestly, I don't know." Beckett leaned back, his hands sinking into the dirt. Despite the harvest being done, the air smelled faintly of apples. The sweet smell tugged a smile from his lips as he thought about all the times Gram would cook or bake with the fruit. He felt her at that moment, surrounding them with her warmth.

Before he could stop himself, he let a morsel of truth slip. "I miss her, and I'm worried about Gramps. They were together for over forty years."

Evan nodded, his voice low. "That's a lot of history, but he's a tough man. He'll rally for you."

Beckett scoffed. "He shouldn't have to rally for me. I need to be strong for him."

"You will be. Don't beat yourself up."

Beckett shook his head, his glasses sliding down his nose. He didn't bother to push them back into place. "I want that, you know."

"What?"

"That kind of earth-shaking love. That feeling that I'm with my person, that the world makes sense."

The fact of the matter was, Beckett knew he already had that with Mallory. Their friendship had morphed over the years into something burgeoning on true love. If things hadn't happened with Gram, he knew he would have told her by now. But after the heart attack, Beckett was all thumbs. He couldn't focus on his job, could barely keep himself sane while Gram neared the end.

"You'll find her, Foxy." Evan was so certain, so quick to say the right thing.

"Thanks." Beckett pondered letting the truth out now. It was high time he told Evan how he felt about his sister, how much he loved Mallory. Plus, he wasn't above using his grief as a shield. No matter his reaction, Evan wouldn't punch him on the same day as his grandmother's funeral.

Pulling in a deep breath, Beckett readied himself. "You know, Lawless, I—"

"I've been thinking," Evan interrupted, sitting up and snagging Beckett's gaze. "It's high time we got you back out there. Ever since we graduated, you've been obsessed with work."

Beckett wasn't sure where this line of conversation was going. "Yeah? It's called a career?" He nudged his buddy, well aware that Evan was in the process of figuring out his own career path. Lucky for Beckett, he'd always been into computers and numbers. Accounting came easily to him, and he liked the life it afforded him. He wasn't going to be a millionaire, but he'd be able to provide for a family. *For Mallory.*

"No, I mean we need to find you a girl. You've been palling around with me and Mal for too long. You need to get out there and find your great love. You won't find it with us."

Beckett couldn't hear much beyond the ringing in his ears. Where was Evan going with this? Did he know the truth about how Mallory and Beckett felt for each other? The rustling of the trees in the wind was the only sound around them as Beckett struggled to find his words.

"And you have a plan?" he asked, hoping to turn the conversation around.

Evan nodded, his trademark grin in place. "Oh, yeah. I say we drive up to Columbus, or even down to Cincy. Let's find some cool places and see who's out there. You can't stay here forever, man."

Beckett wanted to argue, to tell Evan there was, in fact, a lot here for him. But he chickened out. Between his father's appearance and watching Gramps grieve, he couldn't handle the emotional landmines of telling his buddy he wanted to date his sister. Instead, he took the coward's way out, certain the truth wouldn't make it back to Mallory.

"You're right, Lawless. There isn't anyone for me here." The words felt all wrong, bringing a wave of nausea. Beckett rallied, dusting his hands off and clapping Evan on the back. "Give me some time with Gramps, and then we'll find those girls. I need to get out there."

Evan chuckled. "That's the spirit. Your boy is on the case. I am ready to play match maker."

And that was when Mallory chose to reappear, her arms weighed down with a basket, her expression defeated. "Mallory." Beckett sprang to his feet, his heart plummeting down to the orchard floor.

Her expression was pinched, her blue eyes shining in the moonlight. "Here," she said quietly, shoving the basket into his hands. "Thought you might be hungry."

Evan, completely oblivious to the turmoil around him, beamed. "Thanks, Mal. You're the best." He turned to Beckett and threw fuel on the fire. "This is the type of girl you need to find when we go to the city."

Mallory turned on her heels and damn near sprinted to freedom. Beckett took a step to follow, but Evan kept talking. "Heck yes, she brought us some beers and snacks."

Beckett knew he needed to go to Mallory, needed to set the record straight. She had to know he was just bullshitting, that he had no intention of following Evan to the city to pick up strangers. That was not his style and never had been. Mallory was his style, and he had a sinking suspicion he had blown it.

But the universe had other plans. Within a month of Gram's passing, Gramps received his cancer diagnosis. Beckett's world tilted even further off its axis, and Mallory never came back. His carelessness cost him the most important person in his life, and Beckett had spent every waking moment since that damn night regretting his words, regretting his choices, regretting that he didn't run after her. Didn't take a single step toward the woman he loved.

Now fate had thrown them together again. He knew he had a long way to go in making it right, but Beckett would try. Reconnecting with Mallory was the first time Beckett felt like himself in ages, the first time he felt like he was ready to move forward. It had taken them what felt like forever to get here, but he wouldn't lose Mallory again. Beckett didn't know how to do this, but he planned on having both Lawson siblings in his life again…whatever it took.

CHAPTER 6

"You realize I'm a professional nurse, right?" Mallory asked, cradling her youngest nephew in her arms. Her sister, Emily, glowered from the other side of the living room, a permanent crease knitted between her brows. "I can show my transcripts. I got an A in neonatal care, and I'm the head nurse on the evening rotation at the ER." Holding the baby up in her arms she added, "And Tyson isn't even a preemie. He's getting so big; he'll be able to chew steak soon."

"You say that," Emily countered, "but you're not supporting his neck properly." Mallory struggled to hold back an eyeroll as her sister strode over and scooped up Tyson. She looked over her son like he'd just come back from deep sea exploration, studying every hair on his tiny head. "A baby's head is soft and not fully formed for months, you know."

Of course, Mallory knew, as did anyone who ever interacted with a baby, but there was no point interrupting her sister when she was on a roll. Dutifully, she held her tongue and kept her eyes locked on her sister, careful to avoid even a hint of an eyeroll. Emily had been a mother for nearly a year, which naturally made her an expert on all things parenting and babies. Mallory half expected to see her

59

sister pop up on a TED Talk before the end of the week on the importance of napping and balanced diets.

A few weeks ago, over family dinner, she lectured their eldest sister, Sophie, on all the ways she'd raised her children to be serial killers. "Do you have any idea what is in that yogurt?" she had asked, flabbergasted that her niece and nephew were allowed to eat dairy and breathe the same air as the cows that provided it. Sophie had made a few choice hand gestures to end that line of conversation. Mallory only wished she was the older sibling, then she would really tell Emily her thoughts on baby bone density and dairy products.

Glancing at her watch, Mallory willed Evan to show up sooner rather than later. He'd promised to swing by and see their young nephew, but also to save Mallory from another Emily lecture. Her sister caught her checking her watch for the third time in as many minutes and scoffed. "Do you have somewhere better to be?" She angled young Tyson so his pinched face could judge Mallory with all the gusto of an eight-month-old baby. "Look how upset he's getting," Emily said, her voice dripping with disdain. Tyson offered his aunt a gummy smile, his cheeks plumping with the effort.

Mallory pulled herself to her feet and plodded into the kitchen. While only two years apart, her sister had the uncanny ability to sermon at the drop of a hat. "Chill, Em. I'm just checking to see if Evan's almost here."

Tyson made a gurgling sound before closing his eyes and drifting off to sleep. Emily carefully nestled him in the crook of her arm before following Mallory to the fridge. "I'm guessing we won't see him for a while. Isn't Beckett back in town? They're probably off wreaking havoc."

Impressed with herself, Mallory didn't even flinch when Beckett's name was uttered. It was like she was completely in control of her emotions. She grabbed her phone and checked her text messages. "Ev said he'd be here for dinner. He knows you're leaving town tonight." Emily lived a couple of hours away in Indiana, but she came out to Buckeye Falls to visit Mallory and Evan whenever she could. Their oldest sister, Sophie, lived up in Cleveland and the foursome video-called weekly to catch up.

Emily eased Tyson into the pack and play that Mallory kept at her place. After ensuring her son was perfectly positioned for optimal sleep, she tiptoed back to the kitchen and joined Mallory while she diced some vegetables for a salad. "Has it been hard?" Emily asked, her voice low so as not to disturb the baby.

"Has what been hard?" Mallory sensed they were teetering on the edge of sisterly advice. It wasn't that she and Emily weren't close, but they were close in a different way than she and Evan. Emily was the middle daughter, and after taking orders from Sophie for her whole life, she was eager to share the fun with her only younger sister. Normally Mallory didn't mind, but today she feared it would drain her.

Emily tossed a bag of greens into the salad bowl before shaking a bottle of dressing. Her shrewd gaze never left Mallory's face, and her cheeks burned. "I'm going to go easy on you, because I know Evan will barge in here soon."

"Oh, boy." Mallory sighed, nearly chopping her thumb in her haste to finish dicing a cucumber. "Can we just pretend we had this talk and move onto something for fun? Like Dad's upcoming colonoscopy?"

Emily wrinkled her nose. "Eww, gross, Mal. You're about to put me off my appetite."

Mallory hip-checked her out of the way, going in search of salad tongs and hopefully a new line of conversation. "So what is hubby up to while you've been here all day?"

"Pfft, working and enjoying a few hours in a quiet house? Now knock it off and let's get down to business. How are you handling Beckett being back in town?"

Mallory had gone to a lot of trouble keeping her feelings for Beckett hidden. Sophie, bless her heart, had been oblivious to her sisters' crushes growing up, mostly because she was older and had her own matters of the heart to attend to. Emily, on the other hand, lived for this type of drama. Mallory idly wondered if that was where her love of celebrity gossip came from.

On a particularly low day in high school, Mallory had come home in tears when Beckett had asked another girl to join him at the Christmas Jubilee. They'd been dancing around asking each other for weeks, until Beckett surprised her by mentioning bringing another girl. It was clear her infatuation at that point was one-sided, and she broke down. Emily had found her in a very cliched state—eating ice cream directly from the tub and sobbing through her millionth rewatch of Kierra Knightly's *Pride and Prejudice*.

Mallory stabbed the tongs into the bowl, causing the top layer of lettuce to wilt under the pressure. "And don't mess up my salad. I need to make sure I get enough folic acid, or Tyson will grow up crossed-eyed and with a crooked spine."

"Yeah, I'm not even going there with you. Yes, nutrition while breastfeeding is important, but if you miss three pieces of iceberg, you're hardly malnourished."

"Stop stalling," Emily ordered, poking Mallory in the ribs with the blunt end of a butter knife. "Have you seen Beckett? Does he still look like Conan O'Brien's little brother?"

Finally, Mallory let loose a dramatic eye roll. "Really? You're still on that?"

Emily held up her hands and started counting down her reasons. "First, he's tall. Second, he's got red hair."

"Do you have any idea how many tall red-headed men there are in the world? I'm guessing thousands, and they don't all look like Conan."

"Beckett's funny. That's another similarity." Emily smirked, clearly pleased with herself.

"Ugh, I'm not even fighting with you about this."

"Because you know I'm right..." Emily sing-songed as she carried the salad to the table. "Quit stalling and tell me how you feel. You two have the whole will-they-won't-they thing like it's an Olympic sport."

Mallory heaved out another breath before following her to the dining room table. She set out three plates and turned to get utensils.

"Bring back another plate," Emily ordered.

Mallory ignored her sister, carrying back forks for three. Handing them out like playing cards, she said, "Now I really am going to pull the nurse card. Tyson can't have salad and chicken."

Emily flicked Mallory on the elbow, a nasty habit she'd picked up when they were girls.

"Ow," Mallory exclaimed, rubbing the spot and glaring daggers at Emily. "What the hell, Em?"

"Shh, you'll wake up Tyson. I'd like to have at least three bites of my dinner be uninterrupted."

There was a knock at the door, intruding on their sisterly bickering. "I invited Beckett," Emily said quickly. "Evan mentioned they were spending the afternoon together, and I thought it'd be nice to see him."

Another knock sounded at the door, and Mallory went pale. "Why did you invite him?"

Emily shrugged. "Because he's practically family? I haven't seen him since my wedding, and he needs to meet Tyson."

Mallory covered her face with her hands and groaned. "Why didn't you tell me? I look awful." Since she was planning for sibling togetherness, she'd worn old jeans and a tunic that hid her shape completely. She'd be more glamourous wrapped in a trash bag.

"Calm down and go change. I'll handle the guys." Emily pushed her down the hallway. "And put on a little makeup. You look tired."

"Very helpful, Em. You could have just told me you invited him." A third knock sounded from the door, and Mallory wondered why Evan wouldn't use his damned key.

Emily shoved her sister again, this time with more gusto. "My life is very boring right now. It involves a baby and a variety of bodily functions. If watching you squirm and *finally* admit your feelings to Beckett freaking Fox brings me joy, kill me."

"I very well might," Mallory countered, flicking Emily right in the forehead. "And I'm not admitting anything to anyone."

"Suit yourself, but I'm still having fun." Emily turned on her heel and ran to the door.

The last thing Mallory heard before she barricaded herself in her room was Beckett's warm voice as he cooed over the baby. "I might not make it out of here alive," she mused as she scoured her closet for something to wear. Probably something dark to cover the blood stains when she murdered her sister.

*

Mallory didn't know he was coming, Beckett mused as he took in a table set for three. Plus, their hostess hadn't made an appearance for nearly ten minutes. She was either hiding or sick, and he wasn't fond of either option.

Evan asked the question on his mind after he hugged his other sister. "Was Mal abducted by aliens or something?"

Emily flapped her hand in the direction of the hallway, clearly unbothered. "She'll be right out. I spilled salad dressing all over her."

Evan snorted. "Sorry I missed the sisterly bonding."

Peering around her apartment, Beckett saw Mallory in every detail. From the stack of gossip magazines on the coffee table to the family photos on the walls and the comforting lavender candle burning in the corner, it all screamed Mallory. Lost in his musings, he almost missed a tabby cat as it skittered across the floor and right under the sofa. "What was that?" he asked, gesturing in the general direction the beast fled.

"That's Fernando," Evan said over his shoulder, attention focused on the baby in his arms. Head dipped, he muttered something in a high-pitch voice until Tyson giggled. His buddy was a natural with kids, and Beckett knew Evan would have a big family of his own someday. A guy like that had a lot of love to give the world.

"Mal got him a couple of years ago, and I can safely say that darn cat hates anyone but her."

Beckett's heart squeezed at the notion that she finally got her own cat. It was silly really, but there was a part of him that felt better knowing she had followed through on this wish.

Emily joined them with a pitcher of iced tea. She deftly filled each glass and added a fourth plate to the table without looking up. Once her work was done, she joined them in the living room. "Fernando is all right. The trick is to pretend you don't care. Then he'll pop up in your lap and demand belly rubs."

"I've tried to rub his belly every time I come over, and all I get for my effort are scratches and snarls. And let's be honest, everyone likes me," Evan protested.

Emily couldn't stop laughing. "Ev, you literally chase that cat around until you corner it. I think your love is bordering on abuse."

Evan cradled Tyson against his chest and whispered in mock horror. "Don't say that in front of the baby."

Beckett shuffled his feet, unsure where to sit and how to act in this Lawson family tableau. This was far from his first family dinner with the squabbling siblings, but it was the first in two years. A lot could happen in two years, and judging from Mallory's absence, she wasn't thrilled at his presence.

Adjusting his glasses with his thumb, Beckett made a decision. Yes, he wanted to see Mallory and get back to how they used to be. But he also wasn't a bully, and he'd wait for her to come to him. "You know," he said, clearing past the lump in his throat. "I should probably head back to my place. You guys have some family stuff and…" he trailed off, unable to think of a reasonable lie for why he was leaving dinner before they even sat down.

"What are you talking about?" Evan asked, closing the distance between them and hoisting and now-sleeping Tyson into his arms.

Slightly panicked, Beckett fidgeted with his hands until he got Tyson into place. The kid was as hefty as a sack of sand, and his shoulders slumped from the weight of him. "What are you feeding this kid, Emily?" he teased, watching her eyes shine with pride.

"Nothing that isn't doctor approved. I'm still trying to breastfeed every—"

"Nope!" Evan yelped, raising his hands in defense. "Em, you know the rules. I want to know everything about my family, especially my niece and nephews, but I draw the line at body talk. I know you had to have sex once to make Tyson, and that is as far as I'm willing to go on the topic. Now please talk about anything else in the world."

Emily threw her head back and groaned. "You are such a baby, Ev." Reaching out, she pinched his elbow until he wiggled free. It was a patented Lawson family defense strategy, and Beckett learned it at an early age.

"I'm not a baby, I just don't want to know anything about my sisters' personal lives."

"I doubt you're this squeamish with Mal," Emily countered, eyebrow raised. "And if you're going to be ridiculous, I'm going to make you go outside so we can start over."

Evan's lips quirked at her threat.

Evan and Mallory were only eighteen months apart and were practically inseparable as kids, and still were as far as Beckett could tell. While he doubted the pair talked about hormones and their dating exploits, he assumed Evan and Mallory talked about almost every aspect of their lives. Well, except for one very big aspect. Beckett and Evan were thick as thieves, but if Evan knew he'd broken his sister's heart, Beckett would be six feet under.

As if summoning her into the room, Mallory appeared in the hallway. Her hair was styled up and off her face, with tendrils of curls spilling over her shoulders. Even from a distance, Beckett saw a rosy hue to her cheeks and a swipe of deep pink across her lips. He wanted to stride over to her, take her in his arms and kiss that lipstick away.

Instead, since he was in the land of the living, he rearranged the baby and hoped she couldn't see his pulse hammering in his neck. "Hey, Mal." Beckett lamely lifted a hand in greeting, the other arm still nestling Tyson to his chest.

"Hi," Mallory replied, her greeting swallowed up by Evan and Emily's bickering. Her blue eyes darkened at the sight of him, and he hoped he wasn't making her uncomfortable by showing up at her place. If she was angry with him, she covered it well. "I see you've met Tyson," she added, stepping closer until she could reach her nephew. Raising a hand, she gently swiped his fuzzy hair off his forehead. Never one to be jealous of a baby, Beckett suddenly wished she'd do that to him.

But, then again, he was currently holding a baby and thought spontaneous combustion was a bad idea. "Yeah," he choked, clearing past a lump in his throat. He'd seen Mallory a handful of times since coming back to town, but tonight felt different. Maybe it was because he was in her space, maybe it was the baby powder scent of Tyson between them paired with her loving expression, but Beckett had to focus on breathing.

"Please tell me these two haven't started a nuclear war out here." She pitched her head toward her siblings and sighed good-naturedly. "They'll be the death of us all."

For a moment, they stared at each other. Beckett studied her expression like he was practicing for an exam, memorizing every feature and detail for later. Her hair looked so soft; his fingers twitched to feel the strands between his fingers. He had first-hand knowledge of how silky her hair was, and if he wasn't careful, he was about to show how much that memory affected him.

After he cleared his throat again, Emily heard and

misunderstood the situation. "Goodness," she said as she walked to the table. Grabbing one of the glasses, she gave it to Mallory before scooping up Tyson. "That's for you, Beckett. Where are my manners?"

Becket felt the absence of little Tyson immediately, and apparently so did Mallory. Without a human shield between them, she backed away until her butt hit the wall. He stepped closer, not wanting to lose what little closeness they still shared. "Here." Mallory thrust the glass into his hands before falling back against the wall. She opened her mouth to say something else, but the kitchen timer dinged and she sprinted to freedom.

Dinner was delicious, and the conversation flowed well. Mallory sat in the corner, her back ramrod straight and her gaze always directed beyond Beckett's shoulder. He started to fear he was Medusa and would turn Mallory to stone if their eyes locked. Frankly, he'd chance turning to marble if he had just one minute of the old Mallory.

"Thanks for dinner, ladies," Evan said when the last of the meal was devoured. "Take this as high praise when I say it was delicious."

"Given who your fiancée is, I'll take it."

Beckett wasn't sure who knew of Evan's intentions with CeCe, but judging from Emily's expression, the cat was out of the bag. "Oh, my God, Ev!" She squealed and startled Tyson awake. His little arms flailed at his sides; his back arched in protest. Emily covered his head and cooed for a moment before continuing, "You popped the question to CeCe?"

Evan shook his head and gave Mallory a death glare. "Not yet." His words were clipped and very un-Evan-like. "I told Mal last week that I was planning on it, because I needed Nana Lawson's ring."

For a moment, the table went silent. Mallory's already downturned gaze was even more shadowed, and he didn't miss how her fingers toyed with the edge of the table cloth. Her knuckles were whiter than their empty dinner plates, her fingers curled tightly around each other.

Emily looked at Mallory, hesitating a moment before she congratulated her brother. "I know you two will be very happy together. I'm excited for you, Ev." With her free hand, she reached out and swatted Evan's arm. "Now don't keep secrets like this, because you know I thrive on gossip."

"I'll make you a deal," Evan said, leaning back in his chair and crossing his arms over his chest. "You'll be the first person I tell about my next engagement." He winked to punctuate his point and Emily made a lewd gesture in return.

Emily jostled Tyson back to sleep and asked, "So Nana's ring, huh? I didn't think that was CeCe's style."

Beckett couldn't help but agree, yet saying so would likely get his best-man status revoked. Judging from the fact that Mallory hadn't looked up to meet her sister's gaze, Beckett knew this was a complicated subject.

Evan ran a bread crust through a trail of gravy and popped it in his mouth whole. He chewed thoughtfully for a moment before continuing. "I thought about getting another ring, but with Nana's available, I thought it made sense. Plus, Nana would love CeCe."

Mallory silently stacked dishes, seemingly eager to avoid the conversation.

"I have no doubt of that," Emily said, pulling herself to standing.

"Let me help with the dishes," Beckett offered no one in particular.

The news about the ring was making him antsy, and Mallory's reaction hit him in the solar plexus. If she were truly okay with CeCe having that ring, she'd be showing it right now. A happy, excited Mallory was impossible to contain. Instead, she was sullen, gathering dishes and keeping her eyes downcast while Evan chatted animatedly about the plans to propose.

Beckett met Mallory at the sink, placing the stack of plates to her left. "You wash and I'll dry?" he offered, a familiar carry-over from his time at the Lawson household.

Mallory shrugged but didn't decline his offer. When Beckett was certain Evan and Emily weren't joining them, he got right down to business. "Did you approve Evan using that ring?" he asked, his voice low.

At first, he feared Mallory didn't hear him over the gushing faucet, but when he caught her sour expression, he knew she was playing coy. "I don't need to give approval. It's not my ring." Her hands trembled as she handed him a clean plate to dry.

Snatching her hand, Beckett squeezed. "You're allowed to speak up, Mal. It doesn't sound like Evan's particularly in love with the ring. He's more in love with putting it on CeCe's finger."

"Then that is where it belongs," she said with a huff, dropping a serving spoon into the sudsy water with a clatter.

"I don't want to upset you, it's just that—" He stopped his argument when Emily entered the room.

Tyson was in a car seat, hanging from her right arm. "I hate to eat and run, but Zach just texted that he's stuck at work and can't let Baxter out. If I wait too long, I'll come home to a puddle of pee and a cranky baby."

"Baxter is still alive?" Beckett hated asking the question, especially so rudely, but that hound was about ten thousand years old. The last he'd seen him, he could barely bark and had a white snout the color of freshly fallen snow. As children, they used to run after the Lawsons' dog until no one could breathe. That was over fifteen years ago, and Baxter was half in the grave back then.

Evan cackled, doubling over in laughter. "God no, this is Em's new dog."

Emily clapped a hand on Beckett's shoulder and smiled. "I'm touched you remember Baxter One though. He was a sweetheart."

Mallory joined them, sliding a tinfoil-wrapped package into the diaper bag. "Those are brownies for the ride home, and I threw in an extra for Zach."

70

The sisters kissed each other on the cheek before Emily leaned in and whispered something to Mallory. With a quick shake of the head, Mallory stepped back and shoved her hands into her pockets. It didn't take a genius to see the sisters were talking about the ring, and Beckett didn't blame them.

But that didn't mean Beckett wasn't going to bring it up—and the sooner the better. Like a lot of things with Mallory, this didn't sit right with him. He needed to get to the bottom of this conundrum, and fast.

CHAPTER 7

"Em looked good," Evan said from his perch on the couch, socked feet resting on the coffee table. In his haste to get comfortable, a stack of magazines teetered onto the floor. "And Tyson is adorable. I can't believe how big he's gotten."

"Geez, make yourself at home, Ev." Mallory rolled her eyes at Evan's sappy expression. Her brother was currently in love with everything and everyone, and it was starting to be a bit much.

Escaping into the kitchen, she heard Beckett behind her. Even after all these years, she recognized the cadence of his steps. Like the man himself, his steps were sure, yet quiet. "Let me help," he offered, opening the dishwasher and lining up a row of glasses. "Dinner was delicious, by the way."

Mallory clicked the dishwasher shut. "Thanks," she said on a sigh, her lower back tight after a day of work and cooking.

"Are you okay?" Beckett stepped closer, reaching out and caressing her arm. His thumb glided over her skin, working in slow circles. Goosebumps erupted everywhere he touched, and Mallory fought a shudder. On instinct, her body listed toward him, a magnet unable to stop.

"Fine, just a little tired. I picked up a shift this morning for a coworker, then Emily called to say she was coming by for dinner." Mallory covered her mouth as she yawned. "Sorry, it's just catching up to me."

Beckett furrowed his brow, causing his glasses to slide to the bump in his nose. "Evan mentioned you're working a lot. Are you overdoing it?"

Mallory shrugged. "Probably? I mean, I work in the ER. Every day is different. Somedays I come home with blood on my scrubs and a pocketful of some kid's barf, but others it's just a few head colds and minor injuries."

"That's intense," Beckett said, leaning closer still. If Mallory didn't stop herself, she could pull him closer and smell the heat of his skin, adjust his glasses, and then kiss him until the world ended. But this was reality, and her brother was in the other room, so she stayed put and focused on their conversation. The butterflies in her tummy would have to wait.

"It is, but I really like it. I think it's the variety. No two days are alike, and that's what I need."

"You were always very nurturing, so I'm sure that helps get the job done."

Mallory's expression was pinched. "I don't think I'm that nurturing." It was true she cared for her patients, but that felt like an extension of the job—the right thing to do when people were suffering or in need.

Beckett ran a hand through his red hair, causing a few strands to stick up on end. He looked like he did when they were younger, yet his boyish features had morphed into lean muscle and a striking set of cheekbones. Mallory's fingers itched to trace the new lines on his face, to memorize all the ways Beckett had matured.

"You're nurturing, Mal. C'mon." He scoffed, lowering his gaze while he hung up a tea towel. "You just made us all a wonderful dinner, played with your nephew and kept him calm when we couldn't find his teething ring, and I know for a fact that you're always checking up on Evan."

Mallory bristled, and a feeling of unease crept up her spine. "Am I bothering him when I swing by the diner? I thought it was breakfast, but if…" She rested a hand over her chest, feeling her heart kick up. Mallory has always been Evan's buddy, and she never thought of herself as cloying. Maybe her brother was ready to be left alone with his fiancée and their future? Maybe Mallory had officially become the proverbial third wheel?

Beckett peeled her hand away and cradled it in his own. "Listen to me," he hesitated until she caught his gaze. "You are not bothering Evan at all. In fact, he's mentioned that he's glad you still *want* to come over and see him. You could have a place in Columbus, be closer to work, but instead, you're here in Buckeye Falls. That means a lot to Ev, and frankly to me, too."

"Really?"

After squeezing her hand then letting it go, Beckett shoved his hands in his pockets. For a moment, he didn't say anything, just glanced around the kitchen and inventoried the mismatched towels and chipped cupboard. She wondered what he saw when he looked around. "Yeah, Mal. You're one of the reasons I moved to Buckeye Falls."

"I am?" Her question escaped on a whisper, her heart shuddering in her chest.

Changing topics and avoiding her question, Beckett asked, "Why won't you tell Evan the truth about the ring?"

"It's not my ring to keep," she muttered.

"If Evan knew you wanted it, he wouldn't use it. I guarantee it." Certainty dripped from his words, but Mallory wasn't convinced.

Mallory gently shoved Beckett back, feeling if she stayed that close for another second her skin would combust into flames. Couldn't this man see what he did to her? How even a five-minute hushed conversation sent her over the edge?

"I repeat, it's not my ring." She sliced her hand through the air for effect.

Beckett let out a long exhale before pushing his glasses back into place. "Mal, why do you insist on protecting Evan from everything? Let the man know how you feel."

"I don't protect him from things," she spat, her pulse skyrocketing.

"Yes, you do." Beckett countered, taking another step closer until their toes touched. "You always sacrifice yourself for Evan, and he doesn't need it right now. What he needs is the truth from his favorite sister."

Mallory couldn't help but falter at Beckett's admission. He knew Evan loved each of them with his whole heart, but she couldn't deny her and Evan were the closest. They shared everything with each other, except for this one touchy subject. For Mallory to admit her feelings toward the ring, she'd have to admit her feelings toward Beckett. And she sure as hell wasn't about to do that.

"Why does this matter so much to you?" she asked, hoping he had something real to say about it. More than platitudes to make her feel better. "That ring doesn't mean anything to you," she said the last part as a dare, willing him to make her girlhood fantasies come true.

You're right, Mal. I love you and I want to put that ring on your finger. Let's run away and pretend the last two years didn't happen.

Blinking back to reality, Mallory poked Beckett in the chest. "From where I'm standing, you're just trying to stir up trouble. That ring is meant for CeCe, and I'm fine with it." She lifted her chin, hoping she exuded the confidence she lacked.

Beckett licked his lips, collecting his thoughts. "That ring is yours, Mal. It has been for fifteen years."

Mallory gasped, her hand coming up to cover her mouth. Her mind whirled with potential reasons for him to say that, but she came up empty. "What do you mean?" she asked, her hand falling back to her side.

"You heard me." Beckett closed what little distance remained between them. He slowly brought his hands up to cup her cheeks, staring into her soul. "You need to stop pretending that I don't remember when I put that ring on your finger."

"I do?" she asked, completely dumbfounded, her brain now the consistency of day-old oatmeal. "But you said—" She was about to go on a tirade on all the things he told Evan, all the ways he'd broken her heart. But that time wasn't now. She already heard Evan's footfalls growing closer as he walked down the hallway.

Deftly, Beckett tipped her face down so he could plant a kiss on her forehead. "We're not done discussing this," he promised, stepping back and leaving her completely boneless. "I'll call you tomorrow." He turned and walked into the living room. "You ready, Lawless? I've got a busy morning at work and need to get some rest."

Evan shot his friend a thumbs-up before giving Mallory a quick hug. "Thanks for having us. It feels like old times."

Mallory leaned into her brother's embrace, trying to rationalize all her roiling feelings.

How could she love her brother so much and yet be unable to share her feelings about losing their nana's ring?

Even more importantly—how could Beckett freaking Fox still have this hold over her head and her heart? Did he know what he was saying with his words? Did he know how much she'd dreamt of him coming back into her life *just for her*?

"It was a great night. Thanks, Mal." Beckett leaned down to scratch Fernando between the ears, and her heart slammed in her ribcage. Her ornery cat didn't allow strangers to touch her, let alone pet like that. Her houseguests usually left with scratch marks and a healthy fear of the feline community, not gentle purrs from her hellion cat.

Evan strode out first, leaving Beckett and Mallory alone for a moment. Without looking over his shoulder, Beckett walked up and kissed her cheek, lingering a moment to whisper, "I'll call you tomorrow. Please don't shut me out."

The door closed with a snick behind them, and Mallory

fell back onto the couch with a heavy sigh. Narrowly avoiding Fernando, she didn't miss his meows of displeasure at losing his petting companion. "You'll have to get in line there, buddy," she teased the cat, giving him belly rubs for a few minutes.

After all this time, Beckett Fox had the ability to surprise and impress her. Mallory didn't know if she should give him that power or if she needed to hold on to it for herself. It wasn't that she didn't trust her heart with him again, but that she did.

But did falling for the same man again make her a romantic, or just a fool?

*

As soon as they were in the car, Evan cranked up his favorite K-Pop station and rolled down the windows. The summer heat had dwindled down to a hazy evening, and Beckett savored the feeling of the wind in his hair.

Drumming his fingers over his knee, Beckett was uncomfortable. He'd known Evan for basically his whole life, yet this was the first time he didn't know what to say. He wanted to thwack his buddy over the head and scold him for taking his sister's ring, and he also wanted to ask if he was blind for missing the way he and Mallory interacted.

Couldn't Evan see the hearts bugging out of his eyes like a damned Looney Toons character? It was all Beckett could do back there not to throw Mallory over his shoulder and storm off into the night like a Viking. The news of the ring notwithstanding, tonight had been a sheer delight. The loneliness that clung to him was nowhere to be seen, and Beckett treasured the chance to laugh and gossip with friends. Well, with friends who were his family.

There was an instant, when he held Tyson and Mallory joined them, that Beckett saw his future clear as day. He wanted a family, he always had, but he also wanted Mallory to be there. Thoughts of them together had been impossible to avoid for weeks now, but spending time doing domestic chores felt amazing. In fact, it felt so amazing that Beckett had to distract himself before he decked his buddy for taking the ring and breaking Mallory's heart.

"I was thinking about the wedding," Beckett started, striving to find the right way to bring the ring into conversation. Guys didn't talk about this stuff, so coming right out with it would be weird.

Evan nodded, his attention on the road. "So am I, and I think I have some ideas for you."

Beckett posed in the passenger's seat, tilting his head just so. "I think we should do slim fit tuxes, Lawless. I mean, they're practically made for this stunning beanpole frame."

Letting out a cackle, Evan turned onto Beckett's street and put the car in park. He turned down the music and spun to face his friend. "Good to know, Mister Supermodel. But I meant your date."

"My date?" Suddenly, Beckett feared his dinner would make another appearance. Maybe Evan wasn't as clueless as he thought.

"Yeah, I've got some ideas."

"Ideas?" Beckett nudged his glasses back into place, his pulse kicking up. Should he take his glasses off? He didn't think Evan would sock him in the car, but then again, he wasn't certain.

Evan shrugged. "Yeah. I can't have my best man showing up alone. It'll depress me."

Oh no, here they went again. Even though Beckett had never verbalized his loneliness with Evan, or really anyone, his buddy loved to play matchmaker. The only problem, he never played matchmaker when Beckett wanted him to. "I was thinking," Beckett said carefully, his brain roiling with ways to express his desire to go with Mallory. *Hey Lawless, you mind if I finally ask your sister out? I thought that'd be fun. Nothing serious, just the rest of our lives together with a house full of kids.*

"Wait a minute." Evan chuckled. "You are seeing

someone, aren't you? You old dog." He thwacked his buddy on the shoulder. "You do have a dopey look on your face. Here I thought it was just gas."

Beckett snorted. "Real nice, man."

"So who is she?" Evan raised an eyebrow, eager for the answer.

"What? No, I'm not seeing anyone. But..."

"Good. If you're not seeing anyone, CeCe and I have some options."

"Options?" Anxiety swirled through his core, his mouth going dry.

Evan ran a hand through his blond hair, a rogue curl falling back over his forehead. He always managed to look boyish and perfectly disheveled. It was probably one of the reasons he dated a lot more in high school than Beckett. The broad-chested blond guy on the baseball team was a lot hotter than a gangly ginger with glasses who tended to hide in the library or play video games and could never get beyond being the team's bench warmer. But he wasn't complaining. Beckett knew who he was and rolled with it. Besides, he could tell tonight that Mallory wasn't complaining either.

Mallory. Just thinking about her brought heat to his cheeks. Beckett was grateful for the evening lighting, otherwise, Evan would grow suspicious. He turned into a walking carrot when he blushed. If he had a nickel for every Carrot Top comparison he'd received over the years, he could have retired before graduating from college.

Evan continued, completely unaware of his inner turmoil. "CeCe has a few friends that might be good wedding dates, but of course, I haven't asked her yet since I..."

Beckett gleefully interrupted, "Since you still need to pop the question?"

"Haha. I need to find the right time. I want it all to be perfect."

This was it—Beckett's chance to say something about

the ring, or at least get Evan off his back with setting him up. "It will be perfect, Lawless. You'll find the perfect moment."

Evan scratched his chin, brow furrowed in concentration. "I think I need to propose in Buckeye Falls. This is our home. It's where all our memories are. It feels right."

"Then I think you have yourself a plan."

"I do, and we'll find you a date, Foxy." Evan unlocked the door and shot his friend a thumbs-up. "This may be a small town, but there's some cute girls."

The words burned the tip of his tongue, *I don't need to find cute girls—I've found* the *girl.* But apparently, he was a coward, because Beckett shrugged and pulled himself out of the car.

"Pop the question first, then we'll worry about the rest." He winked at his friend before closing the door. Evan honked the horn before driving back down the road, leaving Beckett with a nagging feeling in the pit of his stomach.

He needed to figure out a few things, and they all had to do with Mallory. They'd wasted so much time, and Beckett was ready to make a move and put the past behind them. But he needed to figure out the best way to tell Evan.

Having lost Gramps, Beckett couldn't handle losing the other two people that meant the most to him. Certainly a good friend would be happy for him if he and Mallory finally got together, or this could blow up in his face and he'd be no one's best man—no one's anything.

Beckett hardly slept that night, competing thoughts of the Lawson clan zipping through his head. On one hand, he wanted Mallory more than he wanted his next breath. The older he got, the more he wanted a partner by his side. Coming home to an empty place grew tiresome, and he didn't want to miss the best years of his life—the potential best years of *their* lives. Throw in Gramps's confession and dying wish, and he was about to go out of his mind.

But then there was Evan. The guy had been his best friend forever, and he couldn't stand the notion of a life without his buddy. Evan would understand, right? The man was a walking advertisement for love, so maybe this was the right time to share the truth.

Morning came with no solutions to his problems, so Beckett decided a change of scenery was in order. Sliding behind the wheel, he drove the forty minutes to the farm house. Maybe a day of manual labor would put his head straight. Perhaps strolling through the rows of trees he'd known since boyhood would shift his perspective? Or he could finally fix some of the loose boards and planks on the house? No matter what he'd do at the house, he knew he needed to be there. The memories would be painful, but the pain reminded him he was alive.

Frankly, something had to give. Beckett didn't know how much more he could take.

CHAPTER 8

"You're doing great, Mrs. Henderson," Mallory said, carefully swapping out vials while she drew the older woman's blood. It was Saturday afternoon, and the ER was a madhouse. Screaming children and the wails of those in pain echoed around her, but she was focused on the patient in front of her. When she first became a nurse, she thought she'd hear the noise. Now it merely provided a soundtrack to her career, the din blending into the beige wallpaper.

"You're so sweet, dear," the older woman said, voice shaky with fatigue. "When Gerald told me I wasn't looking right, I hoped you'd be the nurse today."

Mallory carefully removed the needle and folded Mrs. Henderson's arm up. "Keep this elevated for just a minute while I grab a bandage. How are you feeling?" She wasn't happy with the pallor of her skin, and Mallory snagged a small bottle of orange juice. "Why don't you sip on this for a moment?"

Mallory peeled a bandage off and placed it over the puncture mark. Mrs. Henderson gleefully sipped her drink and mused to her husband, "Free juice, Gerald. Isn't this just so nice?"

The older man huffed, muttering something under his

breath that sounded an awful lot like, "That juice is hardly free."

Mallory stifled a grin and handed the man his own juice. "Don't tell anyone," she teased with a wink. Turning back to her patient, she directed her on next steps before ducking back into the chaos of the ER.

Janis, one of the receptionists, met her with a stack of bedding. "We need new sheets in room seven, and the gentleman in room twelve has been asking for you since he arrived. We stopped the bleeding, but he's insisting on seeing you."

Mallory swapped her armful for Janis's and thanked her. "Is this a new patient, or the same gentleman with the head injury?"

Janis took the case of blood vials and shook her head. "No, this is a new guy. Martha tried to help him, but when he heard you were working, he asked for you."

Mallory had no idea what was going on, but she wouldn't waste her time arguing with poor Janis. The woman was the messenger, and it wasn't her fault that patients got attached. Even sweet Mrs. Henderson was a prime example. The woman had type 2 Diabetes and heart disease, coming into the hospital nearly monthly when she lost track of her medications. They'd built a rapport over the years, and Mallory enjoyed their interactions—although she wished the older woman took better care of herself.

As Mallory approached room twelve, a second thought hit her. There were patients who took their interactions as more than a nurse helping a patient. They read too much into a caring glance or a smile. She really hoped it wasn't one of those instances, because the thought of a handsy patient made her blood boil. She was too busy for nonsense today.

Pushing the door open, Mallory glanced to the white board on the wall for the patient's name before she addressed him. "Good afternoon, Mr. Fox," she said, feet faltering as she walked straight into the dresser. Spinning on her heels, she came face to face with Beckett. The man had clearly seen better days. "Beckett? Oh, my God."

Years of training suddenly forgotten, Mallory rushed to his bedside and inventoried his injuries. There were a few scrapes on his cheeks, his red hair was mussed and disheveled, and he looked exhausted. White bandages covered his left arm while his right ankle was elevated and iced.

"Hey, Mal," he said, smile crooked and eyes tired. He lifted his right hand in a wave but grimaced as soon as he moved.

"What happened? Are you in pain?" She swept her gaze up and down his frame until his cheeks turned crimson.

"It really is better than it looks. I had a bit of an accident on the farm."

Mallory eased onto the edge of the bed, taking his uninjured hand in hers and squeezing it harder than she should. "Why were you back at the farm? What happened?"

Beckett lifted a shoulder and sighed. "There's a lot I need to get ready before I put it on the market, and I didn't have plans today, so I thought I'd get cracking. Turns out that using a nail gun on a loose shutter while standing on an old rusty ladder is a recipe for disaster." He chuckled, but it was humorless.

Mallory's heart clenched. "You're not doing that alone," she ordered, shaking her head. "Evan or I will help. It's too dangerous."

Beckett groaned. "I can handle it. The realtor said there's some cosmetic fixes I should do before I sell, and I thought I'd save a few bucks."

Mallory lifted his hand to her mouth and kissed his knuckles, the movement second nature. "I'm glad you're all right." For a moment, neither of them spoke. The beeping of machines kept time with her racing heart.

"I didn't mean to scare you," Beckett said, his voice hoarse. "But when I got in the car and headed toward the hospital, I wanted to see you."

"You drove here?" she asked, aghast. It was bad enough

the man was reckless, but to drive himself was a step too far. "Let me see that," she said, pulling back far enough to see his chart. After flipping the pages back and forth, she gasped and flicked his elbow on instinct.

Beckett yelped and cradled his arm to his chest, a surge of guilt washing over her. "Oh hell, I'm sorry."

Shaking his head, Beckett coughed. "Next time, I'll drive to Buckeye Falls General."

Mallory flinched as if she'd been slapped. While a perfectly fine hospital, it was hardly the state-of-the-art establishment they currently sat in. Columbus had the funds that Buckeye Falls did not, and it showed here in the healthcare industry.

"Next time, you're bringing me to help." She couldn't be sure, but she thought she caught a smile at her inviting herself along.

"Yes, Nurse Lawson." He raised his free hand to salute, but Mallory snatched it before he could put it down.

With a steady hand, she peeled the corner of the bandage free and frowned. Glancing back at the chart, she saw one of her coworkers had done the work. While a nice person, Nurse Martha was hardly known for her tight wrapping skills. "I'm going to get this cleaned again and rewrap it. Looks like Dr. Shuptar wants to discharge you before the shift change."

"And when's that?" Beckett asked, his eyes pinched shut.

"How bad is it?" Mallory washed her hands, pulled on a fresh pair of gloves, and returned with supplies. When the old bandage was removed, she saw a quarter inch wound right through the center of his hand, black stitching holding the skin together. "Oh, my God," she wailed. "You literally shot yourself with the nail gun?"

Beckett winced. "Yes? When the ladder fell out from under me, I was in the middle of nailing the shutter into place. I guess I shot myself on the way back to Earth." He said it like it was common, to shoot a nail through your hand

86

while hanging from a second-story window.

"You're lucky you won't have permanent damage."

"That's what I said," Dr. Shuptar said as he entered the room. He pulled out a pair of glasses from his coat pocket and perched them on the edge of his nose. "Mr. Fox, it looks like the scans were clear, so you're good to go. No permanent ligament damage, and you missed all the bones. I guess if you had to shoot yourself in the hand, you did it the right way." He paused long enough to chuckle at his own joke. "Do you have anyone who can pick you up? I'd like you to rest that hand and ankle for a few days before you drive."

Mallory didn't hesitate. "I'm taking him home."

Dr. Shuptar raised a dark eyebrow, the corner of his lips twitching. "My word, Nurse Lawson. I know you are praised for your bedside manner, but this goes above and beyond."

"We're friends," Beckett said, jumping to her defense. "Mallory wouldn't just take random guys home." He paused a moment before adding, "I think." That earned him a covert elbow pinch, but he didn't seem to mind.

"My shift is done in thirty minutes. I'm happy to drive Mr. Fox home."

After scrawling a couple of notes on the chart, Dr. Shuptar took off his glasses and rested his hands on his hips. "Then you're good to go. Make sure you have someone monitor you tonight, in case you did hit your head on the way down. The scans looked clear, but with potential concussions, we like to follow a strict protocol."

"I'll spend the night," Mallory said, unable to stop the words from pouring out. Lord, she'd thought about that invitation a lot over the years, but obviously under different circumstances. Concussion watch was far less stimulating than she'd like it to be, but a girl can't have everything. Making sure Beckett lived was her top priority, her own feelings be damned.

The doctor seemed satisfied, nodding and backing out of the room. "You're in good hands, Mr. Fox."

As soon as they were alone, Mallory met Beckett's gaze. "I can call Evan, Mal. You really don't need to trouble yourself. And what about Fernando?"

Mention of her cat warmed her for a moment before she flinched at his unwillingness to spend time with her. "First of all, he's a cat and he'll survive a day on his own. And second, you obviously haven't checked your phone." She busied herself with tidying up the room, throwing out the old bandages and jotting her own notes on the chart. Her hand trembled as she documented the wound.

Beckett scoffed and wiggled his limbs. "I've been a little busy today."

Mallory straightened and sighed. "Then I guess I'll be the one to share the good news. Evan couldn't wait and popped the question this morning at the diner. I imagine he'll be a little busy celebrating with CeCe tonight."

When she'd gotten Evan's text, she truly was happy. It was a selfie of him and CeCe in the diner's kitchen, matching smiles on their faces. Held in the foreground of the picture was CeCe's hand, Nana's ring shining for all the world to see. Mallory was happy for her brother, and for CeCe. The woman had become family the minute they met, and she looked forward to having her in her life permanently. But that didn't mean she wasn't still bitter about the ring, and her own cowardice at not sharing her feelings with her brother.

"Oh, wow. Go Lawless," was all Beckett said before nudging her with his toe. "How are you handling this?"

Mallory blinked a few times, willing the tears not to fall. "I'm thrilled for them. Evan's been in love with CeCe since they met, and I cannot think of a better partner for him."

Beckett sighed. "I'm happy for them too, but that doesn't mean you can't be disappointed."

What Beckett could not possibly understand was that she was disappointed, but not only because of the ring. This engagement marked the beginning of Mallory's spinster stage. When Evan was single, it was the two of them against the world—or at least their family's meddling. Last year, her best friend Alice had faked a relationship with her current boyfriend for the same reasons, to get people off her back. Funny enough, it turned out she and James really liked each other and the rest was history.

But Mallory wasn't Alice, and she needed to figure out a way to move beyond her girlhood crush on Beckett. Unfortunately, that would have to wait until she took him back to his place and made sure he didn't die in the middle of the night from an undiagnosed head injury. *Ah, the life of a nurse...*

Mallory checked the time on the wall clock and said, "Give me twenty minutes to check in with my last patient. I'll come by to get you."

Beckett shook his head. "I can call an Uber and—"

She silenced him with a firm shake of the head. "You're not calling anything. I'm taking you home, and that's final." She turned and headed for the door before adding, "And you'll have to leave in a wheelchair. Hospital policy."

"Oh boy, a free ride." Beckett chuckled.

Mallory left, letting the door close behind her. She leaned against it for a moment, willing herself to calm down and focus on the patients who needed her. She could handle a car ride and a night with Beckett. It was purely for medical purposes, and she was a professional, dammit.

Nothing would happen, just like nothing ever seemed to happen between them. This wasn't a movie where the heroine nursed the hero back to health. This was reality with a stupid man who took a careless risk. Mallory would keep him safe, and while she was at it, she'd protect herself. There were not enough stitches in all of Ohio to close the gaping wound on her heart, and she couldn't afford to open it again. Even for Beckett Fox.

*

"Are you sure this is necessary?" Beckett asked, wiggling

89

in the wheelchair as Mallory pushed him into the fading twilight. The hush that surrounded them was in stark contrast to the chaotic melody of the ER. He couldn't believe he'd spent the whole day in the hospital.

The accident had been a careless moment, but that didn't mean he wasn't happy with the result. Well, he wasn't happy about having a hole in his hand and a sprained ankle, but he was thrilled to have some quality time with Mallory. Frankly, this seemed a small price to pay.

"Quit your whining," she ordered as she parked him at the edge of the sidewalk. She pushed her foot down on the brake and held her hand out. "Keys, please."

"What about your car?" he asked, not wanting to put her out more than she already was. Just like any other time he needed her, Mallory didn't hesitate. She offered her time, herself, freely. It was one of many qualities he loved about her.

Mallory shrugged. "I'm in staff parking, so it's free. You're probably getting charged a million dollars an hour while we argue." She wagged her hand in front of him again and added, "Keys, please."

Beckett reached into his pocket and handed her the keys. "It's the—"

"Gray Honda with the World of Warcraft bumper sticker?" She finished his thought, making him both smile and grimace.

"I swear, as soon as I upgrade, the sticker is gone."

Mallory seemed undeterred. "You're not the only gamer in Ohio, Beckett."

"Yeah, but I'm pushing thirty and don't want to look like a nerd."

Mallory blinked, her expression shifting to serious. "But you are a nerd, and I don't think you have anything to be ashamed about."

A surge of warmth coursed through him at her words, but that fire was quickly doused when she added, "And isn't Henry Cavill like a huge gamer?"

"I'll be here," he muttered, leaning back in the wheelchair and throwing his head back in the most dramatic fashion he could muster. If he looked like Superman, he probably wouldn't be driving an old beater car and be single.

A few minutes later, they were in his car and merging onto the highway. "You want to go back to your apartment or the farm house?" She gestured toward the fork in the freeway ahead of them.

Beckett quickly mulled over his options. If he went back to his apartment, there wasn't as much room. The farm house had his grandparents' bed, plus the couch in the living room. By contrast, his apartment had his new IKEA sofa and double bed. Neither of those seemed particularly appealing.

If he was being honest, Beckett wanted Mallory back at the farm house with him, even if just for the night. She hadn't seen the upgrades he and Gramps did before the cancer took over, and he wanted to show off his handiwork. Although his handiwork was also the reason they were in this mess, so she might not be that impressed.

"Um, I kind of need to make a decision here," she said, lightly tapping the brakes as their exits approached.

"Farm house," he said, hoping he wouldn't regret the decision.

He wasn't certain, but he thought he caught Mallory smiling at his directions. Maybe the house held a little magic for her as well.

The Fox family farm was nestled halfway between Columbus and Buckeye Falls. Low rolling hills surrounded the property, which used to be a sheep farm with orchards. As a kid, Beckett's father grew up sheering sheep with his father while his mother tended to groves and groves of apples and peaches. But Mike Fox wasn't cut from the same cloth as his parents. While his parents liked the quiet lifestyle, he chafed at the responsibility and bland routine.

Mike met Beckett's mother, Alison, on one of his many trips down to Cincinnati. They bonded over their shared desire to make it in the world, and quickly fell pregnant with Beckett. They were young and broke, so moving into the small guest house on the farm was their best option.

Beckett didn't have a lot of memories of his parents as a kid, mostly because they pawned him off on his grandparents every chance they got. His father took odd jobs all over Ohio to keep busy, and more importantly for him out of his family's hair. Alison was never really at home with the Foxes, but Beckett had a few memories of them together. When he was getting ready for Kindergarten, they'd played hide and seek in the orchard.

"Come on, Beckett," she'd teased, sprinting between rows of apple trees, their limbs heavy with the upcoming harvest. "You have thirty seconds to find me…"

"Should we get something to eat on the way?" Mallory asked, shaking Beckett from his trip down Memory Lane. "Or do you have food at the farm house?"

Beckett shook his head and adjusted his placement in the passenger seat. His ankle throbbed, but he was grateful it wasn't broken. "No, there's only a case of bottled water and random things. You want to get some Frizz and Freeze?"

Mallory beamed. "Oh, my God, do they still have the malt shakes with the pretzel straws?"

"Pfft, if they don't, I'm not going." Without thinking, he reached out and rested his hand over her knee. He wanted to be closer to her, to share in a memory that wasn't tainted with his parents' abandonment. Mallory didn't pull back, but her leg jerked under his touch, causing the car to briefly lurch forward. Even in the fading light, he saw a flush creep up her neck.

Parking the car right outside the entrance to the old shop, Mallory turned and pointed. "You stay put. Unless you've developed a food allergy, I know what you're getting."

Beckett smirked. "You think you remember the *whole* order?" He was goading her, but he didn't care. Back when they were kids, the three of them would ride their bikes to

Frizz and Freeze and load up on chili fries, malt shakes, and whatever else they could scarf down on their limited allowances.

"This ain't my first rodeo," she said over her shoulder as she closed the door and strode ahead.

Even in her rumpled scrubs, she was a vision. Her dark hair had been styled into a complicated braid that trailed down her spine. Beckett was sure she didn't know she was doing it, but her hips swayed as she walked, the motion far too appealing. After a quick glance around the parking lot, Beckett was relieved not to see any other men checking her out. They'd be fools not to, but he was greedy and wanted Mallory—and her swaying hips—all to himself.

Ten minutes later, Mallory appeared with two paper bags and a drink caddy weighed down with cups. He couldn't fight the smile on his lips as she opened his door and handed him one of the bags. "Don't even think about sneaking a fry without me."

"I wouldn't dream of it." He was a liar. As soon as her back was turned, he opened the bag and shoved three fries in his mouth.

In his haste to quickly chew and swallow before she got in the car, he started to choke. Mallory slid into place and pulled a cup from the paper tray. "I should have known," she chastised him. "Here's your double cherry pop with a lime twist."

The concoction was basically Diabetes in a cup. It was their house-made soda with enough sugar syrups to rot anyone's teeth. Beckett slugged down the sugary drink until his coughs subsided. "Thanks," he muttered, totally busted, lips tinged red with his crime.

"I told you," she sing-songed while pulling back to the main road. In a matter of minutes, they were driving down the farm's long driveway. "I can't wait to see it in the light. It's been ages," she said, mostly to herself.

Beckett wanted to give her the grand tour, or as much as his foot would allow. The crutches the doctor gave him rattled in the back seat, and he was incredibly grateful to Mallory for helping him home. If he didn't think the admission would cause him to burst into tears, he would tell Mallory how scared he was when he first fell. He had called out for Gramps, forgetting in the heat of the moment that no one was there for him. It felt comforting to have Mallory with him now, but he promised himself he wouldn't get used to it.

"All right," Mallory said on a sigh. "We're here." She put his car in park and opened the door. Sidestepping the fallen ladder, Mallory quickly retrieved the nail gun and tossed it closer to the house. Just as she reached the car, thunder barked overhead. She yelped before scurrying over to his door. "Let me get the crutches. I'll handle the food." Her hands shook as she handed him the poles, her face drawn tight.

"I'll get the door. It'll be okay," he promised. Mallory was tough, the bravest person he knew. But she was also petrified of thunderstorms. The last thing he wanted to do was make her anxious when she was already doing so much for him. Was already doing everything for him...

"Thanks." Her gratitude came out in a whisper, but she was fast on her feet. By the time Beckett hopped up the three porch stairs, she was on his heels with their food and her purse. A flash of lightning aided his efforts to find the keyhole, and they were inside before the first raindrop fell.

Once over the threshold, Beckett directed Mallory to the kitchen with their bounty. "I'll lock up and join you."

While Mallory plated their meal, Beckett kicked off his shoes and eased back onto the crutches. When he reached the kitchen, his breath caught at the tableau before him. Mallory had turned on the lights under the cabinets, bringing a soft light to the space. A lock of chocolate curls fell from her braid, tickling her cheek as she set out their food. Her pale cheeks flushed to a rosy hue from her sprint inside, and the color reminded him of peaches at harvest time.

If Beckett died right now and went to heaven, he was certain this was the sight that would greet him beyond the pearly gates. Gramps's words rang through his head on a loop, the chant growing louder the closer he got to Mallory.

Go get your girl… Go get your girl…

"I thought we could share the—" Her words faltered at the sound of his crutches clattering to the floor.

Before he could overthink things, before he could talk himself out of this, Beckett made his move. "I'm going to kiss you now," he said, cupping her cheeks and swiping the rogue lock of hair away with his thumb. "Is that okay?"

Mallory barely nodded before his lips crashed down on hers. She tasted like the mint of her chewing gum, bright and fresh. A tiny moan escaped her, but he swallowed it and angled her head so he could deepen the kiss. Her lips were soft beneath his, and he savored the warmth of her body as she pressed close. Hands roaming, she clutched his T-shirt and stayed flush against him. This was the best kiss of his life.

Every nerve ending was on fire, every cell in his body cheering that he was where he needed to be—here with Mallory.

A crack of thunder sounded above them, causing Mallory to flinch and pull back slightly. Resting his hands on her shoulders, he held her in place. "It's okay, just a little storm."

She nodded, bringing a hand to her mouth. Her lips were swollen from kissing, and he deflated with relief when she smiled. Just as he was about to pull her close, another sound interrupted them. His stomach growled so loudly, he was surprised it didn't drown out the rain falling on the tin roof.

"We should eat," Mallory said, making no move to pull free.

"We should," Beckett agreed, but he wasn't done kissing her yet. Starting slowly, he kissed the corner of her mouth before trailing downward toward her neck. Mallory's head fell back, exposing the pale skin and providing access to more of her—to all of her.

This wasn't their first kiss, and Beckett promised himself it wouldn't be their last. He'd finally gotten a taste of Mallory again, and much like the double cherry pop, he was far from done. He craved her, needed her in his life. Perhaps this injury provided the perfect scenario for them to reconcile. No matter what happened next, Beckett was certain of one thing.

He was going to do Gramps proud. He was going to get his girl. She was here, all he had to do was keep her.

CHAPTER 9

Mallory had a concussion. That was the only plausible explanation for the dreamscape playing out in front of her. She sat in one of her favorite places with the man of her dreams, and could still taste him on her lips. That kiss had been core-shaking, bringing her to the brink of insanity—of a meltdown. Every cell in her body was on fire and begging for more.

How was Beckett so calm right now? Not only was the world ending outside, but they were casually eating like they hadn't just made out like teenagers. God, that kiss. It was hungry and filled with years of tension and longing. That couldn't all have been one-sided, right? He instigated, so clearly he was into her.

Didn't he feel this? Was that kiss the result of too much pain meds and the adrenaline of the day? Why wasn't he spiraling down the rabbit hole like she was? Pulling her briefly from her musings, she felt the warmth of his hand in hers.

Beckett held her hand as he shoveled his second helping of chili fries into his mouth. His thumb gently caressed over her knuckles while he ate like he had been on a deserted island for centuries. And to think, just ten minutes before

97

he was devouring her like that.

She watched him, willing him to say something perfect, something romantic to prove he felt this connection between them. Instead, he turned to her and asked, "Are you going to eat that ranch dressing?"

Mallory couldn't help it, she burst out laughing. The last weeks' worth of muddled emotions spilled out of her in hysterical laughter. Beckett's grasp on her hand loosened and she pulled free to dab at her eyes with a crumpled napkin.

"What's wrong?" he asked, clearly alarmed by her outburst. His mouth hung open so wide, she could have shoved the entire bottle of ranch dressing inside.

Mallory propelled the chair back with a clatter, striding to the sink for a glass of cold water. After chugging half the contents in one go, she let out a long exhale and leaned back on the counter. Once again, he asked, "What's wrong, Mal?"

Her mouth opened to reply, but she didn't have the words. Technically, nothing was wrong. She was eating one of her favorite meals and had just had the best kiss of her life, but there was still so much that needed to be said, so much that needed to happen, before she'd feel completely at peace with their kiss.

Waving her arms around her, Mallory scoffed. "How are you not freaking out right now?"

Beckett frowned, looking outside the kitchen window at the roaring storm. "It'll blow off soon. We're safe here."

"Are we?" she shrieked. Gesturing wildly between them she added, "What did that mean?"

"Huh?" Beckett tossed his napkin on the table and struggled to stand. He attempted weight on both legs before wobbling like a toddler.

She took a step closer and gently pushed on his shoulders, keeping him seated. "Don't get up. You need to stay off your feet for a few days."

"Then you come over here and tell me what the hell is going on."

"You start," she countered, easing back into her seat and facing Beckett. She adopted her 'Nurse Lawson' face, as her coworkers called it. Her stern expression had cut through the nonsense in the ER, yet now it didn't seem to have the desired effect. She wanted answers, or at least a vague explanation to keep her from needing an overnight stay at the psych unit.

His head dipped for a moment while he collected his thoughts. When he raised his head, his glasses were crooked, matching his sheepish grin. "I'm guessing this is about the kiss and not your undying Midwestern love for ranch dressing?"

Mallory snorted. "You could say that."

Beckett reached out with his good hand, snagging hers and keeping it in a vise grip. "I hope I didn't upset you, but I had to do it."

Mallory was incredulous. After the last two years, she couldn't believe her ears. *Maybe he did have a concussion?* "You *had* to?"

Beckett gave a firm nod before soldiering on. "I had to, Mal. I don't know if it's just the craziness of today, of having you here in the farm house, or the last two years of guilt, but I can't do this anymore. I can't pretend you don't drive me crazy. I can't pretend that I don't want to be with you."

"I drive you crazy?"

Letting out a humorless laugh, Beckett squeezed her hand. "I'm so sorry about what happened after Gram's funeral."

The mention of their last time together took the air from her lungs, and Mallory had to focus on breathing. "I don't want to talk about that," she whispered.

Which, of course, was a lie. Not only did Mallory want to talk about it, she wanted to dissect every moment of that interaction. Like the archeologists who found the Rosetta Stone, she needed to decipher every detail until she was satisfied—until she understood what he was talking about.

"Tough, because I do. I'm an absolute ass. I should have

stood up for myself, for us, and told Evan to knock it off with the matchmaking. But I panicked and screwed everything up."

There they were, the words Mallory had waited two long years to hear. And the worst part was, she had no idea what to say or do about it. Swallowing hard, she wondered when this gaping void in her chest would close. It was impossible to deny that his words affected her, but she still felt there was something standing in their way.

"You don't want Evan to know about us." It was a statement, not a question.

Beckett's Adam's apple bobbed a few times as he gulped. Mallory wouldn't say a word until he answered her. She could sit there all night in the farm house's warm kitchen, surrounded by the memories of her childhood and the scents of milkshakes and burgers. If Beckett needed a century to find his words, she'd wait him out. Hell, she felt like she already had.

To punctuate her point, she pulled the last of the milkshake from her cup, the whoosh of air through the straw the only sound between them. Finally, after adjusting his glasses and muttering something under his breath, Beckett snagged her gaze.

"I want to tell Evan about us, but I want to do it right."

Mallory snorted. "What's the wrong way to tell him? Hire a pilot to write it in the sky? Take out an ad in the local paper? Do a viral TikTok?" She really was curious, as it seemed foolish to hide anything now. Everyone was an adult, or at least on paper. Hell, if Evan could get engaged to the love of his life, why couldn't she share a lousy meal with hers?

Wait a minute…she didn't mean love with a capital L, right? It was too soon to fall back into that headspace. Her heart couldn't handle that again, could it?

"Do you still have Gramps's secret stash?" Mallory asked, striding around the table toward the walk-in pantry.

Beckett's chuckle followed her as she went scavenging

for liquid courage. "Third row in the right-hand corner. Behind the cannister of oatmeal."

Mallory returned with a bottle of vodka and two juice glasses. After splashing a generous shot into each, she slid a glass toward Beckett. "To all of those who wish us well," she started, raising her glass to clink.

"And all the rest can go to hell." Beckett finished their toast and downed his vodka in one. His eyes watered, but he rallied. The nurse in her screamed that alcohol with his meds was a bad idea, but so was this entire evening, so she let it ride.

The vodka coursed a hot trail down her throat, and Mallory relished the burn. Beckett nibbled on a cold French fry for a moment before he continued, "I want Evan to know this is real." Shoving the plate aside, he added, "I want *you* to know this is real. Mallory, you're it for me. I've been an absolute idiot for years, and I'd like us to figure this out."

"You mean for real? You'd be my date to family dinners? We'd go to Evan's wedding as a couple? We eventually move in together?" Her voice grew higher with every question.

Beckett nodded, each statement making his smile bigger.

"And if it came to it, you'd want to marry me? Have a family?"

Reaching out, Beckett cupped her cheek. She worried about his injured hand, but she leaned into his touch. The warmth of his skin seeped through the dressings, anchoring them together. How had she gone this long without Beckett touching her; holding her close?

"I want all of that with you. If you'll give me a chance, I'll make it up to you."

Yeah, she needed to get to a doctor. There was no way she heard that right. "Just like that?" she asked, leaning closer so Beckett could cradle her face in both hands. The scratch of the bandages grounded her to the moment—to the potential madness.

Despite his work as an accountant, Beckett's hands were

calloused and worn, like an old pair of work boots. She loved knowing he used his hands to keep the farm house looking nice, that he wasn't afraid to jump into a situation to help. These were hands she trusted, hands she knew intimately.

His voice a low grumble, Beckett said, "It's not just like that, Mal. We've been trying this for years."

Trying—six little letters strung together for maximum impact.

"Yeah, Beckett. We have tried this forever." Unwilling to show her hand, but knowing it needed to be said, she continued. "What if we're not meant to be? What if all of these years of miscommunication were signs we aren't supposed to be more than friends?"

Beckett's hold tightened, but only slightly. "You really think that?"

Mallory shrugged helplessly, unsure what to think. It was all too much right now. Beckett's words, his proximity, the memories this old house held, everything threatened to crush her, leave her broken and begging for mercy. "I don't know what I think anymore. We're basically the human equivalent of a yo-yo."

She didn't want to be negative, but she felt she owed her heart more than a few platitudes and a milkshake. Perhaps Beckett picked up on that too, because he said, "I'll prove to you that this is the right thing. That *we're* right. I promise, Mal. I just want one more chance."

Closing what little distance remained between them, Beckett kissed Mallory. It was a sweet kiss, their lips falling into a familiar rhythm. Mallory's hands ran down his shoulders, coming to rest on his forearms. The bandage tickled her fingers, and she pulled back with a groan. "We should probably check your bandages before sleep."

"My hand is the literal last thing on my mind." Beckett laughed, and Mallory couldn't blame him. But for as eager as she was to explore this newfound connection, her heart pleaded with her to take it slow.

They had a history, and she prayed they had a future, too. Because no matter how things ended before, something felt different this time around. Maybe they were simply more mature, maybe they had nothing to lose. Either way, Mallory wanted to see where this went. She could only hope they wouldn't get lost along the way.

*

"I can make it up the stairs," Beckett said through clenched teeth. His pain meds had worn off, and he grimaced as he climbed each step. His weight was entirely on the railing, and he felt Mallory behind him. "Maybe you should go ahead of me," he suggested. The image of him losing his balance and taking her with him made his stomach sour.

"Pfft, not a chance. I'm tougher than I look." Her hand pressed into his lower back, steadying him as he progressed. His legs wobbled like a newborn calf, and he was grateful for Mallory's medical background. This was probably the least sexy he'd ever been…except maybe that horrible year of acne freshman year.

"I don't doubt it," he replied. Granted he'd only seen her in action at the hospital for a moment, but he saw how respected she was by her peers. It made him so happy that she was following her dreams and making a career for herself. Yet the dark smudges under her eyes gave him pause, the concern that she worked too hard never far from his mind.

When they reached the top of the stairs, he shuffled into his grandparents' room. The room across the hall had been his, but most of the furniture was now at his apartment. Mallory strode ahead and turned on the nightstand light. A warm glow filled the space, and Beckett eased onto the chair in the corner. "I'll get the linens and make the bed. I haven't done anything since Gramps—" but he couldn't say a word.

He hadn't been in this room much since Gramps passed,

103

and he suddenly remembered why. Sitting downstairs with Mallory over dinner, he thought he could handle anything. Things felt more certain, clearer, when she was with him. If he was honest, a tiny part of him had hoped to see the old man sitting in bed yelling at the TV, devastated that the Guardians lost another game.

But the bed was empty, stripped down to the mattress and waiting for its owners to return. Beckett didn't know if he believed in heaven, but he wanted his grandparents to be together, enjoying themselves. His gold standard for happily ever after began with them, and watching Mallory now, he hoped his own happy ending was within reach.

"The linen closet is in the hallway, right?" Mallory took a step toward the door, but Beckett stuck out his crutch to stop her progression.

"Can you, um, wait a second?"

Nurse Mallory jumped into action. "You need your pain meds. I can't believe I forgot." Before he could stop her, she bounded down the stairs and returned a moment later with a glass of water and a fistful of little white pills. "Take two of these, drink all of this, and I'll get you more within six hours."

Ever the dutiful patient, Beckett took the pills and drank the water. As he slid the glass onto the dresser, Mallory snatched his hand. He linked their fingers together and tugged her closer, but it was no use. She pulled free and rested her index finger on his wrist, counting his pulse. "I was trying to have a moment here, Nurse Lawson." He huffed, but she didn't look at him.

"You laugh," she argued, "but all I need is you keeling over. Evan would never forgive me for killing his best man." She winked to soften the blow, finally leaning down to kiss his cheek. "Any dizziness or pain in your neck or head?"

Beckett blew a raspberry with his tongue. "Mallory, come on!"

She flicked his forehead and groaned. "Are you going to be a bad patient?"

Beckett beamed. "I'm planning on besting your top patient, but first I want a kiss."

"Scandalous! I'm telling Dr. Shuptar." Mallory knelt in front of him.

Using his good hand, Beckett traced a line of freckles from her ear down to her collarbone. She shivered at the contact. "You need your rest," she protested weakly, inching closer to savor the heat of his touch.

"And so do you."

"I'll stay up here with you, but no funny business."

Beckett replaced his finger with his mouth, kissing a pattern down her neck. The tart aroma of her perfume drew him in, beckoning memories of summer berry picking and sun-kissed skin. "I've never been called funny a day in my life."

Mallory giggled. "I don't know, Emily still thinks you look like Conan O'Brien."

He couldn't help himself, Beckett let out a bark of laughter. "Wow, way to kill the mood, Mal. Here I am trying to seduce you, and you bring up my least favorite celebrity comparison." He needed this, the feeling of Mallory against his skin, the taste of her burning his lips…he craved a distraction from it all. He craved Mallory, full stop.

"You love it," she teased, poking him in the side. "How many nights did we stay up and watch him?"

"Doesn't mean I want Conan on the brain when I'm trying to woo you." He held her as close as he could without hurting his hand.

Mallory pulled back and shook her head. "You are ridiculous. We already agreed we need to take things slow."

"We will, but that doesn't mean we can't—" Another clap of thunder shook the house. A moment later, the room filled with a flash of lightning. Even in the dim light, Beckett saw Mallory pale. It was no secret that she hated thunderstorms, and it broke his heart to see her so frazzled. The woman had been through enough today.

"I better make the bed while we still have power." She

pushed to her feet and started for the doorway. Beckett watched her go, but when she returned with sheets, he panicked. No one had touched that bed since Gramps died, and he didn't think he could muster even one night tucked into the familiar space.

The last time he was in the bed, he held his grandfather's hand while he drifted away. The hospice team had been so kind, so patient while he broke down in the aftermath. Looking at the bed now, Beckett did not want to be close to those painful moments. Avoiding them was pointless, but that didn't mean he literally needed to nestle into them.

Mallory unfolded the fitted sheet, shaking the fabric apart. "Stop!" he practically shouted, startling Mallory so much she dropped the sheet.

Splaying her hand over her chest, she gasped. "You scared the hell out of me." She bent to retrieve the sheet and start again, but Beckett couldn't handle it.

"Please, Mal." His voice broke, and his eyes began to water. "I don't think I can—" His words were lost to the sob that escaped his lips. "I can't." He covered his face, knocking his glasses loose and tumbling to the floor.

Through the ringing in his ears, he heard Mallory approach. She pulled him to her in a bone-crushing hug, muttering words of encouragement as the tears fell. This was hardly the first time he'd broken down since Gramps died, but it was the first time he'd been truly comforted by someone he loved.

"We don't have to stay up here," she promised, rubbing comforting circles on his back. "If memory serves, that couch is pretty damn comfy."

Beckett choked out a laugh, his arms still tight around Mallory's waist. Their little trio had built countless forts on the downstairs couch, and right now, he couldn't think of anywhere else he wanted to be.

"Let's bring the sheets. I think it's high time we built a fort." Wiping at his eyes with the backs of his hands, he looked around for his glasses. He didn't have to squint long before he felt the frames slide over his ears. In the blink of an eye, Mallory was in sharp focus in front of him, a loving expression on her gorgeous face.

"I call the extra pillow," she teased, kissing his forehead before leading the way back downstairs, a set of sheets tucked under her arm.

By the time they reached the bottom of the stairs, Mallory had her arm around him, and his head rested on her shoulder. The only sounds were the rain on the tin roof and the distance whoosh of wind around the house. It was simultaneously comforting and life affirming.

"Thanks for coming back down here. I know you're not a fan of storms, but I couldn't stay up there."

"It's okay," she promised, steering them toward the kitchen. Dropping the bedding on the counter, she headed to the pantry. "When I found Gramps's vodka stash, I also found Gram's tea basket. How about a cup of chamomile before we build the fort to end all forts?"

Beckett shuffled to the kitchen table and took a seat, careful to prop his foot on the opposite chair. "Tea sounds perfect."

Mallory went to work putting a kettle on the stove and flitting around looking for mugs and sugar. When the tea was ready, she carried everything over to the table. After sliding a cup to his side, she closed the distance and knelt in front of him. Beckett's heart lodged in his throat at the sight of her, so relaxed in his presence. If it had been any other time, he would have her in his lap and kissing like their lives depended on it. Yet now, surrounded by the distant surge of grief that threatened to pull him under, Beckett couldn't think of a better place to be.

This all felt right to him, even down to the farm house. While they sat in companionable silence sipping tea, Beckett wondered if perhaps he made a rash decision by moving out of the old house. This felt like home more than a stuffy apartment in Buckeye Falls, no matter how close his best friend was.

Perhaps he was too hasty and it was time to come home. Then again, maybe he had suffered a head injury and was hallucinating a future that did not exist. As Mallory gathered their mugs to put in the sink he made a decision. This would not be the last time they spent an evening together on the farm. If he played his cards right, they would sleep in each other's arms like in his wildest dreams. Beckett would make some changes—he was coming home. And he was bringing Mallory with him.

CHAPTER 10

Mallory wasn't going to scream, she wasn't. She was a grown-ass woman who wasn't afraid of thunderstorms or the dark...or the churning in her gut. Nope, she could handle this. A boom of thunder sounded overhead, shaking the farm house, the vibrations coursing to the soles of her sneakers.

Beckett reached out, snatching her hand, and tugging her to this side. "We're going to lose power in a second," he warned, fumbling in his pocket with his good hand for his cell phone. By the time he turned on the flashlight app, another clap of thunder echoed overhead. Before Mallory could react, a bolt of lightning coursed through the sky. The room lit up for an instant, long enough for her to see the worried expression on Beckett's face.

"It'll be fine," she said, mostly to calm herself. She wasn't going to be a baby about this, she wasn't. When a third round of thunder and lightning hit, the house went dark and Mallory yelped.

Wasting no time, Beckett shone his phone's light around them. "Grab the sheets, Mal. I think it's time for that fort." Never releasing her hand, he hobbled to the couch and moved a stack of newspapers onto the floor with an

109

unceremonious thud. Mallory side-stepped the pile and joined him, careful to stay close enough so he didn't drop her hand. It was childish, but she'd savor any contact with Beckett.

Once they were settled, he turned off the light and opened his weather app. The blue light reflected off his glasses, which were again slightly crooked. Using her free hand, Mallory tilted them back into place without a word. Beckett was so lost in his musings he hadn't noticed. It was probably for the best, she told herself. Platonic friends don't make a habit of touching each other's faces. *They also don't hold hands or kiss passionately over cheeseburgers, and yet here we are...*

Beckett muttered a curse before pocketing his cell phone. "Looks like it's a really bad storm. That cold front is going to mess with things all night." He flopped back onto the cushion and huffed a sigh, but he still held her hand.

Mallory tucked her feet under herself and followed suit, nestling as close to Beckett as she could without being obvious. Thank the Lord the man wasn't a mind reader, otherwise, he'd probably bolt out into the heart of the storm to get away from her love-starved actions. They needed to be smart about whatever this was. It's like hiking in the woods without a map. They needed to stay on the trail or risk getting lost and eaten by a grizzly bear. Well, that wasn't the best analogy, but Mallory was exhausted.

For a moment, neither of them moved. They were as still as marble statues in a museum. Finally, Beckett's thumb traced lazy circles over her knuckles. The pattern was known only to him, but she shivered at his touch. "Are you cold?" he asked, sitting up and releasing her hand. She missed the contact instantly.

"Not really. I guess I'm still a big baby about thunderstorms." She laughed, but it sounded hollow.

Beckett stood and stumbled over to a stack of boxes by the door. It was clear he favored his good leg, and Mallory cursed her subpar nursing skills as he made his way around the room. At first, she feared he was going to run outside for something, but instead, he pulled out a hoodie and joined her back on the couch. "Here. It's one of my old college hoodies." Without asking permission, he unzipped it and draped it around her. His hands rested on her shoulders a moment longer than necessary, as if he wasn't done sharing space with her either.

"Thank you," Mallory said, covertly sniffing the fabric for any hint of Beckett. Even when they were kids, he had this warm, cedar scent that clung to him. The sweatshirt smelled faintly of detergent, and she tried not to be disappointed.

"You're welcome," he replied, his voice husky. Instead of sliding back to his cushion, he flung his arm over the back of the couch and leaned in until their legs touched. Mallory forced herself not to react, just in case he'd spook and pull away. She didn't think she could handle not having him close right now.

Call it the storm, or maybe it was just being back in this old house with him, but Mallory never wanted to leave. She was desperate to cling to whatever part of Beckett he was willing to give her until he moved on. Because wasn't that what always happened? Just when it seemed like they were on the same page, he'd up and leave town for one reason or another. In some ways she couldn't fault him. She knew she was lucky growing up in a home with siblings and parents who loved her. Granted their version of love sometimes felt cloying, but they were her family. Now with Gramps gone, Beckett really didn't have anyone. *He has you,* her traitorous heart chanted. *He's always had you.*

Resting her head on Beckett's shoulder, she asked the one question that had been on the tip of her tongue since they arrived. "How are you holding up?"

"Fine." His response was too quick to be genuine, but Mallory wasn't letting him off the hook.

"It's okay if you're not fine, you know. I know you want to help Evan with the wedding and everything, but you're allowed to grieve."

Staying silent for what felt like an eternity, Beckett finally cleared his throat. "I miss them." His voice was so quiet, Mallory could hardly hear him over the pelting rain against the window. He didn't often open up about his feelings, but when he did, it was best not to interrupt. Even the slightest distraction was an excuse to stop talking. So Mallory leaned closer and held her breath, knowing he'd fill in the gaps when he was ready.

*

The sun rose as it always did, filling the farm house with ribbons of sunlight. Bird song filled the air, proving the storm was long gone. Beckett woke with a headache that nearly blinded him and a sore ankle he'd love to forget. More importantly, Mallory was still plastered beside him. Her quiet snores mixed with the whistles from the birds, creating a symphony Beckett committed to memory.

Being back at the house was surreal. Beckett kept blinking, waiting for Gramps to saunter in from the kitchen, a can of his favorite beer in hand. Within thirty seconds of popping the top, Gram was by his side with a pot of herbal tea and a scowl on her face. "That's not good for your heart," she'd chide as she filled a mug they all knew Gramps wouldn't touch.

"C'mon, woman, it's been a day." That was always Gramps's excuse. Whether it was a good day or a bad day, the man wanted a beer with his nighttime TV watching.

Closing his eyes, Beckett rested his head on top of Mallory's. She'd nestled against him, anchoring him to the present. He couldn't lie, it was a good place to be. Sure, he wished his grandparents were here, but having his girl by his side certainly made the task of moving up bearable.

Go get your girl...

Gramps's words ricocheted through his skull on a loop, as if the old man himself were sitting with them.

112

"The only consolation is that they're together now," he muttered on an exhale. Mallory didn't react, just like he knew she would. Back when they were kids, Evan and Beckett would talk about all sorts of things. He never felt like Evan couldn't handle the heavy stuff, but Mallory would listen. Evan had the right responses, platitudes that boys told each other to get onto the next thing. Mallory would hold your hand or sit next to you while you opened a vein and shared painful truths.

The biggest truth of the moment was that Beckett was lonely. The solace he got from knowing his grandparents were reunited in the Great Beyond was tainted by the fact that he was now alone. After the funerals, his father barely contacted him. Gramps's will was iron clad, confirming everything was left to Beckett. The farm, the house, what little money remained…it all went to Beckett.

He remembered the look on the lawyer's face when he read it, surprised that their only son didn't receive a dime. For as shocked as Beckett was, his father was not. Unlike with his mother's death, Mike Fox hadn't bothered to show up. His attorney had contacted the estate's attorney, and when he learned the truth, he didn't bother coming back to Ohio.

Despite how painful their interaction at Gram's funeral had been, Beckett wanted to see his father at Gramp's. He'd hoped the shock of losing both parents would jump start a paternal gene in his father; that he'd want to come out and check on his boy. It was almost like the death of his parents freed Beckett's own father from coming back to Ohio—and Beckett still didn't know how to feel about that. Was no father better than a callous one?

In a weak moment the day before the funeral, Beckett reached out to his mom. He thought him calling would be enough for her to take it seriously, but she let his calls go to voicemail. Rather than calling her son to see how he was doing, she sent a few text messages lamenting her busy schedule with his half-brothers and step-dad. Message received; she didn't care about what her firstborn needed.

Beckett shuddered at the memory, feeling the prickle of tears behind his eyes. He really didn't want to cry right now, especially in front of Mallory. She'd seen him cry before, but he wasn't in the mood for it now.

"Morning," she muttered, yawning into his chest as she wiggled awake.

Beckett didn't overthink, leaning down to kiss her temple. The flyaway hairs from her braid tickled his nose, but he didn't care. "Good morning." He breathed the words into her skin, loving the warmth seeping into his body.

"How are you feeling?" she asked, raising an eyebrow as she flexed his hand.

It was impossible to hide the grimace as his muscles flexed and his injury woke up. "Fine," he said through clenched teeth.

Mallory made to get up, trying to push off the couch despite his arm being wrapped firmly around her shoulder. "Let me get you some pain meds and ice for your ankle."

"In a minute," he held tight and she soon gave up the fight, falling back against the couch cushions.

"You're a horrible patient," she teased, her words holding no heat.

"I'm enjoying the moment," he admitted, blinking awake and truly taking in the scene before them.

The house was half full, a mix of Gram's antique furniture and Beckett's odds and ends. He knew he needed to do more to get the house ready to sell, but that felt like a Herculean task. What wasn't a stretch was spending a few quiet moments with Mallory.

Picking up on his mood, Mallory sighed. "It's so nice being back here, but it does feel different."

Mallory was like a truth serum. Her proximity pulled honesty from deep down, regardless of if Beckett wanted to utter the words. Despite the dry eyes, Beckett couldn't keep his thoughts from pouring out. "I'm alone, Mal. They're gone, my parents aren't coming back, and I'm truly alone."

There, that wasn't so hard. He'd shared his painful truth, and now Mallory could laugh in his face and leave him to pick up the pieces. It was what he deserved, and Beckett wouldn't blame her a moment or two of schadenfreude.

Mallory took his hand and squeezed it so hard he felt her rings dig into his skin. Her fierce response was surprising but not unwelcome. "You're not alone, Beckett. You have friends, people who care."

"Pfft," Beckett snorted. "I'm hardly a social butterfly."

"That doesn't mean you don't have people in your corner." Mallory insisted.

Beckett blinked, trying to picture this spectacular social circle. His coworkers in finance mustered up enough effort to send a sympathy card when Gramps passed. Although, thinking back, one of his workers called him *Bernard*.

Granted, he had his gamer friends, virtual friendships that were hardly deep or taxing. Some of those guys had been in his internet circle since the first time he logged into World of Warcraft in high school. He enjoyed his time with that crew, but they weren't here picking apples or holding the ladder so he didn't shoot himself in the hand.

"I don't know," he grumbled.

Mallory wasn't having it. "You have Evan and most importantly, you have me."

"Do I?" He turned to face her, hoping the morning light would hide the fear in his own gaze. "Because we're friends?"

He couldn't be sure, but Mallory's expression flashed to a look of fear before she blinked and squeezed his hand again. "Yes, because we're friends, but Beckett…"

Mallory's words faltered, her eyes falling closed. She tensed beside him, and he pulled her flush against his frame. A hint of her tart perfume hit his nostrils, and Beckett had to focus on breathing. Being this close to Mallory was a new form of torture. He wanted to pull her closer and kiss her senseless. He wanted to put into action how he felt about her. He wanted everything from Mallory, and it scared the hell out of him.

"But what?"

"But…" Her explanation died on her lips when he turned her to face him. Staring at her through his smudged glasses, he was gob smacked by how beautiful she was. Even in her rumpled scrubs and limp ponytail, she was a sight to behold. Her eyes shone with concern and something else. The apples of her cheeks were pink, and her lips were plump and so kissable Beckett wanted to scream.

Why was he such a coward? Why couldn't he tell her the truth? That he was in love with her and had been for as long as he could remember. He'd been in love with her that day on the hill out back, holding her hand and seeing the future in her cornflower eyes. He'd been in love with her at the middle school dances, when they'd swayed to horrible pop music in the gymnasium. He'd been in love with her in high school, when they'd sneak out of study hall to practice kissing under the bleachers. He'd been in love with her after college, when he'd lied to his best friend and broke all their hearts. God, if only he could turn back time…

Mallory blinked and leaned forward to grab the stack of sheets at her feet. "Well, I think we should find your meds and…"

Beckett watched helplessly as Mallory went back into nurse mode and pushed to her feet.

"Let me help," he offered, but Mallory pushed him down by the shoulder.

"Nope. I'm more than capable of cleaning up a fort. I'm not that rusty." She sidestepped the couch and pulled the bedding free. In their haste to avoid the effects of the thunderstorm, Beckett had forgotten about their pile of sheets and pillows. All that he cared about was the woman under the covers…the woman pulling away from him now.

Within minutes, the couch was transformed back to its original boring state. Beckett tried to hide his frown, but it was no use. "You and Evan still do Kung-fu movie nights, don't you?" He smiled at the memory, even though he wished he'd been there. When he'd ghosted Mallory, he had lost more than just her. He missed countless memories they could have shared. It gutted him still.

"Is that even a reasonable question?" She mocked him, helping him ease back onto the pillow stack.

Beckett snaked his hand around her wrist, stopping her from retreating. "What's the rush? Sit with me." Her lips quirked at the invitation, and he was relieved that she didn't automatically say no. "My pain pills can wait another few minutes." She still didn't say anything, so Beckett went in with the big guns. "I'm lonely."

He watched her face sag as his words hit their target. "Okay, but no funny business." She wagged a finger at him before crawling back onto the couch.

Over the years, Beckett had laid awake and fantasized about this very moment. Okay, in his fantasies he didn't have a gimpy leg and a bum hand, but Mallory was always there. Now she wiggled into place, her rump grazing his torso, sending a bolt of awareness to places that need to stay calm. Now was not the time to act like a pubescent boy. *Think about baseball...*

Mallory's breathing slowed and she whispered, "I missed you, Beckett."

Before he could stop himself or think rationally, Beckett angled himself so he could see her profile. Her eyes were closed, giving him the confidence he needed. Without hesitating, he leaned down and brushed his lips on her temple. It was far from the passionate kiss the night before, but it was perfect nonetheless. "I missed you too, Mal."

Resting her head on his shoulder, she exhaled two years' worth of doubts. "What are we doing?" she asked, her question nearly swallowed up by his racing heart.

Beckett wished he was cool; one of those guys who said something suave and had women falling at his feet. But that was never him. Since he knew he couldn't give her the answers she wanted, he gave her the truth. "I have no idea."

She chuckled, angling closer to his middle as she draped

her arm over his stomach. "I can't lose you again."

"I can't lose you again either, Mal. You're too damn important."

For a while, no one spoke. As the birds carried on with their chorus outside, Mallory drifted off to sleep in Beckett's embrace. Her breathing evened out, her mouth slightly agape.

Beckett flexed his hand and rested it over her shoulder, keeping her close. "I love you," he whispered into her hair, careful not to wake her.

It could have been his imagination or the remaining medications in his system, but he thought he heard Mallory say, "I love you, too."

A guy could dream, right?

CHAPTER 11

Thin Lizzy's "The Boys are Back in Town" blasted from across the room. The chorus repeated three times before stopping and starting again. "Arg..." Beckett muttered as he flopped back over and tried to go back to sleep.

His whole body ached, but especially his hand. As he nestled back into his pillow, he got a mouthful of hair. Coughing, he opened his eyes to find a dream come true. Mallory was there, her hair a mess after a night in their pillow fort. He carefully tucked a lock of hair behind her ear before the damn song started again.

Beckett cursed the day he let Evan change his ringtone, and he made himself a promise to return the favor the next time he saw his buddy. As carefully as he could, he slid off the couch and hobbled over to his phone.

"Hey, Lawless," Beckett yawned into the phone.

"Foxy, finally!" Evan's voice boomed. "I'm at your apartment. Let me in."

Beside him, Mallory slept on the couch, her cheek smooshed against a pillow. A tiny snore escaped and his heart clenched. "Give me a sec," he said, pulling free and shuffling into the kitchen.

His ankle felt better. The swelling was down and he

could put weight on it without yelping in pain. His hand was another matter, itchy under the dressings and providing a dull ache anytime he moved it.

"Dude, are you alive? The place is dark."

When Beckett was finally out of earshot, he told Evan the truth, or as much of it as he would over the phone. "I'm not there."

"Huh? Where are you?"

Beckett stalked to the pantry for the bag of coffee beans and started his morning ritual. "I'm at the farm house. I was doing some work over the weekend and thought I'd stay." He wouldn't mention his injuries now, mostly because they weren't that bad. And he had a special helper who would ensure they didn't get worse.

"You should have said something. I could have come out to help."

Beckett snorted. "Judging from your texts, you've been a little busy. Congratulations, Lawless. I'm really happy for you."

"Thanks, man. I had this whole elaborate thing planned, but then I got caught up in the moment. CeCe and I were alone at the diner, and she was making a batch of cheesy bites and I thought it was perfect."

Beckett filled the carafe with water and clicked the machine on, eager for a caffeine fix to match his friend's buoyant mood. "Sounds perfect for you two."

"It was," Evan replied, the sound of his footfalls coming through the line. "You want me to come out to help this morning? I'm not due to the diner until dinner and don't have any contracts this week."

Any other time, Beckett would love to have Evan by his side for some chores, especially now in his current state. But Mallory was here, clad in his old college hoodie and a look of pure satisfaction. There would be a lot to explain, and he wasn't ready yet.

Their time since his accident had been magical, pretty much perfect. While he knew he needed to tell his friend, he was still afraid. Being up in Gramps's room, feeling that surge of loneliness, still clung to him, a shadow he couldn't shake free. There was a chance that Evan would hate him for dating his sister, would go into protective brother mode and shove aside a lifetime of friendship.

On one hand, Beckett wanted that for Mallory— demanded it really. She deserved to have people in her corner protecting her from life's assholes. Unfortunately, right now he felt like one of those assholes.

Mallory deserved a man who would shout their love from the highest rooftop, would tell everyone who asked who loved her and would sing her praises. Yet here he stood, hunching down and whispering into his phone like he was having a torrid affair.

"Thanks, but I'm okay."

"I don't mind," Evan countered, oblivious to his friend's inner turmoil.

"I know, but the place is a mess and I've got it. I'll pull you in when it's time to go through the old shed."

Evan chuckled, the familiar sound bolstering Beckett's decision to stay mum. "Deal, but only if you buy the chili cheese fries."

Beckett gripped the back of his neck, centering himself so he didn't think about their night in the house. He could still feel Mallory in his arms, still taste her on his lips. The last thing he needed was to get turned on while talking to his best friend. "Sure thing, Lawless."

For a few moments, they discussed mundane topics, nothing that would show his hand or his feelings for Mallory. After a moment, Evan asked, "Have you heard from Mal at all? It's not like her to miss breakfast at the diner on weekends, and no one has seen her."

"I'm sure she's fine. Probably had a hot date." As soon as the words left his mouth, he regretted them. Evan would reach out to Mallory pronto for answers, especially since he liked to get the gossip first. He may tease his sisters for their love of celebrity trash news, but he was also chomping at the bit for details when anyone had something exciting happening in their lives.

"Hot date? I don't think Mal's had a date since that loser last year."

While he figured Mallory wasn't locked up in a tower somewhere waiting on his return to her life, it felt like a sucker punch to learn she'd been out with other men. Worse, to be out with subpar men that didn't treat her right.

"What loser? The married one?"

Evan scoffed. "Naw, another douche bag. I can't remember his name, but he was a liar. Tried to sell her a bill of goods before she did some Googling and discovered he was hardly the golden boy he put on his dating profile."

"Jesus, I hope you kicked his ass."

"Tried to," Evan said with a chuckle, "but Mal told me to back off, that she can fight her own battles."

"I don't doubt it," Beckett replied, and he meant it.

"We need to find you guys good people. It kills me that my two favorite people are so unlucky in love."

You don't know the half of it, Beckett wanted to scream. "Yeah, I guess."

Evan wasn't done with his argument. A man so clearly in love he wanted to share the joy with everyone. Any other time Beckett would enjoy it, but now it felt as cloying as a peanut butter sandwich without milk. "No, I mean it. We need to find you someone, Foxy. You're a catch, and I'm sure there's a girl who will treat you right."

"Yeah," Beckett sighed.

"Now that the cat's out of the bag, let me check with CeCe. She's got some single friends out there." He paused a moment and added, "Well, not in town but out in the world."

Repeating their familiar dating conversation before coffee knocked the wind from Beckett's sails. "Lawless, don't worry about it."

"You say that, but I hate to see you by yourself." Evan's words were like a shove to the chest, and he knew his friend didn't know how true his words really were.

"I'm not alone."

"I thought you weren't seeing anyone?" Evan persisted; his normal golden retriever personality morphed into a German shepherd on the case.

"No, I'm not seeing anyone. But that doesn't mean I'm looking. When I'm ready to start dating, you'll be the first person I tell. Okay?"

"Fine, I'll drop it for now. But you need to bring a date to the wedding festivities. CeCe and I want a short engagement, so chop chop, Foxy."

"Yeah, yeah. I'll call you tomorrow." Beckett disconnected and tossed the phone onto the table. It landed with a sad thud, but he didn't care.

Just as he pulled himself to his feet, he caught the reflection of Mallory in the kitchen window. The happy, rosy demeanor from the night before was replaced with an ashen expression. "Not seeing anyone?" she asked, hands balled into fists at her sides.

Beckett blanched, feeling caught in a trap like a hunted rabbit. "Mal, come on. What was I supposed to say?"

"How about the truth?"

"What? 'Sorry Lawless, your sister's been here nursing me back to health. I hope you don't mind us fooling around behind your back for the last decade."

Mallory's gaze fell to the floor. "That's all this is to you, a little fooling around?"

"What? No, look, you didn't hear me right." He was blowing this, and somehow worse than he ever had before. "I just mean that I'm not going to break the news to Evan over the phone. I need to come up with a plan."

Mallory tossed her hands in the air and groaned. "We, Beckett. *We* should tell him together. There doesn't need to be a grand plan. Why does this need to be so complicated?"

"Because I don't want to lose my best friend, okay?"

Stumbling back, Mallory gripped the edge of the counter to steady herself. He took a step toward her, but she shook her head. "Don't touch me," she warned, and Beckett froze.

"Mal, I—"

"No, I'm done."

White-hot fear surged through Beckett as bile crept up his throat. The last time he'd felt this level of panic was their last day in the orchard, and he wasn't sure he could survive it twice. He forced himself to ask the question he didn't want to ask. "Done with what?"

"With this," she said on a sigh. It was a tired sigh, the sigh of a woman who'd been passed through the wringer one too many times. He hated that he'd been the man to make her this tired. "I'm going to go." She spun on her heels and ran upstairs. He heard the bathroom door shut before he'd made it to the base of the stairs.

Just as he started the climb on his good foot, she appeared in her rumpled scrubs. Her blue eyes shone with tears and her chin trembled.

"Mal, please wait."

His request was obviously the wrong one, as she pushed past him to the living room. She grabbed her purse and phone and shook her head. "I'm done waiting, Beckett. I'm done being your dirty secret when you have nothing better to do. I literally cannot take this anymore."

"I just need a little more time," he pleaded, running to her as fast as his ankle would allow. Pain shot up his leg, but Beckett didn't care. All that mattered at that moment was getting Mallory to stay, to hear him out.

"More time for what?" she countered.

"To—" but he didn't have the words. Any explanation sounded lame in his head, and he knew Mallory deserved it all. But how could he explain that he'd lost everyone he ever loved? If he came out about their relationship to Evan and it went badly, he'd have no one left. Mallory would never cut her brother out of her life, and Beckett wouldn't ask her to.

"You know what I think?" she asked, not bothering to wait for his reply. "I think you need to decide whose heart you're going to break. You seem to think you can't have it all, that I'm not worth the risk of your friendship with Evan. And if that is the truth"—her voice caught, breaking his heart all over again—"then tell me. I cannot do this yo-yo routine anymore, Beckett. I can't keep waiting for you to decide I'm worth the risk."

She yanked the front door open and squeezed her eyes shut. "Make sure you check your bandages twice a day, and take your meds with food." She shook her head and didn't meet his gaze before bounding down the stairs. Only then did she remember her car was at the hospital and she froze. "Let me drive you," he offered, trying to get to her before she ran away.

"I'll get an Uber," she said over her shoulder, taking the steps two-at-a-time and gaining distance between them.

"Don't be ridiculous, let me help."

Finally, Mallory spun around and caught his gaze. Even through his smudged glasses, he saw the pain in her expression. Yet again, he was breaking her heart. God, he hated himself.

"Do not follow me. If I have to walk back to Buckeye Falls, I will."

At that moment, Beckett had no doubt. "Mal, I promise I'll—"

"Your promises don't mean anything to me anymore," she said, turning away and stomping down the gravel driveway, her rumpled braid bouncing off her back. He watched her until she was out of sight, barely a dot on the horizon.

Beckett decided to listen to her request, not following her as she stormed off like a bad dream. After twenty minutes, he plodded back into the house. His appetite gone, he pulled himself up to the bathroom and took a long hot shower. Only when he was out and dressed did he see his hoodie folded neatly at the foot of Gramps's bed.

Picking it up, he sniffed the fabric and felt Mallory's warmth, smelled her blackberry scent. "Jesus," he muttered, sliding to the floor in a heap. "I made a mess of it, Gramps," he said to the empty room.

Beckett didn't know what to do. He couldn't keep yanking Mallory around like this, but he also didn't want to end up completely alone. Could it really be as simple as Mallory made it sound? Could he tell Evan the truth and the three of them move on like nothing was different?

He wasn't ready to gamble his entire future on a boyhood crush, on a fantasy made in the orchards fifteen years ago. The trouble was, as Beckett clutched the hoodie to his chest, he feared he already had. Mallory was gone, and he had no one to blame but himself. He needed to make this right, but he wasn't sure he knew how to. Gramps would be so disappointed in him.

CHAPTER 12

Over the last fifteen years, Mallory had a host of people she could lean on.

Evan.

Emily.

Sophie.

Her parents.

Beckett.

But none of them could help her now. She was angry at her brother for a situation that wasn't his fault; a situation that could have been straightened up with a little honesty. *No, Ev. Please don't take Nana's ring, the last token of my girlhood fantasy.*

She couldn't reach out to her sisters, who were busy with their own lives and families. Not to mention, they would scold her for not being upfront with their brother, who let's face it, needed to be spoon-fed details he didn't want to hear. Emily was already disappointed in her, and she knew Sophie would follow suit. Those two were peas in a pod when it came to casting judgments on their little sister.

And she certainly couldn't go to Beckett, the source of her heartbreak and unease. Were they making a mistake by sneaking around? *Probably.* Was she a total lunatic to stay at the farm and nurse him back to health? *Certainly*. Would she get her heart broken again? *Most definitely*.

After retrieving her car from work—how did anyone ever survive before rideshare apps?—she spent the day fumbling around. She avoided the diner, instead eating dry cereal on the couch while Fernando slept in her lap. She mindlessly rubbed his belly as she binged Colin Firth's *Pride and Prejudice* for what felt like the trillionth time. Maybe she should just move overseas and find her own Darcy. But then she'd have to pack and attempt to get Fernando in his crate, and that seemed like a lot of effort to be disappointed by men with accents.

When the streaming service asked, *Are you still there?*, Mallory jumped into action. She couldn't handle another moment in her apartment with her fat cat and cliched moping. She couldn't turn to family for support, but she certainly had a friend who would help her.

So as the sun hung low in the sky, she eased her car down a road she'd only traveled a few times. When she arrived at her destination, she hoped her friend would be there, because Mallory was about to lose her cool and needed a shoulder to cry on.

Checking her phone before she got out of the car, Mallory found missed calls from Beckett, a text from Evan with a meme of a cat stuck in a tree, and a photo of Tyson in the siblings' group chat. It also showed the time was too late to show up at a friend's house uninvited, yet here she was.

Mallory pulled herself from the car, walking on shaking feet to the door. She took a deep breath and rang the bell, hoping she wasn't about to get scolded for being irrational. Fortunately, she didn't have to wait long for a reply.

A bleary-eyed James Gibson answered the door, clad in his signature paint-splattered T-shirt and jeans. "Mallory?" he asked, leaning against the doorframe with a worried expression. "Is everything okay?"

Mallory let out a cackle that sounded far too demented

to her own ears. "Um, not really?" she asked, even though it was clearly a statement of fact. She was having a nervous breakdown. Sweat pooled under her arms, and a surge of heat flamed her cheeks, despite the cool evening temperatures.

Before James could finish opening the door, Alice was there. "Who's at the door?" she asked as her footfalls grew nearer.

Mallory exhaled, her knees wobbled. "Alice?" she asked, voice cracking.

"Holy crap, Mallory!" Alice exclaimed as she pushed past her boyfriend and threw her arms around her friend. "What's going on?"

James dutifully opened the door wider and ushered both women inside. "Take her to the living room. I'll get some drinks." Whether it was from nerves or concern, Mallory was grateful for his quick thinking and privacy.

By the time she and Alice were settled on the large couch, James appeared with two glasses of water, a bottle of Riesling, and a box of Oreos. "I have no idea what's going on, but I thought this would cover any situation in Buckeye Falls." He turned to leave and added over his shoulder, "if I need to call any of my connections in New York to bury a body, just let me know."

"Thanks, babe," Alice said, a smile tugging on her lips.

"You're a saint, James," Mallory added as she wiped a snot bubble from her nose. Yeah, this was truly not her greatest moment. Despite always being a fan of the artist, Mallory saw her bestie's boyfriend in a whole new light. He was truly a god among men.

Alice wasted no time pulling the cork from the wine and filling both glasses to the brim. "Before you say anything, I need to know. Are you physically hurt? I don't want to ply you with booze if you're about to have a medical issue."

"I might die of a heart attack by the time I'm done telling you this story, but the wine can only help speed up the process."

Her friend pressed her wine into her waiting hand, hiding her signature smirk behind her own glass. "Then get talking. And before you worry, there's a guest room with clean sheets with your name on it. James is on deadline, so he'll be in the studio all night. It's just us girls."

Mallory slugged back a third of her wine, then covered her mouth with a belch. "Sorry about that," she muttered. "And I'm sorry to just randomly show up here at nine thirty."

Alice waved her off and sipped from her glass. "Screw the hour, Mal. I'm worried about you. What the hell is going on?"

Rubbing the back of her neck, she willed herself to calm down long enough to form coherent sentences. Mallory felt like she was living in a carnival ride, her emotions rolling back and forth without her consent. "Remember when you came to the hospital last year? When you thought James was cheating on you?"

Alice nodded slowly, reaching for her glass to take another sip. "Yeah. Not my finest hour."

Mallory frantically gestured to her current state and snorted. "Yeah, I'm not here to judge you on that." Motioning toward the rear of the house where James's studio was, she added, "And clearly it all worked out and you had no reason to worry."

"I suspect you're telling me this so I go easy on you?"

Shoulders slumping, Mallory sighed. "Yes, please. I'm about to dump two decades of drama in your lap, and I need your help."

Alice leaned over to grab the pack of Oreos. After ripping the wrapper with her teeth, she pulled out a handful of cookies and handed them to Mallory. "Start talking," she ordered.

For nearly half an hour, Mallory let it all loose. Her and Beckett's past as friends, her ebbing and flowing feelings toward the man, his hesitations to tell Evan the truth, and her fear that she was about to risk it all for a man who wasn't going to follow through on his promises. Letting out all her frustrations felt cathartic and freeing, like taking off your bra after a long day at work.

"Good Lord," Alice gasped when Mallory finally came up for air. "Um, that's a lot."

Mallory drained the last of her glass and waved it in the air. "Yep, I'm aware. Is there any more liquid courage in this house?" She was officially the worst houseguest, showing up uninvited and then drinking a nice, and likely expensive, bottle of wine.

"I'll get your liquid courage," Alice countered, "but first I need you to drink this." She handed a water to Mallory before sliding the Oreos closer. "And I'm sure mixing wine with cookies is only making the situation worse, but go whole hog."

"You're the best."

Alice winked. "It's what besties do." For a moment, the pair sat in silence while Mallory chugged her water and Alice surveyed her friend. "I'm going to ask you a question, and I don't want to hurt your feelings."

Mallory held up her hands, curling them toward her in invitation. "Give me your worst."

Tucking a lock of hair behind her ear, Alice blinked a few times. "I'm just wondering, why haven't you mentioned Beckett before? We've been friends for over a year, and he's never come up once."

"Yeah, I'm going to need that wine now." Mallory deadpanned, grabbing a pillow and covering her face.

"You get a two-minute reprieve while I find more wine, but I'm serious. I want answers."

"That's fair." Mallory's reply was muffled under her pillow mask.

When Alice returned, she handed Mallory a fresh glass of wine and said, "I think you mentioned something when I came to the hospital last year. About your heart being broken? I'm guessing that was Beckett."

"It's always been him, Alice. Every guy I date is always

compared to Beckett. What his smile is like, is he kind to animals. Does he have glasses that never seem to stay on straight?" Mallory tossed the pillow across the living room, a sad thud the only reply. "I probably shouldn't have done that. I feel like everything in this house is worth more than my monthly rent payment."

Alice scoffed. "I got that at Frick and Frack with you over the holidays. How drunk are you?"

Mallory smiled briefly, remembering their frequent trips to the local consignment shop. "Oh, yeah. I guess it looks different when it's in James Gibson's house."

"Here we go again. You knew he was a pseudo celebrity when we started dating."

Mallory held up her finger to stop her friend. "Fake dating, I remember how that all went down."

"People in glass houses," Alice warned, but her smile betrayed her words. "I'm pretty sure keeping a secret like Beckett Fox from me is pretty comparable."

"You're right, and I'm an asshole." Mallory took a long pull from her glass, savoring the sweet punch of the wine. "And thank you for offering your guest room. I'm already half in the bag."

Alice muttered under her breath, "I'm pretty sure you're at the bottom of the bag, honey."

"Blah, I hate men."

"I know, most of them suck. But my question for you is, do you think Beckett is one of the baddies?"

Mallory wracked her brain for the answer to that very astute question. "I don't think he is, or at least that he doesn't mean to be."

"You mentioned something about his family," Alice offered, refilling both their glasses. "Do you think it really is as simple as he doesn't want to risk losing you and Evan if things go south?"

"Evan will always side with Beckett. They've been best friends forever."

Alice chortled. "Yeah, I don't think your brother will

turn his back on his favorite sister. You can spout whatever nonsense you want, but he's protective of you, Mal. As a sister with a protective brother, I promise Evan will always be on Team Mallory."

Mallory groaned and groped around for another pillow to hide under. "I don't know," she mumbled into the soft fabric.

Tapping her shoulder, Alice said, "I wouldn't be so sure. I think you *do* know, and that's why you're here freaking out."

"Damn you, Alice Snyder. Stop making sense."

"Pfft, come on. You know I'm usually the drama queen. Let me have my moment."

Mallory took a second to think, to attempt to put herself in Beckett's shoes. She trusted that he felt the same way about her that she did about him, but why wasn't that enough? They'd been tiptoeing around each other and their feelings since they were in puberty. She was tired of hiding, tired of lying, and most importantly, tired of not living the life she wanted.

"Why aren't I enough?" she asked, tears pooling in her blue eyes. She thought she'd cried herself out between binging Oreos, yet here she was bawling like a leaky ship.

Alice draped her arm over her shoulder, pulling her to her side. "Oh honey, you are more than enough. Maybe it's time to really talk to Beckett. You gave me the same advice last year, and I'd say it turned out great."

Mallory wiped at her face and elbowed her friend. "This is a really bad time to rub your hot, successful boyfriend in my face, you know."

Alice shrugged. "Oh, come on. Maybe just a little?"

Mallory chuckled, unable to hold her frown. "Fine, you can be happy. And you know I am happy for you, right?"

"Yes, but we're not here to talk about me. We're here to get to the bottom of your Beckett conundrum."

"Can't I just live here and hide away from my life for a while?"

Alice cocked her head, pretending to mull it over. "Sure. I'll just tell James to start charging you rent when the wine rack is empty."

"Deal."

Rubbing Mallory's back, Alice nibbled on her lip.

"Uh oh, I know that look. You're about to drop some wisdom on me."

"Maybe, but I had a thought."

"Hit me with it already. I need answers, and you're the only woman for the job."

Alice huffed. "What a scary thought."

"Stop selling yourself short, Ms. Future-Best-Selling-Author." She loved her friend dearly, but Mallory knew Alice could get down on herself. She was funny, accomplished, and brilliant, but that didn't stop her anxiety from showing.

"Pfft." Alice waved off her friend's kindness. "Hear me out, what if Beckett is afraid of failing you? It could be that he's so stuck in his head that he can't see the forest for the trees. He obviously broke your heart before, and it's possible he doesn't want to do it again."

"Then why kiss me? Why make promises he doesn't intend to keep?"

Alice shrugged, a very unhelpful movement that Mallory hated. "I think he does intend to keep his promise, but he knows he might lose his best friend in the process. After losing the last of his family, maybe the poor man wants to protect his heart?"

"But I don't think Evan would cut Beckett off! If we were happy, then he would be happy."

Alice raised an eyebrow, daring her friend to read her mind. "Um, if that's the case, why haven't *you* said anything to him? From where I'm sitting, you might be just as bad as Beckett with lying to your brother."

"Okay, now I need you to be a little nicer." Mallory grimaced, knowing full well her friend was right. She had no leg to stand on when it came to giving Evan the truth. Both his best friend and sister were lying to him, and it wasn't right. It wasn't how they were—the Lawsons were better than that. And frankly, so was Beckett.

"I'm not saying things with Anthony have always been smooth sailing," Alice started with a sigh, "but I know that over the last two years, we've gotten a lot closer, and that's because we're being honest." She snorted and added, "Still snarky as hell, but honest."

"I need to tell Evan, don't I?"

Alice took her hand and squeezed it. "I think you both need to tell him. But first, you need to confirm with Beckett *what* you're going to tell him. If you guys are just having a little fun, then it's probably not worth rocking the boat. But if you're serious about each other, and it sounds like you are, then sit down with him and spell it out. I'm sure you've been through more than this, and Evan will want to know."

"Dammit, you're right."

"It's surprising, I know."

James emerged from the studio, a streak of blue paint on his cheek. "Sorry to interrupt, but I'm heading to bed." He ducked down to kiss Alice on the forehead before turning to Mallory. "I'm sure Alice already told you, but the guest room is yours. I'll see you girls in the morning."

Alice swatted his butt as he walked past and shouted, "I love you."

"Love you more," he returned over his shoulder.

"God, I want that," Mallory sighed.

"Can't have him," Alice replied, poking her friend in the side until she giggled. "But you can have that with Beckett if you put yourself out there."

"I'm tired of putting myself out there," Mallory whined like a bratty child.

"Then you might have to get used to being single, my dear. I learned the hard way that nothing is worth keeping if you don't fight for it."

"I think you're right, again."

Alice pulled herself to her feet and stretched. "I know,

now let's get some sleep. Nothing you can do now except enjoy the impending hangover."

That wasn't entirely true, as Mallory lay awake for hours staring at the ceiling. Images of her past with Beckett sped through her mind at warp speed—the good, the bad, and the beautiful moments. When he kissed her at the farm house, she felt a piece of herself clink into place for the first time in years. Being with Beckett felt like being home, and she knew she had to fight for that if she wanted to move forward with him in her life.

It was all easier said than done, and Mallory knew they had to talk to Evan. Her brother meant the world to her, and she hated the notion that she was hurting him with her secrets. Yet it seemed like poor form to stress the groom out before his wedding, although the pang in her chest told her that might be inevitable. It was time to break the Beckett cycle, to decide if they were worth fighting for.

Mallory had her answer, and she could only hope Beckett had his.

CHAPTER 13

Mallory had ignored his calls and texts for a full twenty-four hours, and Beckett could not blame her. Not one bit. He was a coward of the highest order, and hated himself. The only saving grace was that he could hobble around without the blasted crutches and drive himself again. It was a small victory, but he'd take it.

Beckett's job as a virtual accountant was perfect for times like these—days when all he wanted to do was bury himself in work and hide away from the rest of the world. The sun hung low outside the kitchen window, and Beckett felt his stomach growl. Unlike his time with Mallory, he knew he couldn't survive on takeout alone. Not to mention, there was no way in hell he'd be able to stomach Frizz and Freeze until they were back on solid ground. Just the thought of it made his body revolt.

Tidying up his work, Beckett attempted to make the kitchen a kitchen again. When Gramps was on the decline, he kept his office upstairs in his room. He wanted to be close by in case the older man needed anything. Now he was downstairs hiding away from all possible memories of the past, and it suited him fine.

Well, maybe not his back. In his haste to avoid his

137

grandparent's room, he slept on the couch last night. At least when Mallory was there it was fun and cozy—and very sexy. But a guy nearing thirty couldn't pretend his back was invincible. Much like his heart, he needed to give it extra care. What a depressing reality.

The sound of gravel crunching alerted him to a visitor. Unable to play it cool, Beckett sprinted toward the front door, only to trip over one of his sneakers and tumble against the wall. Unfortunately, it was his busted hand that broke his fall, and a bolt of pain shot right up his arm. A few choice profanities later, and he was back on his feet. It was Mallory, it had to be. There was no way she wouldn't come back and check on him, right? Didn't nurses have to follow the Hippocratic oath?

"Foxy!" Evan's voice boomed from beyond the door, and Beckett grimaced. He loved his buddy, like a brother, but right now, he wasn't in the mood for sunshine vibes. He was in the mood for sulking and beating himself up. *Although if Evan knew why I was hiding out, he'd probably take care of the beating-up part...*

Beckett ran his hands through his red hair, attempting to make it look less disheveled. His glasses had a smear of ketchup on the left lens, but he wasn't worrying about that now. Throwing the door open, he was greeted to the aroma of chili cheese fries and cholesterol.

"Hey, man." Evan shoved past with a literal armload of food. "I swung by your place and saw it was still dark, so I thought I'd take a field trip."

Evan strode into the kitchen and made himself at home, pulling out plates and glasses while he set up their spread. Despite wanting anything but more fried food—and painful memories—Beckett took his seat at the table and moved a stack of files to the side. "Thanks, I was just about to search for dinner."

"I gotta ask, man," Evan said, pouring a variety of sodas and shakes into glasses. "Why not stay out here? Granted I love having you closer in Buckeye Falls, but if this is your home, you should stay."

Beckett reached out for one of the cups of pop, touched that Evan bought one of all their favorite soda combinations. Eventually their metabolism will catch up to them, but that was hopefully a decade away. "I don't know," he replied, uneasy at opening yet another wound. He himself couldn't fully explain the need to leave this house, despite the fact it was truly the only home he ever had.

No matter what happened with his parents, no matter how his grandparents passed, he'd always felt like he could come back here and feel safe, feel protected from the world. Now, with everyone gone, it felt like he was trying to wear someone else's skin.

Before he could continue his lame explanation, Evan grabbed his forearm and tugged him closer. "What the hell is this?" He wiggled Beckett's limb and frowned. "Are you hurt?"

Beckett muttered under his breath, "I guess we're doing this now." He sighed and shook his head. Turning to Evan, he said, "Yeah. I sort of shot a nail through my hand on Saturday."

Evan snorted, dropping his friend's hand and looking incredulous. "I'm sorry, what?"

Regaling Evan with the story didn't take long, especially since he didn't mention Mallory once. The impetus for his seclusion was based on the fact he couldn't mention her to Evan without turning as red as a tomato and stumbling over his words. He'd spent time with Mallory, kissed her, and held her like she belonged to him—like he'd always wanted. How was he supposed to come back to reality after stepping through heaven?

"Did you go to Buckeye Falls General?"

There it was, the out Beckett needed. He could lie to his best friend, and tell him that he'd stayed local and avoided his sister like the plague. Yet as strong as the urge to lie was, Beckett wanted to be honest. Evan was family, and he was tired of tiptoeing around the truth like it was landmines.

"No, actually. I went to Columbus."

Evan frowned. "You should have called. I could have driven you." He took a handful of fries and dipped them in ranch before shoving them in his mouth. "Did you see Mal while you were there?"

Beckett's neck grew hot as he flushed crimson. The infernal blush rose until he was practically as red as his double cherry cola. Damn his Irish heritage...

"Yeah, she was my nurse." He cleared his throat and coughed, a dribble of soda sliding down his chin.

"No way, what a coincidence."

Sure, a coincidence that Beckett orchestrated by asking for Nurse Lawson every five minutes until she finally arrived. He'd feared at one point that security would throw him out for being a creep, but he didn't care. As soon as he'd fallen off that ladder and shot himself with the nail gun, he'd wanted Mallory—and not just because of her nursing degree.

Changing topics, Evan asked, "Have you seen Mal recently? I know she picked up some extra shifts this week, but she's been radio silent for days. Even when she's slammed at work, I'll get a handful of memes about animals or some crap. Something's up."

Beckett took a huge bite of his BBQ mushroom burger, enjoying the savory tang of the sauce as he chewed. If they kept eating, he could avoid more thoughtful conversations, right? "I'm sure it's just work."

Evan wiped his hands on a wad of napkins and tossed them onto the table. "I don't know. This reminds me of a couple of years ago."

Beckett's throat tightened, and he nearly choked on his burger. "Oh, yeah?"

"Yeah. I didn't want to bother you with it back then, since Gram had just passed, but she was really down for a while. Like hiding in her apartment and eating cookie dough from the tub depressed."

What little food Beckett had managed to eat turned to

cement in his gut. He'd done that to Mallory. He'd been the one to break her heart. "It was that bad?" he asked, already knowing the answer.

Evan's head was down, studying the cooling stack of onion rings between them. "She doesn't get that like, Foxy. Mal's always the one to make us laugh and keep us on our toes. She never gave me details, but I think some asshole broke her heart. I mean, why else would she shut people out?"

"Does Mal date a lot?" Beckett knew the answer, or at least thought he did. Mallory wasn't exactly living the life of a nun, but she always was selective when it came to dating. She wouldn't spend her time with just any Tom, Dick, or Harry.

"I guess? We've always been close, so I think I know when she's dating. There was that one loser last year. They lasted about five minutes. It was the married guy." The vein in Evan's temple pulsed at the memory.

"I still can't get over that," Beckett shoved his chair back, unable to sit and listen to this story another minute. He strode into the pantry for Gramp's secret stash and returned with the vodka bottle and a pronounced limp. He'd likely march himself back to the hospital with a compound fracture at this point. Without asking, he splashed a shot into each of their pop glasses before falling back into his chair, his shoulders sagging with guilt.

Evan raised an eyebrow at his friend's reaction. "Calm down, man. I took care of it. You think I'd let any asshole get away with treating Mal poorly?"

"I guess not," Beckett said, unable to hide the fact he was pouting like a toddler. "What did you do?"

Evan smirked, the curve of his lips devilish. Evan wasn't a guy who gave brotherly enforcer vibes, mostly because he usually smiled like he'd just celebrated Christmas. But this look was a little scary, and Beckett squirmed in his seat. "I invited him to the diner and pretended I didn't know what he did. We chatted for a while and then I offered to walk him out."

"Yeah?" Beckett asked, his fingers digging into his palms.

"Then I sucker punched him in the stomach. He fell down like a sack of potatoes. I probably would have done more, but Max came out and stopped me." He shook his head, clearly upset he didn't get to finish his—clearly justifiable—ass kicking.

"Jesus, Lawless. That's awesome."

Evan shrugged. "That clown deserved more, but Max was right. It wasn't worth me getting arrested for attempted murder."

Beckett waited for Evan to chuckle, to give a sign he wasn't serious, but the edge in his jaw and the tension radiating off him proved he was still mad as hell. "I'm getting those vibes now, man. I feel helpless. Here I am, engaged to the best woman in the freaking world, and Mal's moping about some jackass. What the hell can I do?"

Clearing his throat, Beckett asked, "And you asked her what's going on?"

Evan snagged a balled-up napkin and tossed it at Beckett's head. "No Foxy, I'm taking mindreading lessons at the community college. Hopefully I can just read her mind and get to the bottom of this. Yes, I've asked her. She said she's fine, and we all know women aren't fine when they say they are." Evan drained his glass and grimaced when the vodka hit. "I guess that's the benefit of growing up with three older sisters. I've become very good at reading moods, or at least knowing when to hide from them."

Beckett's neck thrummed. A tension headache threatened to knock him to his knees. There was a pink elephant in the room, sitting between them and their melting milkshakes. The truth burned the tip of his tongue, begging to be unleashed. *Hey Lawless, funny story. Turns out I've been breaking your sister's heart for the last fifteen years. But don't kill me, because I'm going to be your best man.*

Shaking his head, Evan pulled himself to standing and

collected empty plates. "Let's change the subject. I didn't come over here to be angry and depressed. I came to help with the house and talk about my *fiancée*." He put extra emphasis on the last word, his signature grin sliding back into place.

"I don't need much help with the house tonight," Beckett said, putting the leftovers in the fridge. "But I'm sure there's wedding stuff I should be doing? Have you guys set a date yet?"

Evan wiped down the table and gestured toward the living room. "Let's sit by the window. I love watching the sunset from the front of the house."

Beckett said a silent prayer of thanks that he'd had the forethought to put away the pillow fort he and Mallory built. Granted he'd slept in that fort like a lovesick loser, but self-preservation won out in the nick of time. The Lawsons were well known for their pillow forts, and Evan would recognize his sister's handiwork. *At least I have a set of crutches ready for when Evan breaks my legs...*

Evan flopped down on the far side and draped his arm over the back of the couch. Beckett took the other end and propped his busted foot onto the coffee table. "So, what's the plan?"

"We're thinking a short engagement."

Beckett didn't know the first thing about engagement periods, but short sounded good to him. The idea of years of wedding planning made him antsy. "Sounds reasonable."

"Yeah, I mean, we're still young, but we're thinking about the future. We want to get a house and have kids, and it seems foolish to wait."

The weight of his statement settled around the friends, and Beckett felt his eyes sting. There had never been a doubt that Evan would be an excellent family man, but that always seemed so far ahead in the future. Yet now, he was spitting distance to living the American Dream. "Wow, Lawless. I'm really excited for you guys."

Evan reached out and flicked Beckett's elbow, causing

143

him to yelp. "Thanks, Foxy. But let's not get all emotional about it. I already cried on the way over here, so I should be good until tomorrow." He winked before settling back on his side of the sofa. "What I will need help with is an engagement party."

"I love a good party." Beckett waggled his eyebrows.

"We're thinking lowkey, honestly probably at the diner. We just want our immediate family and close friends there. Nothing too fancy, just really good food and the people we love."

"Sounds perfect to me," Beckett said, meaning every word. Being a man, he'd never obsessed about the perfect wedding day. The more he thought about that fact, the more he realized it was because he'd already had the perfect wedding day. It was intimate and sweet, just the woman he loved and his best friend.

"Dude, are you okay? You're as white as a sheet."

Beckett waved off his friend's concern. "Absolutely. I think it was too many onion rings. I hate to say it, but I might be getting too old for that much fried food in one sitting." He rubbed his belly to illustrate his point, and fortunately, Evan bought it.

"Well, I won't take up your whole night. I'll text the dates we're thinking, and I thought you and Mal could help me with the planning."

"Of course." Beckett tried not to get too excited over the prospect of seeing Mallory again, especially since it meant she couldn't avoid him for all eternity.

Evan pulled himself to his feet, pausing for a moment to watch the sunset outside. The sky had turned orange and pink, like someone had left rainbow sherbet out to melt. The colorful light cut through the rows of apple trees, still bearing fruit despite being ignored for the season.

"God, it's gorgeous here."

"No argument here."

"You should get married here," Evan said, his smile infectious. "We're going to find you a nice girl and you'll live here and then our kids can be friends."

"Probably need to find a date to your engagement party first, Lawless. Maybe there's someone in Buckeye Falls." Beckett hoped his voice wasn't shaking. It was as if Evan had jumped inside his brain and found the truth. *Maybe he had taken mindreading classes?*

"Pfft, yeah right. The only ones I can think of are married or Mallory. And we all know that'd be a terrible idea."

Beckett froze, unable to hold back his follow-up question. "And why is that a terrible idea?"

Evan was incredulous. "Um, are you serious?"

Unable to stop himself, Beckett puffed out his chest. "I mean, now I am. You don't think I'm good enough for your sister?"

"I'm not saying that, but I think it's a horrible idea. I can't have my best friend and sister fooling around. When you guys break up, I'd have to pick sides, and that sounds terrible." He chuckled, clearly not picking up on Beckett's inner turmoil. "I'll find you someone for the wedding. Don't worry about it. You won't have to resort to taking Mallory. I know you guys used to be each other's backups, but we can do better."

"If you say so," Beckett mumbled, following his friend out into the cooling evening air. "Say hi to CeCe for me. Tell her if she wants to change her mind, I'm still available."

Evan threw back his head and laughed before flipping him the bird and getting behind the wheel. The sound of his favorite K-Pop station blasted from the open window as he drove back to the woman he loved.

Beckett could barely get himself back inside before he collapsed onto the couch and covered his face. There had been his chance to tell Evan the truth, and he'd blown it. Worse still, Evan made it perfectly clear how he felt about Beckett and Mallory together. In fact, it was crystal clear. Perhaps this was the universe telling him to give it up. Pack up the farm house and figure out his next move. He'd be damned if he lost his friendship with Evan.

Judging from what Evan said, he already blew it with Mallory. Beckett hadn't felt this low in months, and he yearned for just five more minutes with Gramps. The old man's advice would go a long way now, especially since his directive was too simple. Beckett couldn't just get the girl, he needed to get a time machine.

CHAPTER 14

After a week of not hearing from Beckett, Mallory's curiosity got the better of her. He'd stopped texting and calling after three days of being ignored, and she couldn't blame him. Yet she herself hadn't come to a decision on how to move forward. Evan had happily informed her of the impending engagement party and his expectations for her and Beckett to plan it. She needed to find a way to talk with him that would not drive her up the wall with nerves.

As luck would have it, Beckett was due back for a follow-up appointment for his wound, and she decided to take matters into her own hands—literally. Mallory cornered Janis at her desk when she arrived for her shift. Did she put a little extra effort into her appearance? Maybe. Did she hope Beckett would notice? Definitely. Did she think this was a fool's errand? Hell yes.

"Hey, hun," Janis greeted from her perch, four different pens stuck in her up-do. Since it was the beginning of her shift, she was involved in a complicated array of spreadsheets.

Janis was a little older than Mallory and had fallen into the older-sister role on the job. She looked out for Mallory, but also knew when to have a little fun. They were overdue for a drink after work, and Mallory made a mental note to not close herself off again. Having friends was important, no matter her dating status.

"Hey, Janis. Can I ask a favor?" Mallory held a clipboard with the day's schedule and a hopeful expression.

At her words, Janis looked up and blinked. "Someone is all dolled up today. Did I miss your birthday?"

Mallory laughed. "No, just thought I would wear a little makeup." Any by a little, she meant mascara, lip liner, and some highlighter she borrowed from Alice. Her chocolate hair was braided into a complicated twist that gathered in a halo around her crown. Compared to her normal top knot and chapstick, she looked like she was ready for the prom. *I'm an idiot,* she mused.

"Well, you look lovely. What can I do for you?"

Mallory warmed at Janis's compliment and brandished the clipboard. "There's a patient coming in this afternoon for a follow-up from last weekend. I see that Nancy is listed as helping Dr. Shuptar, but I was hoping you could swap our bookings. It's Mr. Fox at four o'clock." She offered a smile that probably looked more deranged than friendly, but Janis didn't seem to notice.

"No skin off my back." Janis clicked away on her screen for a moment before turning around and retrieving a stack of papers from the small printer at her desk. "You mind updating everyone's clipboards? The digital calendar is set."

"You're the best, Janis." Mallory greedily took the sheets and spun around on her heels. Before she ran away, she hastily added, "You want to grab a coffee next week after a shift?"

Janis winked. "Sure thing, hun. That'd be nice." Mallory was three paces away when she added, "Unless you're busy with Mr. Fox."

Busted. Mallory stifled a giggle and ran to her first patient of the day.

Her first patient was an elderly man with a nasty cut on his arm from a "complicated fight with a lawnmower." It took her and another nurse nearly an hour to stitch him up and stop the bleeding. Next it was a little girl who had shoved twelve peas up her tiny nose. Her mother was scolding her in between tears, but the girl only shrugged. "I was trying to beat my record. Last week it was only ten." She held up her chubby hands to count her progress. Before her lunch break, she helped with a horrible automobile crash that looked like a scene from an episode of *ER*.

By the time Beckett's appointment rolled around, Mallory felt her makeup deserved an industry award for staying power. Although her braid required a few extra pins, she was externally as ready as she would be. The exam room door was closed with a red tag hanging from the handle. It was the hospital's way of alerting staff that a patient was inside. After taking another long breath, she knocked on the door and stepped inside.

Beckett was seated on the exam table, his long legs dangling from the edge. Much like herself, he'd put a little work into his appearance. His red hair was slicked back, his glasses were clear of smudges, and he wore an Oxford shirt that looked like it had seen an iron in the last week.

At first, neither of them spoke, the only sound in the room that of the door snicking shut behind her. Mallory held her clipboard to her chest like a shield. "Hi," she said simply, unable to think of any other words in the English language.

Beckett raised a hand in greeting. "Hey."

"Hi," she repeated, feeling like a first-class moron. These two shared decades of history, and all she could muster were repeated one-word greetings. *This is going really well...*

"I'm glad it's you," Beckett hurriedly added. "I mean, I wasn't sure if you would want to see me. I contemplated fixing the shutters again, but I thought with my luck I'd fall to my death." He snorted and rolled his eyes, shoving his glasses up his nose. Even with the distance between them, she could see a thumbprint from where she stood. She felt better knowing he was this nervous. It was a good sign,

149

right?

"I don't want you falling to your death," she added, shaking her head. "Obviously."

"That's good." Beckett nodded, wiggling around on the exam table, the sound of crinkling paper echoing in the tiny room. "How are you?"

"Pfft, I should be asking you that question. Any swelling, discoloration, pain, or joint issues?" This was safe, medical questions were safe territory.

Beckett frowned. "Mal…"

"Because we should be mindful of any signs of infection or permanent damage to your hand."

"I don't care about my hand," he said, color rising in his cheeks. "I didn't come here for my hand." He held it up for her to see, the bandage gone and a small Band-aid in its place. He flexed his fingers to prove his point. "I came here to see you. I'm not kidding. If you weren't here, I would have borrowed one of the crayons from a kid in the lobby and shoved it up my nose." He chuckled at his own joke and Mallory wondered if the little girl with the peas had moved on to bigger challenges.

"Beckett." Simply saying his name brought her pulse skyrocketing. Despite everything that happened last weekend, she missed him deeply. Since having him back in her life, every day without him felt hollow and boring, like a mozzarella stick without the cheese.

"I want to talk about the engagement party."

His words drew her back a step, bringing her crashing down to earth. "You want to talk about Evan and CeCe's wedding?"

Beckett held up both his hands. "No! Crap, this is not coming out right at all."

Before he could continue, Dr. Shuptar came in. A man in his late forties, he was no-nonsense but also kindhearted. "Sorry to keep you waiting, Mr. Fox. Let's look at your hand. I appreciate you coming in. Since you don't have your primary care physician set up, we like to have a professional

150

stay on top of wound care." Glancing up from this tablet, he caught the expression between Mallory and Beckett. "Is everything okay?"

Dr. Shuptar had helped another nurse the month before with a very grabby patient who misunderstood the request of "I need you to take your top off" as an invitation to take off all his clothes. He'd handled the situation beautifully, managing not to humiliate the nurse but also keep everyone safe.

Fearing that was where his mind was going now, Mallory blurted out, "Beckett is not a pervert."

Both men looked at her like she'd sprouted another head, and frankly, she wished she had. Perhaps a second brain would help her out of her current conundrum. "Huh?" Beckett asked, his cheeks flashing his trademark red. If the situation didn't improve soon, he'd probably be admitted for a flushing problem. He was as red as a tomato.

Dr. Shuptar's lip quirked and he shook his head. "Noted. I'll update Mr. Fox's file."

Beckett scratched the back of his neck. "Am I missing something?"

Mallory wheeled over a stand with examination tools and turned up the lights. "Just erm, standard hospital documentation." Now it was her turn to change colors, her face flashing an unflattering shade of violet. Maybe she'd get lucky and the ground would open up and swallow her whole.

Five minutes later, Dr. Shuptar confirmed that Beckett's hand had, in fact, healed nicely. His ankle was also on the upswing, barely swollen under his socks. He was given basic care instructions and discharged. "Come back and see us if you run into any other issues, and I recommend hiring professionals for those home improvement projects." The doctor smirked and left them alone again.

As soon as the door was closed, Beckett jumped off the exam table and strode toward Mallory. "Beckett's not a pervert? I guess I'm relieved to hear that."

Mallory peeled off her rubber gloves and tossed them in the trash. "I thought it was worth noting."

"Was it a real concern?"

She nearly felt guilty for the look on his face, but then she remembered their last interaction and shook away the guilt. "You wouldn't believe some of the characters that come to the ER. Sadly, it's worth noting when patients aren't Ted Bundy."

Beckett took a step closer, shoving his hands in his pockets as if he was afraid to get too close. "Sometimes I really worry about you, Mal. Are you safe here?" His eyes were unblinking, a pensive expression on his freckled face.

Mallory warmed at his concern but soldiered on. "Yes, as safe as anyone is anymore. The hospital has great security, and all the doctors are receptive to our concerns when we have them."

"That's something at least," he muttered. He kicked at the tiled floor, scuffing his shoe.

An alarm sounded outside their room, and Mallory knew it was all hands on deck. "I have to go. That's a code red." She threw the door open and took a step before she felt Beckett's hand on her shoulder.

"Have dinner with me tonight." It wasn't a question, and she wished she had the time to dissect this new expression on his face. Was that hope she saw through his crooked glasses?

"I—" Alarms rang all around them, and Mallory cursed her job of saving lives. Right now the person in dire need of medical attention was her.

"Please, Mal."

Nurses and doctors raced past them, and Mallory had to move. "I don't know if I have time to come out to the house."

Beckett shook his head. "I'm back at my apartment. Stop by whenever you're off work, I'll be there."

"Nurse Lawson!" someone shouted beyond them, and Mallory reluctantly pulled free of Beckett's hold.

"I get off at six, but that's only if this isn't pure chaos."

"Whenever you're ready. I'll be there."

Mallory offered a quick tip of her head before she turned and ran toward the admissions area. As horrible as the scene was that greeted her, she was relieved to have a reprieve from Beckett—and his touch. Even his fingers grazing her shoulder had burned her like a branding. Her heart told her to stay away from him, to keep things platonic and focus on the wedding planning. But there was something about his tone, something about the soft expression behind his smudged gaze that drew her back in.

Once again, Mallory was powerless to stop the pull to Beckett Fox. At least she worked with one of the top medical teams in the Midwest. Perhaps it was time to find a cardiologist to address the issue of her erratic heart.

*

When Beckett got back to his apartment, he immediately slumped onto the couch. The apartment was nice, or nice enough, but after spending so much time back at the farm house, he wondered what the hell he was doing. It wasn't that he was past his grief, far from it, but being back at the old place wasn't as painful as he thought it would be. Granted there was a five-foot-four distraction with chocolate braids that helped, but she wasn't there now.

But she would be here soon, and that was something.

Understanding that they couldn't live on takeout alone, Beckett had stopped by the market for a few things to make dinner. He chopped vegetables for a salad and got the fixings for French bread pizza together. Was this a ploy for Mallory to lower her guard? Absolutely. Was he ashamed of his methods? Absolutely not. If the nostalgia of bread and cheese made her smile, he'd make it for her every day of his life.

When dinner was prepped and ready, Beckett's watch told him he still had an hour until her shift was over. Unable to focus on the television, he booted up his laptop and logged into World of Warcraft and kicked up his feet. Getting lost in a world of magic and warriors felt like a vacation right about now.

His gaming buddy WickedWarri0rBr0 was on, and Beckett typed out a message.

FoxyMage96: *Hey man, got time for a quick raid?*

WickedWarri0rBr0: *For you, Foxy, of course.*

Beckett's lips quirked as the nickname, knowing this stranger and Evan had never met. There was something to be said for having connections like this one, anonymous people who shared a hobby and generally kept the drama low. There were no expectations—save from keeping each other's characters alive—and that was what Beckett loved about it.

When his parents divorced, they'd bought him a gaming console as a consolation prize at the end of his childhood. Within hours of logging into his first game, Beckett was hooked. As a pre-teen boy with a newfound distrust of the world, being able to kill faceless enemies made him feel alive. What he didn't expect, and to this day still enjoyed, were the online friendships. WickedWarri0rBr0 was just one of the guys he'd met along the way, and he felt like a virtual version of Evan. Although there was one big exception— Evan didn't know he was in love with Mallory.

WickedWarri0rBr0: *What's your plans tonight? Can't imagine a single guy wants to spend all night on WoW.*

FoxyMage96: *You'd be surprised. I only have an hour. A friend's coming over for dinner.*

WickedWarri0rBr0: *A friend or a* friend. He helpfully added some NSFW emojis, causing Beckett to snort.

FoxyMage96: *I wish, man. She's really just a friend.*

But even as Beckett typed the words, he knew they weren't true. Mallory had always been more, and it was becoming impossible to pretend otherwise. His life made sense when she was in it, and not just as the sidekick to his and Evan's shenanigans.

WickedWarri0rBr0: *Uh oh, please tell me it's Mallory.*

FoxyMage96: *And what if it is?*

WickedWarri0rBr0: *Then I say log off right now and get ready, dude. When I met my wife, I did everything I could to impress her. Flowers, food…clean T-shirts. Once I even wowed her with aftershave.*

FoxyMage96: *LOL. Wow, you're a prince among men.*

WickedWarri0rBr0: ::king emoji::

FoxyMage96: *Already have dinner prepped. I'm not a total slouch.*

WickedWarri0rBr0: *What's the plan? You going to tell her how you feel?*

FoxyMage96: *Yeah, because that's gone well in the past.* ::laughing while crying emoji:: ::face palm emoji::

WickedWarri0rBr0: *Not to get all philosophical on you, but love is a lot like this raid we're on.*

He paused long enough to kill a dragon, helping Beckett cast a spell on another incoming foe.

WickedWarri0rBr0: *You need to put the work into it and trust your partner. Tell her you're all in, and then go from there.*

Beckett frowned, knowing his buddy spoke the truth. But offering platitudes was a hell of a lot easier than putting your heart on the line with the woman you'd shattered before. Their relationship had always been about timing. When one of them was all in, the other wasn't. Or worse, they were chicken and too afraid to commit. Needless to say, Beckett was the chicken in this scenario.

FoxyMage96: *Appreciate the advice, man. I better log off and get ready.*

WickedWarri0rBr0: *You've got this, Foxy. Just being your charming self. If that doesn't work, cast a love spell.* ::winky face emoji::

FoxyMage96: *I'll do my best.*

Beckett logged off and tidied up the apartment. It was sparsely decorated, but at least it was neat. He wasn't much for a cluttered space, until the clutter meant something. Gram's old sugar bowls and tea pots filled the farm house with a cozy warmth, but they would look ludicrous on his

155

IKEA bookshelf.

Idly, he wondered if Mallory wanted them. She'd always enjoyed tea parties with Gram as a girl, and it would make Gram happy to know they were getting used and loved instead of spending eternity in storage. Much like himself, but he wasn't going there now.

Twenty minutes later, he heard a quiet knock at the front door. Beckett checked his appearance on his phone before jogging to the door. His glasses, for once, were clean and his hair was as tame as his curls would allow. Not wanting to appear too eager, he'd opted for jeans and a T-shirt. Swinging the door open, he was knocked back on his heels by Mallory. She'd changed since the hospital, wearing a pair of leggings and a curve-hugging blouse that his fingers itched to unbutton. *Real gentlemanly, Foxy.*

"Hey," Mallory said with a wave, a timid smile on her lips.

"Hi." His response came in a husky whisper. The fading sunlight cast Mallory in a glow that looked better suited for his videogames than the real world, golden flecks popping in her hair. Gripping the door handle, Beckett tried to think of unsexy things like baseball or taxes—anything to keep himself in check. They had to talk, then he'd kiss the hell out of her.

Mallory held up a bottle of wine. "I brought wine."

Good, liquid courage was good. "Good," he stammered, feeling like an idiot. How had they ever managed full conversations over the last fifteen years?

"Good," she replied, blinking at him like he'd officially lost his sanity. "Um…" She held up the bottle, waggling her eyebrows. "How about you invite me in and we have some?"

Muttering a curse, Beckett stepped back and let Mallory pass. Her signature blackberry scent followed her into his apartment, and his knees nearly buckled. He needed to get a grip, and fast.

Becket led the way into the kitchen and pulled out a

chair. "Have a seat. I'll get the cork screw."

Mallory giggled. "No need. I went fancy and got a twist top." She punctuated her point by opening the bottle and dropping the cap with a clatter to the table. "I assumed this low rent Pinot Noir goes with French bread pizza," she said casually.

Beckett grabbed a pair of glasses before bumping into his chair. In his haste to sit, Mallory had to catch the bottle as it threatened to tip over. "Am I that predictable?"

Mallory smirked. "I'm not saying it's a bad thing." She poured the wine and handed him a glass. Their fingers grazed, and Beckett felt a jolt of awareness bolt through him. That was always how it was with Mallory, simmering heat that followed him like a shadow. "To your clean bill of health," she toasted.

Beckett dutifully clinked glasses. "We're not sending people to hell tonight? How boring."

"The night is young, and this is only our first glass." She gave him a look he needed the Rosetta Stone to decipher. Her blue eyes sparkled, like she was in a joke and he was the punchline. Mallory's shoulders were relaxed, her legs crossed and posture casual. She seemed at home with him, and he could feel it in his bones.

"Should I put our predictable dinner in the oven? I made a salad too, just to throw you off your game." He winked, hoping it looked more flirtatious than squinty.

Mallory sipped and nodded. "Yes, please. I missed lunch today, and I'm about to devour this stack of napkins."

"How bad was that code red?" he asked, busying himself with finishing dinner. When Mallory tried to stand to set the table, he gently pushed her back into her chair. "And don't even think about helping. How was work?"

For a moment, she didn't respond, and he had to turn around to make sure she was listening. A funny expression flitted across her lovely face before she recovered and took another sip. "Well, it was a multi-car collision from 70. Fortunately, everyone made it, including the staff. When there's that much chaos, that much noise and adrenaline, I almost fear one of us will pass out from the stress. But we always rally, support each other. It's a good team, and I'm lucky to be there."

Beckett diced a tomato and added it to the salad bowl before joining her at the table. "I think you're pretty amazing, handling that kind of work day in and day out. You're a superhero, Mal."

"Pfft, just doing my job."

Beckett slid her salad to her, taking a moment to linger. Cupping her cheek, he tilted her head up and snagged her gaze. "Don't do that," he ordered.

"Do what?" she asked, her voice barely audible.

"Diminish your career, how hard you work. Very few people can handle that kind of stress, let alone thrive in it. You're amazing."

"Oh." It was all she could manage, her mouth forming the letter as she leaned into his touch. His thumb slid over her bottom lip, which was tinged a plum purple from the wine. He passed his thumb over the plump skin again, this time rewarded with a quick nibble.

Beckett's knees gave out, and he knelt before her. Mallory swiveled in her seat until they were facing each other. She mussed his hair, her hand sliding down until it rested on his shoulders. "What are we doing?"

Beckett closed the distance and swallowed her question. He didn't have answers, but he did have an undying need to taste the wine on her lips.

The kiss was hungry, frantic. Mallory pulled him closer, grasping his shirt in an unforgiving fist. Beckett cupped her face and deepened the kiss. Her lips tasted like a mix of her cinnamon gum and the spicy wine. A tiny moan escaped her, and Beckett felt his skin combust.

The truth was, he had no idea what they were doing, and he didn't care. Having Mallory back in his space, sitting in his tiny kitchen doing the most mundane routine of any couple, he couldn't fathom life without her. He wanted to hear about her days every night over a bottle of wine. He wanted to support her, laugh with her, love her like she deserved. But right now, this kiss was more than enough, and judging from the way Mallory clawed at him, she was enjoying the moment too. That was enough for Beckett, at least for the moment. He had bigger plans, plans that included their current activity every day.

CHAPTER 15

You came here to talk!
You came here to talk!

You came here to talk... Mallory's brain chanted as she yanked Beckett closer. His long legs banged into the table, but she didn't care. Judging from the animalistic growl as he trailed kisses down her neck, he didn't care either.

This felt amazing, this felt like home, this felt like a mistake. They had so much to talk about, and kissing him without a care felt wrong. She would put a stop to this as soon as dinner was ready.

The oven timer beeped, cutting through their lust-filled moment. "Dinner's ready," Mallory breathed, anchoring Beckett in place as he stumbled.

"Yeah," he said in a daze, his mouth swollen from their make-out session.

The oven beeped again until he got to his feet. As he pulled out two of the most gorgeous pieces of pizza she'd ever seen, she was happy they paused for food. It was truly a testament to her love of nostalgia that she didn't jump on Beckett again, but her growling stomach won the argument.

Beckett plodded to the fridge and came back with two types of ranch dressing. "Being a good Midwestern boy, I

161

have two ranch options for you this evening." He brandished the bottles like he was a sommelier tempting her with the season's newest merlot offering from France. "Tonight for the lady, we have a spicy ranch from the Hidden Valley or a regular ranch," he faltered for a moment, biting back a grin, "also from the Hidden Valley."

Mallory tapped the second bottle. "I'm afraid I'm a bit boring."

Beckett dipped down and planted a kiss on her temple. "Mallory Lawson, boring? Hardly."

Sliding into his seat, the pair devoured their meal. Mallory truly was that hungry, but she also wanted to get back to the good stuff. And by good stuff, she meant Beckett's lips. Those lips were currently smirking in between bites. "Do I have a string of cheese on my face or something?" He made a show of swatting at his face, like there was a fly attacking him.

Mallory gestured at her own face. "You have a little something here," she said, pointing to her chin. "And here," she added, pointing to her forehead. "And maybe a little sauce over here." She leaned forward and poked at his glasses with her napkin.

"Oh, wow!" He exclaimed, splaying a hand over his chest. "Beckett Fox has something on his glasses? Alert the media."

It was a poorly kept secret Beckett had been battling eye glasses for most of his life. No matter the situation, no matter the frame, they always ended up smudged, cockeyed, lost, or broken by the end of the day.

"I take it the contacts are still a no go?"

Beckett scoffed, trailing his pizza crust through a puddle of ranch dressing. "Um, have you met me? You know I hate touching my eyes." He shuddered like Edward Scissorhands was his optometrist.

Mallory laughed. "Have you tried since that last time in high school?"

She remembered the day well. She'd shown up at lunch

162

at their usual spot. Evan was talking to someone who looked like Beckett's alien clone. His gray eyes were cloudy, and he kept blinking like he was about to cry or throw up. Beckett cringed at the memory. "Yeah, a couple of times over the years, but it's always the same result. Within three hours, one of them miraculously pops out, and the other gets stuck like it's setting up shop. By the time I get my glasses back on, I'm an emotional wreck."

Mallory covered her mouth to hide her smile, still charmed by this man. "Well, I like your glasses. Frankly, they're as much a part of you as your red hair."

Beckett was incredulous. He reached out to snag her forgotten pizza crust and popped it in his mouth. "That's exactly what men want to hear," he said around the dough, "Red heads with glasses are stone-cold foxes."

Mallory raised an eyebrow in challenge. "That's what I see. You're suddenly going to inform me otherwise?"

Beckett gulped, nearly choking on the stolen crust. "Are you trying to kill me?"

"Potentially. We haven't actually talked about our future, so it's a distinct possibility."

After grabbing the wine bottle, Beckett topped off both their glasses before leading the way to the living room and the comfort of the couch. "If we're going to decide our futures, I at least want to be comfortable."

Mallory followed, trying hard not to stare at his backside in those jeans. She failed, miserably.

Despite wanting to talk, Mallory's gut churned. It was fun playing house, sitting in the kitchen while the man of her dreams cooked and kissed her like she was more important than oxygen. In those moments, these stolen slices of time, she pretended they could have this. She pretended that Beckett wasn't afraid, that he would be brave for her—for them.

Mallory plopped down on the couch, hugging her wine glass to her chest for protection. Beckett sat on the edge of his cushion before jumping to his feet and pacing in front of her. "I can't do this," he muttered, running his hands through his curls.

The meal that only moments ago filled her with joy turned to cement in her belly. "Can't do what?" she asked, taking two long pulls from her glass before thinking better of it. She couldn't get drunk if she needed to make an escape.

Sensing her confusion, Beckett stalked to her and knelt in front of her. He took her glass and put it on the coffee table with shaking hands. "I can't lie anymore, Mal. I can't stand this. Aren't you going insane?"

"Right now, yes," she agreed, wondering what the hell this man was going on about.

Beckett gently gripped her by the shoulders, his gaze sharp behind his lenses. "Mal, I want us. I'm sick of pretending that I'm not—" He stopped himself but didn't loosen his grip.

"Pretending that you're not what?" Mallory's breath hitched, fear a sharp knife over her throat. Was he going to end whatever they had right now? Was inviting her over just a means to go back to friends? She would keep Beckett in her life anyway she could, but it wasn't what she wanted.

"I'm sick of pretending that I'm not in love with you, Mallory."

He hadn't called her Mal, that was the first thing that registered in my muddled brain. Not the "L" word, not the hungry, yet desperate, look on his handsome face, but the fact that he didn't use her nickname.

Throat closing with all the words she wanted to say in response, Mallory was at a loss. "You love me?"

"Yes, for about a million years."

Mallory felt both heavy with dread and light as a feather. "But what are we going to do about it?" They'd done this dance before, mastered the steps until one of them was left alone and hurting, the other having stomped on their hopes for the future.

"I want us to date." Beckett suggested so freely, so easily, she wanted to laugh. Or vomit, she hadn't officially decided.

"You want us to date?" Now it was her turn to be incredulous. "Beckett, I'm pretty sure you've said this before. What about Evan?"

Throwing her brother into the conversation was tantamount to dousing a grease fire in water, things only got scarier and a whole lot messier. "Our feelings don't seem to matter when it comes to coming out to my brother."

"Our feelings," Beckett clarified. "You feel the same way?"

Mallory rolled her eyes and threw her head back in a cackle. "Really, Beckett? You really don't think I love you?" Recovering, she reached out and flicked him on the forehead. "You're an idiot."

Beckett covered the sore spot but smiled. "True, but you're the one in love with an idiot." That earned him another flick before he could dodge away. "Ow."

"You're going to keep getting those until you tell me how we're going to do this."

Hope flashed in Beckett's eyes. "So you're in?"

"Yes, of course, I'm in."

Beckett reached out and tucked a lock of hair behind her ear. "It was the pizza, wasn't it? I knew I'd pull you in with the promise of unlimited cheese and bread."

"You certainly know the way to my heart, you goofball." Mallory kissed Beckett, sweetly and with all her heart. Their lips grazed each other as a feeling of utter contentment washed over her. This felt so right, but she knew they still had work to do. Pulling back, she broke the kiss on a sigh. "We need to tell Evan. I can't keep pretending I like hiding, of being hidden." Her admission cost a lot, and she hoped Beckett realized how much she'd been hurting since his Gram's funeral.

"The engagement party is in two weeks," Beckett started, licking his lips as he continued his plan. "I know I'm weak, but I don't want to upset Evan or stress him out." Mallory couldn't necessarily disagree, but she thought

Beckett might be selling her brother short.

"You think he'd be that upset, and what? Call off the wedding?"

Now it was Mallory's turn for a flick, right on the shoulder. "No, but I don't want to steal anyone's thunder. Us showing up as a couple in front of your sisters and parents will draw attention away from Evan and CeCe, and I don't want that. I want our moment to be our moment, and theirs to be theirs."

"Dammit, you have a point." Just as Beckett started to look too arrogant, she added, "Finally."

"We'll still go to the party as each other's dates, but it'll be as friends."

"You're telling me you want to test the waters?" Mallory asked, her expression pinched. "I hate to state the obvious, but haven't we already done that?"

Beckett ran a hand down his face, knocking his glasses off. Mallory's reflexes were quick, and she snatched them before they could clatter to the floor. "I know this is ridiculous, but hear me out. In a matter of months, this will all be over." Sensing she misunderstood what he meant, he quickly added, "I mean the wedding stuff. Let's go on dates, real ones in the meantime. And we'll go to the engagement party and wedding as each other's dates."

Mallory toyed with the edge of his collar, rubbing the cotton between her fingers as she thought. "But you really want to date me? You want to come to my place and vice versa?"

"Yes, Mal. I want to date you. I want to parade you around town on my arm. I want to get matching outfits for the party, and I want to hold you in my arms while we dance at the reception."

With a snort, Mallory let her hand drop. "Matching outfits will not be required, but I'm liking the sound of the rest of this."

But there was one big issue they needed to address. "Beckett, what happens if you tell Evan and he's upset?

You've always said his friendship is too important to lose."

Beckett let out a breath, but he didn't back away. "He's the closest thing I have to a brother. It would hurt to lose him, but it's worth the risk. Frankly, I can't keep doing this with you, Mal. I can't keep pretending I don't want to spend every waking moment with you. As soon as they're married, we're going to go public. I want the fanfare, and I want you."

It was everything she'd wanted to hear, but she was still nervous. She trusted Beckett and could sense his words were based on contemplation and planning. He was working his way toward a future that hopefully had it all.

"Let's do it," she said, closing the distance to seal their ridiculous plan with a kiss.

"You mean it?" Beckett asked, tracing a line down her cheek until his hand rested over her heart. "I love you, Mallory. I want to make this a reality."

And it was all she wanted too. Mallory had waited forever for Beckett Fox. Surely she could wait a few more weeks.

CHAPTER 16

It had been a whopping twenty-four hours since Beckett and Mallory agreed to secretly date—a term that Beckett both loved and loathed. After they cleaned up dinner, they cuddled on the couch, watching a random Netflix documentary. When Mallory yawned and made to get up, Beckett pulled her back down to the couch.

"Yeah, I don't think so," he grumbled, kissing her temple and imprinting her scent to his memory. "You're spending the night."

Mallory melted into him, humming her approval of the invitation. "I'm not complaining, but how do you know I don't have to work?"

Beckett wasn't about to be a creep and admit he'd memorized her schedule, so instead, he said, "Lucky guess?"

"Uh-huh." She nestled further into his arms and fell asleep in a matter of minutes. Beckett couldn't think of anything better than this. Mallory in his space—literally in his arms—and nowhere they needed to be. He would do right by her, he would. They'd find a way to tell Evan that would salvage everything; he wouldn't lose anyone else that he loved.

Their current tableau reminded Beckett of their earliest

farm house sleepover. Beckett invited Evan for a regular sleepover, no big deal. But when Mr. Lawson arrived with his son, they had a stowaway. "You don't mind if Mallory tags along?" he'd asked Gramps, already handing the older man his daughter's pink duffle bag.

"Not at all. The more the merrier." Gramps had slung that bag over his shoulder and reached out for Mallory's hand. "C'mon in, sweetheart. I think Beckett's Gram is finishing up some cookies."

And that had been that. Mallory would cook and bake with Gram, and then run around with him and Evan. They'd build forts in the living room, play hide and seek in the orchards, and watch scary movies until someone screamed. As they grew older, Mallory continued to follow Evan on his playdates to Beckett's, and whenever Beckett would hang out at the Lawson house, Mallory wasn't far behind.

There had been so many little moments as kids, and especially as teenagers, that stacked up into this moment now. Mallory belonged with Beckett, and he'd known that since their first kiss in the orchard, the first time they shared a cookie fresh out of the oven, the first time he went to find her first instead of Evan.

They'd shared all their important firsts together, and now, Beckett was ready to be Mallory's last. He didn't want her doing this with anyone else, and the thought of another woman in his arms made him flinch. They had to figure this out, they just had to.

Mallory stirred, rolling over to face him on the couch. "We should probably go to bed," she said, her voice coated in sleep. "No funny business," she warned as she stumbled to standing.

Beckett rose and guided her toward his bedroom, his heart racing. "I'm a complete gentleman."

Mallory leaned into him, his arm wrapped around her waist. "I know, and sometime in the very near future, I won't ask you to be."

Her words caused his footsteps to falter, and he walked

right into the doorframe, stubbing his toe. "Oof." He grunted, leaning down to rub his bare foot.

Instantly slipping into nurse mode, Mallory knelt to get a better look, all traces of sleep gone. "Let me see," she ordered, peeling back his fingers, exposing a red welt. With his pale skin, it looked more menacing than it probably was, but Beckett wasn't about to complain about the extra contact. Her fingers deftly moved over his foot until she was satisfied. "You'll live." She stood and faced him, placing a tender kiss on his cheek. "I'll keep the bedroom talk to a minimum to avoid further injury."

"I don't care if I end up in a body cast, don't stop on my account." Beckett kissed her with more gusto than was warranted this late at night, but he didn't care—and judging from how Mallory looped her arms around his neck, she wasn't upset about it either.

In between kisses, Mallory said, "Maybe we should attempt some sleep? I think my day just caught up with me."

Beckett pulled back, wrapping her in a hug before ushering her to the bathroom. "I keep forgetting you don't get the luxury of working in your pajamas."

"Can't save lives virtually." She shrugged. "Although that does sound tempting. It's a shame I can't do math."

Beckett's job was more than just math, but he knew Mallory could handle it. "You realize I do people's taxes, and you need to figure out medications, measurements, and stuff I can't even think about. Like blood, gross."

"I guess that means you won't tag along to bring-your-boyfriend-to-work day," she teased.

"Say it again."

Mallory frowned, clearly not picking up on what she'd just said. How could she call him her boyfriend so casually? He felt like he'd float away on a cloud of happiness if he wasn't careful.

"Call me your boyfriend again."

A devilish grin crossed her face and she licked her lips. What a minx. "You're my boyfriend, Beckett. As long as you'll have me."

How about forever? He wanted to ask, but now wasn't the time. They'd come such a long way already, and he wasn't about to rush the moment. Since he didn't have the words, he used his mouth in other ways, kissing her until he remembered they were still in the hallway.

"All right, girlfriend. Let me get you a toothbrush and some PJs."

"You have an extra toothbrush? You're such an adult."

Beckett opened a drawer and fumbled until he found the pink toothbrush he'd bought when he'd moved to Buckeye Falls. It was silly really, buying something with Mallory in mind before he'd ever seen her. But in his gut, he knew they'd get to this moment, this moment of true intimacy of a nightly routine.

Clearing past the lump in his throat, he handed her the brush. Mallory's lip quirked when she saw it was bubblegum pink, her favorite color as a girl. "I'm going to tell myself this is just a pink toothbrush, not a pink toothbrush you keep on hand for your dates."

Play it cool, man! his brain chanted, willing him not to be the awkward guy he tended to be. But when wasn't Beckett himself? "I got it for you."

Mallory blinked at the admission, but she didn't look upset.

"I don't want to be a creep, but when I was at the drug store, I saw it and I thought what if Mal and I work out and she comes over, and then it snowballed from there."

Mallory held the toothbrush to her chest, as if it was a diamond necklace and not an off-brand toothbrush from the dollar bin. "How did it snowball?" Her question escaped on a whisper.

Beckett rubbed the back of his neck, a red flush creeping up his skin. In a matter of seconds, he went from Snow White to Elmo. Using his uninjured toe, he flipped open the cabinet under the sink. "I, uh, got you a few things."

Mallory dipped down to inventory his secret stash, her

172

hands picking through shampoo, lotion, and even her preferred brand of tampons. "I assumed you used the same stuff."

Did she love this or hate it? A toothbrush was one thing, but Beckett feared he'd overplayed his hand. Was planning for your best friend/ex/best friend's sister disturbing or endearing? Judging from Mallory's watery gaze, he thought he chose wisely.

"You're not going to break my heart," was all Mallory said before she crashed her lips against his. For a moment, he was too stunned to reciprocate. When they came up for air, Mallory cupped his cheeks and stared up into his eyes. "You're a good man, Beckett Fox. I'm not going to let this fizzle, you hear me? We're going to figure this out with Evan."

Beckett nodded, his grip on her hips tightening. "We will."

"Now get out of here so I can get ready for bed." She playfully shoved Beckett out of the bathroom and closed the door. He wasted no time getting her a set of pajamas. He said a silent prayer of thanks to the heavens that he'd washed his sheets that morning. He wanted everything to be perfect for Mallory. This was their first adult sleepover in far, far too long. No pillow forts, no playing nurse, just two people sharing a bed.

Mallory emerged sans makeup with rosy cheeks and her brown hair piled into a knot at the top of her head. Beckett itched to take her hair down, to feel the silky strands between his fingers. Mallory's hair had always been beautiful; thick and shiny. When they were kids, her mother would put her in double braids, and as she grew, the braids became more complicated and stunning. But Beckett liked Mallory when she was at her most relaxed, with chocolate waves framing her lovely face.

Standing there slack-jawed, Beckett finally offered Mallory her pajamas. "Here you go," he said with a wave at the stack of clothes. "Help yourself. I'll be right back."

Beckett sprinted to the bathroom and splashed a gallon's worth of cold water on his face. He needed to calm down. They said they were going slow, and he needed to remember that. When he returned to the bedroom, Mallory was already tucked in, curled into a ball.

"I took your old baseball shirt, and it's so soft it's basically mine now." Her words were muffled from behind her pillow. "Now turn off the light and hop in." She wiggled, making room for him to spoon her. He didn't need to be asked twice. He turned off the light and catapulted in beside her.

Wrapping an arm around her, Beckett exhaled and melted into the mattress. The sensation of Mallory being with him, the scent of her lotion and the warmth of her skin, made Beckett want to cry. He made a promise to himself to remember how wonderful this moment was, because it was worth fighting for—worth keeping forever.

He loved Mallory, and he would treat her well. Evan would understand that. He had to because Beckett wasn't going to choose a Lawson. He would make Gramps proud because he'd gotten the girl. And he intended to keep her.

CHAPTER 17

Any chill Mallory had about their secret dating evaporated the millisecond her brother arrived unannounced at Beckett's place. She and Beckett had shared a perfect morning of cuddles and coffee, and were now idly scrolling on their phones to the sound of a quiet Saturday morning. Mallory didn't often get weekends off, so she planned to enjoy this bonus time...with her boyfriend.

The moniker felt strange, yet wonderful, to her ears. She'd woken up twisted in the sheets and covered in Beckett. One of his long legs was draped over hers, and an arm had her plastered to his chest. She was so smitten, even his snores were adorable. Did she mind sharing her space with a symphony provided by a certain redhead? Hell. No.

Now they were nestled together on the couch, her head resting on Beckett's lap. She'd taken her hair down, and he was mindlessly running his fingers through the strands. The soothing sensation threatened to put her back to sleep until the sound of K-Pop music snapped them both to attention.

She sat bolt upright, eyes growing to the size of baseballs. "Oh crap, were you expecting him?"

Beckett scoffed. "If I did, you'd think we'd still be in our PJs?"

"Crap!" Mallory exclaimed as she sprinted to the bedroom, Beckett hot on her heels. "What time is it?"

"Ten thirty," Beckett replied as he hastily pulled on a pair of jeans. His red hair was mussed and he looked like he'd been lounging around all morning. She knew from her own brushed-out locks that there would be no hiding the truth from Evan.

"He's going to know something's up," she whined as she straightened yesterday's shirt and pinched color into her cheeks.

Beckett shook his head, a rueful smile tugging his lips. "Mal, I don't think you need to worry. We'll just say you stopped by for coffee and to check on my hand."

Mallory deflated, arms falling to her sides. "I'm a nurse. You have an injury. You might be a genius."

Beckett cocked an eyebrow. "Might?"

Tugging him by the hem of his shirt, she plastered a wet kiss on his cheek. "Don't act so smug."

"You like it," he teased, holding her close. Dipping his head, he kissed her temple and sighed. "To be continued."

"That a fact?" She wiggled free and pulled on her shoes.

Beckett smacked her bottom on his way past. "It's a promise, Mal."

The pair sprinted back to the living room and flopped back on the couch just as Evan knocked on the door. "Yo, Foxy!" his familiar voice boomed through the door.

Beckett strode over, running his hands through his hair. Throwing the door open, he clapped his hand on Evan's shoulder. "Perfect timing, Lawless. Mal just got here."

The lie slid off his tongue so flawlessly, Mallory was impressed. "Hey, Ev." She gave a wave from the couch, sitting on her other hand so her brother couldn't see it tremble.

Evan beamed and clapped his hands together. "Perfect. That saves me a trip."

"Oh, yeah?" Beckett asked as he went to the kitchen for another coffee.

"Yeah." Evan took the coffee with a nod and shoved Mallory over to sit on the couch. Sibling dynamics never changed. "My *fiancée* and I were talking." He paused to chuckle at his word choice. If she didn't love her brother so much, she'd gag at how in love he was. "And we think the four of us should do dinner or something." Turning to Beckett, he added, "She hardly knows you, Foxy. I need my people to be comfortable together." He flapped his hand in the air, the other bringing his coffee up for a sip.

"Aww, that's really sweet." Mallory covered her heart.

"Sounds good to me. I'd like to get to know the woman who tamed Lawless." He winked and Mallory groaned.

"You two are ridiculous."

"But you love us anyway," Beckett countered. Damn, he certainly had her there.

Evan leaned back and surveyed the apartment. Mallory held her breath, convinced he could sense the shift between his sister and friend. Beckett, on the other hand, reclined in his chair with a happy expression. How could he be so calm in a time like this?

"You're off at the diner today?" Beckett asked, his tone carefree.

After shaking his head, Evan drained his mug. "Nah, just in the break between breakfast and lunch. Max hired some new wait staff, so I have some time off."

"That's good. You'll need it with wedding planning." Mallory understood their desire for a shorter engagement, but she was also keenly aware of how complicated weddings can get. She was a bridesmaid for both her sisters, and it was an ordeal to say the least.

"You and CeCe can get game planning later. You guys free for dinner tonight?" Evan laughed at himself, shaking his head. "Listen to me, acting like you're a couple." He looked at Beckett and asked, "Any hot dates tonight I need to avoid? I don't want to cramp your style."

Beckett made a show of rolling his eyes. "Why don't you all come here? We can order takeout and maybe play some games."

Mallory shot them a thumbs-up. "Sounds good to me." She was impressed with herself for not shaking as she held up her arms... or slapping her idiot brother. Progress!

Evan turned to leave before hesitating a moment. "Wait a minute." He spun back and put his hands on his hips, his brow furrowed. "What are you doing here, Mal?"

Mallory was ready for this, and she squared her shoulders. "I was out running errands and thought I'd check on Beckett's hand."

A little too eagerly, Beckett held up his hands and exclaimed, "All good. I'm healing like a champ." He did jazz hands for a moment before catching Mallory's eye. A Broadway dancer wouldn't have done that move with more enthusiasm.

Seemingly satisfied, Evan shrugged and strode to the door. "Cool. I'll text you guys the timing after CeCe's off. Later."

And then her clueless brother bounded back to his car. "Wow, you were right. That was surprisingly easy. I'm almost nervous the guy is that unaware of his surroundings."

"I hate lying," Beckett said, his tone dry. "I mean, I do have a hot date later." He reached out, yanking Mallory close until they were chest-to-chest in an embrace. Hugging had never been something Mallory thought about much before, but now it was one of her favorite things. Snuggling Beckett felt like an event, something special that was meant to savor.

"I'm a little offended he didn't ask if I had a hot date." She sighed, leaning further into Beckett's arms. They were fused together like LEGO.

"I love you with your hair down." He breathed the compliment into her neck, and she shivered at the contact. God, this man.

Maybe it was a good thing her brother was so aloof, because Mallory wanted more times like this—moments with just her and Beckett. She'd waited forever for these stolen moments, and she wasn't ready to share him yet.

*

Evan and CeCe were due at his place in a matter of minutes, and Beckett was a nervous wreck. How would he be able to hide his attraction to Mallory? Now that they'd come to their secret dating arrangement, he couldn't get enough of her.

In true Mallory fashion, she arrived early to help him get dinner ready. She'd brought a six-pack of Evan's favorite beer, a bottle of wine, and a cheese tray. "What would I do without you?" he asked, pulling her in for a kiss the second her hands were free of her bounty. Their lips lingered a moment while Beckett caught his breath.

"You'd throw subpar dinner parties." Mallory answered between gasps, her skin turning a gorgeous pink hue as he trailed his lips down her neck. "As much as I'm loving this"—her voice hitched as he nipped at her earlobe—"they're due here any second."

"So?" Beckett didn't care about anything beyond the line of freckles dissecting his girlfriend's skin, a line of dots he promised he'd explore fully when they weren't about to be interrupted.

God, his girlfriend. Mallory had always felt like that in his heart, but knowing they were both on the same page did funny things inside his ribcage. The sensation was slightly soured by the fact that he couldn't share this fact outside his apartment. He wanted to tell the whole damn world, despite fearing the consequences. Beckett would be lying if he said Evan's dismissal of him and Mallory dating didn't sting. It more than stung. It felt like his buddy had ripped out his heart and threw it back in his face. From where he stood, wrapped around the woman he loved, this made perfect sense. Why not base a future on a friendship with someone that made his heart sing?

Go get your girl...

Gramps's words rang through his head, pleading with him to man up and tell Evan the truth. But the thought of Gramps brought an ache to his chest he wanted to avoid. He'd already lost too many people in his life, and he couldn't think of losing his best friend. Although it would be worth it to keep Mallory in his arms, right?

The sound of two car doors slamming brought him back to the moment, and he reluctantly stepped back from Mallory. Arms falling to his sides, he suddenly felt hollow without her warmth, without her skin pressed to his. God, it was going to be a long night.

"Show time," Mallory said, her cheeks flushed and her blue eyes shining. He tucked a loose lock of hair behind her ear and tried to look enthusiastic for their evening. Spending more time with CeCe had been top on his list of things to do, yet now Beckett wanted to spend time with *his* girl.

Mallory made herself scarce and set up the cheese tray and drinks. "I hope you don't mind cheese for dinner. The only downside of Evan marrying a chef is that my already subpar culinary skills feel exposed."

Beckett put out a stack of plates and laughed. "Um, this at least is fancy. I have a feeling French bread pizza won't impress anyone outside our little trio." He winked and warmed at Mallory's expression.

"She doesn't know what she's missing."

A knock at the door was the only thing stopping Beckett from throwing Mallory over his shoulders like a caveman. He needed more of her, all of her. These stolen moments were never going to be enough to fill his quota of Mallory Lawson.

The knob jiggled before Evan let himself in, CeCe close on his heels. "Foxy," he called out, smiling like the happiest man on earth. And he probably was the happiest man on earth, because he was engaged to the love of his life...publicly.

The lady in question playfully shoved Evan out of the

way and strode over to Beckett and Mallory. "Thanks so much for having us," she said, pulling Mallory into a quick hug before doing the same to Beckett. "And forgive my fiancé's lack of manners."

Evan scoffed. "This is Foxy," he insisted. "There are no locked doors between us." He clapped his friend on the back before giving his sister a one-armed hug. "What's up, Mal?"

"Hey, goofball," she replied, flicking him in the arm. "What can I get everyone to drink?" She played hostess, popping beer bottles and pouring generous glasses of wine. "Ev, I got that new IPA you like." She tossed a look over her shoulder and asked, "CeCe, you feeling wine or beer?"

CeCe had already walked over to the kitchen table, sneaking a peek at the array of cheese and fruits that Mallory brought. "I'll have the wine; it'll go great with this brie." Not waiting for an invitation, she sliced a wedge and popped it in her mouth. "This is delicious. Is this from the market?"

Mallory pressed a glass of wine into her waiting hand and shook her head. "Nah, I picked these up last week after work. There's a new specialty market in Columbus. We should do a girls' day trip and check it out."

Beckett watched the ladies exchange *ooh*s and *ahh*s over the cheeseboard. Just as he was about to glance away, he saw Mallory's face fall for an instant before she recovered. CeCe's left hand moved animatedly between them, her engagement ring flashing like a lighthouse. "A girls' trip sounds fun."

If he didn't know Mallory well, Beckett wouldn't think anything of her tone. But he knew she was missing part of her sparkle, part of the excitement he knew she felt for her brother and his future bride.

Evan shook Beckett back to the moment with a jab in the arm. "You listening, Foxy?"

Shaking his head, Beckett turned his back to the ladies, knowing it was the only way he'd be able to focus on Evan. "Sorry, distracted by all the cheese talk. What's up?"

"I said, why don't we head to the tux place early next week."

"Sounds good." Beckett agreed, knowing it was the right thing to say. He wished he knew how to bring up the issue of the engagement ring with Evan, despite knowing Mallory would skin him alive for spilling her secret. It wasn't his place to say anything, but he didn't know if he could handle an eternity of Mallory's hurt expression every time CeCe was around.

Mallory ushered everyone around the table with the promise of more food. "I also picked up some salami and olives, have a seat."

CeCe joined her at the counter, offering to slice and arrange the rest of their meal. Mallory seemed to be back to normal, as she excitedly discussed color palates with the bride. "What colors are you two thinking?"

"Something warm since it will be an early fall wedding. Maybe creams and oranges?" Glancing back at the guys, she added, "But I don't know if that's the best color for Beckett." She winked, a clear reference to his fire-engine-red hair. Ah, the joys of being a ginger...

"Pfft, I'm not basing our color scheme on my buddy's hair." Evan reached out and ruffled Beckett's curls loose. "No offense, Foxy."

CeCe carried the tray over to the table and chuckled. "I thought your nickname was because of your hair. I didn't realize your last name was Fox."

Mallory followed closely behind, laying a stack of napkins on the table. On her way to her chair, she paused to run her hands through his hair, putting the curls back in place. Her touch lingered a moment before she pulled back. It was such a reflex, he didn't think anything of it, until he caught CeCe watching them. She blinked and took her seat next to Evan. Despite not saying anything, CeCe was clearly curious.

Oblivious to her own actions, Mallory plopped down and sipped from her glass. "You two and your nicknames.

Frankly, I've always thought it was hilarious. Ev's like the most lawful person I've met."

CeCe pursed her lips and struggled not to laugh. "I wasn't going to say anything, but…" She poked Evan in the side and beamed. "You're pretty much the nicest guy on the planet, babe."

"You ladies wound me." Evan threw his head back in a moment of theatrics.

The foursome chatted about wedding planning, life at the diner, and how Beckett was settling into his new place. "It's definitely nice living closer to everything. I was temporarily at another place after Gramps passed, but I hated feeling so isolated."

Evan popped an olive in his mouth and nodded. "I'm so glad you're here. Not that I mind the drive to the farm house, but you're basically down the street."

"No arguments here," Mallory chimed in, reaching out with a cheese-laden cracker. Beckett opened his mouth and ate the proffered treat, completely unaware that CeCe was gawking.

Mallory seemed to realize her mistake a moment too soon, dropping her hand so quickly she tipped her wine glass over, spilling the remains of the pale-yellow liquid across the table. "Oh crap." She bolted upright and dashed into the kitchen for a towel. "Sorry about that."

CeCe jumped up to help with cleanup, but Evan stayed behind with Beckett. Slowly, he turned to see if his friend saw that interaction, but he was too busy frowning at his beer bottle. "Did you see they no longer brew this in Ohio? They've moved the brewery up to Michigan. That's blasphemy."

Beckett chuckled, both relieved and shocked at his friend's lack of awareness. Maybe he and Mallory had nothing to worry about with the secret dating. If Evan missed his sister manhandling his best friend *and* feeding him, they would probably be all right. Wouldn't they?

CHAPTER 18

Good Lord, why did she just hand-feed Beckett cheese and crackers? Was she insane? And then she decided to cover by spilling wine all over the table. Not only was that a waste of really good wine, but she knew CeCe was suspicious.

"Let me get a wet rag," CeCe said as she fumbled with the sink's faucet. "At least it's white wine and won't stain."

"Thanks. I'm such a klutz." And an idiot, but Mallory wouldn't provide CeCe with more ammo.

CeCe raised an eyebrow, and Mallory wilted under her scrutiny. "Uh-huh." The other woman wasn't known for holding her tongue, and that was one of the reasons she loved her future sister-in-law. Evan didn't get away with his nonsense. Unfortunately, it appeared that attitude translated to all Lawsons. "You want to tell me anything?" she asked, voice hushed.

"No." Mallory flinched; her lie came too quickly to be genuine. To distract herself, she tidied a stack of already tidied napkins.

"Uh-huh," CeCe repeated, her lips pressed in a suppressed smile. "You know what I love about you, Mal?"

"My ability to make a good cheese tray?"

CeCe nudged her with her elbow while she cleaned up the wine. Thankfully Beckett and Evan had migrated to the couch and were currently watching a baseball game. "Okay, I guess there's two things."

Mallory collected the dirty dishes and strode back in the kitchen, head held high like she wasn't weighed down with secrets and lies. Why did she think she could handle this? They'd been in the presence of other people for less than thirty minutes before the secrets were exposed.

Struggling to distract CeCe, Mallory attempted a change in topic. "My ability to save lives under stressful situations?"

CeCe wrung out the towel in the sink before draping it over the spigot. "That's worth an honorable mention." Her lips quirked. "What I meant was that you're the worst liar in the world. Like, it's impressive how bad you are." She turned to face Mallory, arms crossed over her chest. "What's going on with you?"

"Nothing." Mallory flinched again. She really was bad at this. "Just, uh, tired after a crazy stretch at work." She flapped her hands in front of her, as if batting away the wildness of the week.

"Hmmm, are you sure it's not from…" Her voice trailed off as she motioned toward the living room. True to form, Evan was yammering on about something that Beckett listened to intently, his head tipped in concentration.

"Beckett and I are just friends." The statement landed with a thud between them, and Mallory knew the conversation was far from over.

CeCe picked up the bottle of wine and held it up to the light. "You boys don't mind if I borrow Mallory? I've got some wedding stuff to discuss, and this wine is begging for some fresh air." Not bothering to wait on a reply, CeCe looped her arm through Mallory's and yanked her out onto the tiny balcony.

Mallory grabbed their glasses on the way past, shooting Beckett an expression she hoped wasn't terrified. As soon as they were outside, CeCe pulled the door closed and topped off both glasses.

"We've got about ten minutes before Evan feels left out and joins us."

Mallory snorted. "You're giving him ten whole minutes before FOMO takes over? I was thinking five at best."

CeCe raised an eyebrow, a gesture designed with maximum impact. "You're probably right, but he knows we have girly wedding things to discuss. That'll scare him enough." She waved at the empty chair beside her, and Mallory tried not to frown as Nana's ring caught the fading sunlight. Red and white sparkles flickered like a firework on the 4th of July. *You need to get past this, Mal…*

"So what do you want to talk about? Bridesmaids' dresses, the menu, invitations?" Her voice trailed off, heart hammering. "Oh! What about flowers!" Mallory nearly shouted the last word, the sound of her voice echoing off the neighboring apartments.

"Well, I guess we have two things to discuss. The first is a request, and I hope you don't mind." CeCe's expression was sober, not teasing. If this was about Beckett, Mallory had no idea where the conversation would go.

"What is it?"

CeCe sipped from her drink, looking out at the sunset with a faint smile. "I really do love it here. When I moved, I had no intention of staying, as I'm sure Evan's told you."

Mallory leaned back in her chair, relieved from the reprieve of her own drama. "Yeah, he's mentioned it. But after everything happened with—" She let the sentence hang, knowing the reasoning behind CeCe's frequent moves was a sore subject.

"You can mention my ex. Eric's name no longer turns me to stone." CeCe sat tall, clearly unaffected by her beast of an ex. When he finally got his comeuppance, Mallory and most of the free world cheered. That manipulative asshole was a far cry from her little brother, and she was so pleased he and CeCe found each other. She deserved a happily ever after.

187

"I want you to know, I'm glad Evan got his head out of ass and asked you out last year."

CeCe smirked, the look of a satisfied woman. "Me too." She drained the last of her glass and placed it on the small table between them. Beckett hadn't bothered with more than a pair of folding chairs and a questionable end table he found at a thrift store. Mallory didn't have the heart to tell him it was uglier than the box it came in.

"Anyway," CeCe said, pulling them back to the moment. "When I moved here, the people of Buckeye Falls were surprisingly welcoming. At first I thought just Max was a nice guy, but then I realized it was damn near everyone."

Mallory liked Max, the diner's owner and technically Evan and CeCe's boss. Although he never acted like that, the man was a gooey cinnamon roll through and through. "Max and Evan might be two of the nicest people, you don't need to convince me of that."

"I know, but they aren't the only ones that make me feel included, feel like there's more to this town than baking and winning food competitions." She turned in her chair and pierced Mallory with a look that should scare her, but it didn't. CeCe had this natural intensity that Mallory admired. She was no-nonsense but had a good heart. She was the perfect balance to her brother's sunny disposition. "Mal, you made me feel included in the Lawson clan right away. Not only are you important to Evan, but you've become family to me."

Mallory took CeCe's hand and squeezed, keeping their fingers linked. "You're already like a sister to me, and you know that's saying something."

"And not having any siblings of my own, I appreciate that, more than you know." CeCe tightened her hold and asked, "I'd like you to be my maid of honor, Mal. It's more than my wedding day, it's about having family beside you. I'd love to have *you* by my side. If you don't mind, that is." CeCe's certainty faltered a moment as Mallory blinked.

Mallory's heart skittered in her ribcage and her blue eyes

pooled with tears. "Mind?" she asked, her voice barely a whisper. "That's the nicest invitation I've ever received." She tugged CeCe closer until they were hugging and both holding back tears. "I'd be honored."

CeCe patted Mallory's back and choked back a sob. "Good. Then it's settled."

When they pulled apart, both women dabbed at their wet eyes with their sleeves. "But I have to tell you something," CeCe added, sniffling as she smiled. "I can't have secrets on my bride squad."

Mallory stilled, her gaze not quite meeting CeCe's. "Oh, yeah?"

"Yeah." CeCe scoffed, reaching out and flicking Mallory on the arm.

"Ouch." Mallory covered her arm. "When did Evan show you the Lawson flick?"

CeCe did it again, this time right on Mallory's forehead. "I'm a fast learner, and you need to spill the beans. What is going on with you and Beckett? I know I'm new to this crew, but there is certainly something going on between you two."

"No, there isn't," Mallory said, sounding like a teenager. "We're just friends."

"Pfft, yeah right. And I'm Gordon Ramsay. Something is going on there, sister. The looks you two were flashing each other could have melted the cheese board. And don't think I missed you *feeding* him. Friends don't feed each other, or at least my friends don't. I'm pretty sure I'd cut off Max's hand if he ever tried that move on me."

Mallory's face flamed and her tongue felt heavy. She reached for her glass, only to grimace when it came up empty. Damn, she really could use some liquid courage right about now. "We've known each other for like twenty years."

CeCe arched an eyebrow. "And how long have you been in love with each other?" She held up her hand when Mallory opened her mouth. "Don't bother denying it, Miss Maid of Dishonor. I know what I saw, so cut the crap."

Mallory covered her face in her hands. "Does Evan know?"

CeCe threw her head back and cackled so loudly, Mallory feared half the town would hear. "Are you serious? Oh, Mal. I love that man to death, but he is clearly clueless. All he talks about is finding Beckett a date for our wedding. If he got a whiff of what's going on between you, it'd be all he talked about."

"We don't want him to know," Mallory said, hating that their secret dating had lasted all of twenty-four hours. Beckett would be furious, but she didn't have time to dwell.

"Why not?" The humor was gone from CeCe's tone. Instead, she looked concerned. "You're actually afraid to tell him, aren't you?"

Mallory shook her head. "I'm not, but Beckett is." She let out a lungful of air, happy to deflate and share this burden with someone else. "He's afraid Evan will end their friendship if he found out. Like some bro code or something."

"Evan loves that man like a brother." CeCe was incredulous. "You really think he'd react so poorly?"

Throwing her hands in the air, Mallory sighed. "I don't know. Beckett is convinced it'll end their friendship, which will then end our relationship. Honestly, I don't know how he'll react, but I get Beckett's reasoning. Or at least I'm trying to. He lost his grandparents in the last couple of years, and they were his last remaining family."

CeCe frowned. "What about his parents?"

Mallory scoffed, hating that she had to share the hurtful truth of Beckett's past without his permission, but needing CeCe to understand the full story. "They got divorced when Beckett was eight. They left Ohio, and him, without a backward glance."

Letting out a gasp, CeCe covered her mouth. "That's horrible. Poor Beckett."

"So, you see the issue? If we come out as a couple and things go south, he's afraid he won't have anyone left."

CeCe took Mallory's hand, Nana's ring digging into her skin. "I can't make any sweeping promises of how this will work out, but it's clear this isn't some childhood crush. You two seem really into each other, and I think Evan would hate to keep you apart."

"That's all well and good, but Beckett needs to make that call." Mallory pulled her hands free and covered her face again, feeling the need to hide away from life and all its complications. "I just need to be patient."

CeCe didn't say anything but patted Mallory's arm and sighed. For a few minutes, they listened to the late summer cicadas. "You should trust Evan with the truth of your relationship. I can't imagine him cutting Beckett out of his life, and he certainly wouldn't do that to his favorite sister."

Mallory smiled at CeCe's words, hoping they were true. "But in the meantime, can you please not tell him?"

"Ouch, I hate keeping secrets from Ev. We know how well that worked out last year." Both women recoiled at the memory, and Mallory hated herself a little for asking this of CeCe.

"If it helps, I hate that I'm asking this of you. We just need a little time." She held up two fingers pinched together, barely a sliver of evening light between them.

CeCe huffed and pulled herself to standing. "I'll do my best, but please don't make me wait too long. I don't want to walk down the aisle with a secret literally surrounding us at the altar."

Before Mallory could respond, Evan pulled open the sliding door and walked outside, Beckett on his heels. "All right, are you girls done? I'm feeling a little left out."

Beckett snorted and nudged Evan with his elbow. "He's been pouting for the last ten minutes, convinced you're having more fun."

CeCe wrapped her arms around Evan's neck and pulled him down for a quick kiss. "Babe, you need to calm down. You know I save all the big fun for you." A look passed between them that siblings should never witness, and

Mallory fought the urge to gag. Evan and CeCe could be in love, but she didn't need a front-row seat.

Striving to change the subject, Mallory clapped her hands and announced, "CeCe asked me to be her maid of honor."

Evan whooped and picked up CeCe, twirling her around the cramped balcony until her sneakered foot hit Beckett on the hip. "Oof," he exhaled and tried to duck from another kick.

"Put me down," CeCe ordered, giggling as Evan placed her back on the floor. "Let's not injure the best man in the meantime, huh?"

"Thanks, CeCe." Beckett rubbed his hip. "If this continues, I'll need a wheelchair to get me down the aisle."

Mallory ushered everyone back inside for dessert, which was sadly a store-bought pie. "I know it's poor form to offer this to a pastry chef, but I was short on time."

CeCe took her slice and beamed. "And I will never say no to free pie, especially from family."

Mallory's eyes misted and she shook her head. "No more sweet words, ma'am. I'm really trying not to cry."

Beckett passed out spoons and the foursome fell back into safer conversation topics like the engagement party. "The party is next week," Evan said between bites. "Foxy, you think you can help me make a playlist? CeCe and I have the food covered, but we're thinking it'll be nice for something to play in the background." Turning to his sister he added, "And Mal, can you help me with the invites?"

"Absolutely. Should be easy since everyone is local."

Evan wiped his mouth with the back of his hand and nodded. "Exactly. The only unknowns are your and Foxy's dates."

Like a scene from a movie, CeCe, Beckett, and Mallory all froze. CeCe's fork stalled on the way to her mouth and the piece of pie landed with a sad splat on her plate. Mallory looked to Beckett, who was about to choke on his dessert. "Well, I was thinking," Mallory started, striving to sound casual and not rehearsed. "Beckett and I would go together."

Evan rolled his eyes. "Geez, Mal. Maybe he's got a better offer?" Despite Evan not knowing the truth, his words stung. Why couldn't *she* be the better offer?

"C'mon, man," Beckett said, his brow creased in frustration. "Lay off, Mal."

Ever the diplomat, CeCe covered Evan's hand with hers and added, "I'm with Beckett. Let's be reasonable. If they want to go together, why not? The party's next week."

Evan shrugged and moved on, although Mallory wasn't going to recover so quickly. They needed to find a way to resolve this, because she could not handle many more digs from Evan. She understood that from where he was sitting, these two had just been fallback options for each other. *Oh, how wrong he was...*

But the question remained, how would they convince him that they were a good idea? How could Evan see them in a new light if they didn't shine in public? Mallory tried to catch Beckett's eye, to see what he was thinking, but it was no use. Since Evan's dismissal of their date, he'd been quiet. CeCe, for her part, tried to steer the conversation to other topics, but the mood had shifted.

By the time Evan and CeCe left, Mallory felt wrung out. Beckett snatched her hand as soon as the door closed, pulling her close and cradling her against his chest. "I'm sorry about that," he muttered, his hold on her only tightening. "What did CeCe say?"

Mallory fought the urge to lie, knowing it would stress him out. "She knows about us." Beckett tensed around her, but he didn't pull back. "She's not going to tell Evan, at least not yet."

"I hate that she has to lie," Beckett said, and she agreed. This was no way for CeCe to start her engagement, but Mallory wasn't sure what the answer was.

Well, that was another lie. Mallory knew exactly what the answer was, she just needed Beckett to get on board with the truth. If they were going to do this, they might as well get started. There was no better time than the present, because this secret threatened to hurt them all.

CHAPTER 19

The engagement party was mere days away, and Beckett had never expected to be this stressed. Over the course of a few days, he and Evan basically turned into chicks. One minute they were watching baseball and talking about video games, the next they're comparing color swatches for bowties, looking at floral arrangements, and deciding on the best playlist to set a mood. And per Evan, it couldn't be just any mood. It needed to be the balance between sappy love songs and upbeat pop music—yet it had to be palatable to everyone attending the party. *Sure thing, man, no problem...*

When he wasn't wearing his best man hat, Beckett spent all his free time with Mallory. They had spent the night at each other's apartments a couple of times that week, and every time surpassed his wildest expectations.

During his first sleepover at Mallory's place, she had warned him about her little body guard, also known as Fernando. The relationship between feline and human was not, in fact, the disaster Mallory anticipated. Within five minutes of arriving and kicking off his shoes, Fernando had jumped onto the couch and curled up on Beckett's lap. After five more minutes of belly rubs, he was snoring so loudly they had to turn the TV up.

"I still can't believe it," Mallory said, her mouth hanging open in wonder. "It usually takes Fernando at least a month to warm up to someone. Even me!"

Beckett shrugged, a smile tugging his lips. "I guess I'm just a likeable guy."

"Pfft, I don't know about that." She winked and curled into his side. By the time the opening credits scrolled on the documentary they were watching, both cat and girlfriend were comfortably surrounding him. It was hard to be lonely when he was cocooned like this. Beckett was in heaven.

A knock at the door jolted everyone to the moment, but it was just a delivery driver with food from the diner. "I'll get it," Beckett said, padding over to the door. Throwing the door open, he was greeted to the sight of Evan, bag in hand, eyebrow raised in question. "Lawless?"

Behind him, Beckett heard Mallory rolling off the couch and running to join him. Thankfully they weren't caught in a compromising position, but he cursed himself for being careless. Why did they order from the diner?

"Foxy," Evan said, pushing past him and into the living room. Mallory waved awkwardly at her brother.

"What are you doing here, Ev?"

Evan plopped the bag down on the coffee table and crossed his arms over his chest. "I don't know, Mal. I'm wrapping up a to-go order and hear Helen give the driver the address."

Beckett gulped, unsure how to intervene. "Then I'm thinking, why is Mal ordering all of my favorites to her place?" A huge grin cracked his handsome face as Evan beamed. He threw his arms wide before falling back onto the couch. "Then it occurred to me that CeCe told you she's out of town tonight. You guys wanted to keep me company."

Beckett's entire body slumped with relief as his buddy settled into the spot previously occupied by their little trio. While he was relieved not to be caught, he was a little annoyed that his and Mallory's evening was being interrupted. It was hard to snuggle up to a cult documentary—don't judge his comfort viewing—and the woman he loved when his best friend was literally sitting between them.

Mallory groaned but covered it quickly. "I'll get some plates," she said to no one in particular as she stomped into the kitchen.

"I'll grab drinks," Beckett offered, hot on her heels.

Evan picked up the remote and kicked his feet out. "And I'll find something good to watch on TV. Are you two trying to depress yourselves with this crap?"

Beckett grabbed a few cans of seltzers as Mallory pulled down a stack of plates. While she pulled out utensils, she muttered, "I will not stab my brother, I will not stab my brother…"

Glancing quickly into the living room, Beckett confirmed Evan was in his own world, messing with Fernando and finding something to watch that didn't involve brainwashing and murder. He reached out and smoothed Mallory's hair off her neck. Dipping down, he peppered the tender skin with kisses until she moaned. "You're trying to get us caught?" Her question was husky and dripping with need.

He felt that sensation tight in his gut. Frankly, he wasn't certain he could survive a whole night without touching Mallory. "I'm sorry," he said, not really meaning it. His mouth continued its path up her neck and ended at her lips with a chaste kiss. "I can't stay away from you."

Mallory's head dipped forward until their foreheads were touching. "I can't stay away from you either."

Their private tableau was interrupted by the sound of ripping paper and hissing. "Fernando!" Evan yelled as Mallory sprinted back into the living room.

Beckett was right behind her, stumbling when he found the mess the cat created. Strips of paper were strewn all over the living room floor; the sad remains of some of Mallory's gossip magazines. Fernando hissed, his back arched, as

Evan tried to pick him up. "Come here, fella," Evan cooed, but the cat wasn't interested in being cornered.

Mallory strode between them and scooped up Fernando, holding him at arm's length to avoid scratches. "We've been over this, big guy." She chastised the cat as she stormed into her bedroom. Beckett followed her, opening the crate door as she put the cat in time out. "You get out when you can behave with company."

"I'm sorry, Mal. I'll help with the mess." Beckett took her hand and pulled her to his chest for a far-too-quick embrace.

By the time they joined Evan again, the living room was tidied up. The only evidence that anything had happened was the smaller stack of magazines propped up by the sofa. Mallory sighed. "Why does Fernando always go for the new ones? Now I'll never know who that new Netflix star is dating."

Evan snorted. "Yeah, it's a shame no one invented the internet." He was rewarded for his quip with a flick to the forehead. "Ow," he muttered as he followed Beckett and Mallory back to the kitchen for plates.

Beckett did the honors of unpacking the bag, discovering that Evan in fact threw in an extra sandwich for himself. He couldn't help it, but Beckett bristled at this. It wasn't that the trio didn't hang out together often, but lately, it felt like Evan was inserting himself into every possible private moment with Mallory. Was he reading too much into this? Was it simply Evan's excitement over having his best friend back in town?

Beckett registered the moment Mallory realized Evan brought food for himself. Their eyes locked over a box of tater tots, and she rolled her eyes. As if reading their minds, Evan asked, "Did I remember to throw in some of Max's homemade ranch?"

Mallory retrieved three small ramekins of the heavenly sauce. "The short answer is yes, but that's only if you're planning on sharing."

Evan snatched a ramekin and stalked out to the couch. By the time Beckett and Mallory joined him, they were stationed at the far corners of the sofa. The TV had a paused screen with a favorite martial arts movie. "Oh, hell yeah!" Beckett exclaimed as he eased back onto the cushion and popped a tater tot into his mouth.

"I haven't seen this one in a while." Mallory agreed, taking a bite from a delicious-looking hoagie. Beckett tried to hide his annoyance that they were supposed to be sharing sandwiches, but they couldn't do that now. Sharing food was a couple thing, something intimate that crossed a line of regular friendship.

"Yeah, one of the streaming services picked up the whole series. I've been watching them with CeCe."

They watched the movie in companionable silence until the ending credits. Mallory stood and collected the dishes, but Evan offered to do the cleanup. As he clattered in the kitchen, Beckett reached out and snatched her hand, bringing it to his lips to kiss her knuckles.

"He's going to want to leave with you," Mallory said, her expression unreadable.

Beckett's shoulders slumped and he shook his head. "Maybe not? Or I could always come back?"

Mallory didn't have a chance to answer as the man in question bounded back into the room. "I just realized how late it is. We should probably head out, Foxy." Evan's big hand clapped Beckett on the back, causing him to stagger. Turning to his sister, he added, "Thanks for hosting. It was like old times."

"It was." Mallory gave her brother a quick hug and turned to Beckett. If this would have been before, she'd punch his arm and send him on his way. But this time, she didn't. Mallory strode forward and pulled Beckett in for a hug that crushed his ribs. "Thanks for coming over, Beckett," she whispered in his ear, her nose bumping his glasses out of place.

"C'mon, Foxy," Evan said, shoving his friend through

the door. "Let's give Mal and Fernando some peace."

Beckett felt his feet move without his consent, bringing him all the way to his car. When he turned back to Mallory's door, it was already closed, the front light turned off. If that wasn't a message, he didn't know what was.

Sighing, he yanked his door open and was about to turn on the car when Evan joined him. "Hey, quick question."

Stiffening, Beckett prepared for a question about Mallory. *Hey Foxy, why are you constantly hanging out with my sister? Hey man, any reason you're man-handling my sister while I'm in the other room?*

"What's up?"

Evan shoved his hands in his pockets and rocked back on his sneakered heels. "Any progress with a date for the engagement party?"

Not this again. Beckett squeezed his eyes shut so they didn't roll into the back of his skull. "No man, I told you. Mallory and I will go together. I haven't caught up with the rest of the Lawson clan much, so it'll be nice to mingle."

Scratching his chin, Evan nodded, seemingly satisfied. "Good point."

Before he could stop himself, Beckett mumbled, "I thought so."

Evan took a step back so Beckett could close the driver's door. "See you in a couple of days. Thanks again for all your help, man."

"Of course, anytime, Lawless." Beckett pulled out and headed toward his apartment. It was the last place he wanted to go, but he didn't have the energy for sneaking around. As soon as he got home, he texted Mallory.

I'm sorry about tonight. Want me to come back over later?

He didn't have to wait long for her reply. *Don't worry about it. Fernando and I are having another 'conversation'. ::skull emoji:: ::cat emoji::*

Good luck. Can I swing by tomorrow after your shift?

::thumbs up emoji::

Well, that certainly wasn't the conversation he wanted to

have with Mallory tonight, but there he was. After changing into his sweatpants and making a mug of herbal tea, Beckett booted up his laptop and logged into World of Warcraft.

Within two minutes, his buddy DMed him.

WickedWarri0rBr0: *Long time, no see. You have time for a quick raid?*

Beckett couldn't fight the smile on his lips. While online friendships weren't as important as in-person ones, he couldn't deny that having a network of gamers always put him in a good mood.

FoxyMage96: *Yes, please. Tonight didn't turn out as planned, and I need a distraction.*

WickedWarri0rBr0: *Lady trouble?* ::skull emoji::

FoxyMage96: *Is there any other kind?* ::eye roll emoji::

WickedWarri0rBr0: *We have a few minutes before we reach the dungeon. Want to talk about it?*

He really did, and seeing as how his best friend couldn't be part of this conversation, Beckett unloaded on poor WickedWarri0rBr0.

FoxyMage96: *OK, but you asked for it.*

WickedWarri0rBr0: *I'm tougher than I look.* ::winky face emoji

FoxyMage96: *So you know Mallory?*

WickedWarri0rBr0: *AKA the love of your life? Yeah man, I'm familiar.*

FoxyMage96: *Well, we're sort of…secretly dating.*

WickedWarri0rBr0: *I know we're not on audio, but trust that I just snorted at this. What the hell is secret dating? She's not married, is she?*

FoxyMage96: *God no, we're both single. We're also both insane for keeping this a secret from her brother – AKA my best friend.*

WickedWarri0rBr0: *You gotta come clean, bro. Nothing good can come from lying. Just ask my ex-wives.* ::laughing while crying emoji::

FoxyMage96: *Yeah, I know. I'm afraid I'll lose them both if we come clean.*

WickedWarri0rBr0: *That's a possibility, but you could also lose them both if you keep hiding. Someone is going to get hurt. Might as well try to be honest out of the gate.*

FoxyMage96: *When the hell did you get so wise?*

WickedWarri0rBr0: *About twenty raids ago when we brought down that other guild?* ::winky face emoji::

Beckett spent the rest of his night lost in a fantasy world and pondering WickedWarri0rBr0's advice. Granted the guy's been married three times, but he seemed happy enough with his current wife. And he'd been listening to Beckett drone on about Mallory for what felt like an eternity. Hell, Beckett probably owed the guy a few hundred bucks for therapy services rendered.

Just as he turned off his computer, he heard a knock at the door. Glancing at the clock on the stove, he saw it was nearly midnight. After striding over to the peephole, he saw a familiar halo of hair. Beckett pulled open the door to find Mallory in her pajamas, her purse slung over her shoulder. "I couldn't sleep," she said in greeting, handing her bag off to him as she pushed inside.

"Me either." He followed her to the bedroom and couldn't hide his smile as she pulled back the sheets and dove inside. "I need to be up in six hours, but I needed a dose of Vitamin B." She patted the mattress beside her and wiggled back. "I know we have a lot to discuss after tonight, but right now I just want to cuddle."

Beckett yanked his T-shirt off over his head and catapulted beside her. "You've got it." They immediately clicked into place, Beckett's arm draped over her middle as she nestled into the pillow. "I'm glad you're here," he whispered, meaning every word. He'd been looking forward to their sleepover, and he didn't realize how disappointed he was until she was back in his arms.

"Night, Beckett." Mallory's words were heavy with sleep, and she was snoring before he had a chance to close his eyes.

They would figure this out, he knew it in his bones. This felt too right not to savor and keep forever. Evan was a smart guy and a good friend. As soon as the engagement party was over, they'd come clean. No more secrets, no more hiding. Simple, right?

Then why did Beckett fall asleep with a knot in his stomach?

CHAPTER 20

A week into their sneaking around, Mallory pulled up to her apartment with just enough time to shower and change before work. She really needed to remember to bring more than a hairbrush and pajamas to Beckett's place. The notion brought a goofy grin to her mouth.

Striding up the pathway to her apartment, Mallory was so lost in her musings that she didn't see the figure leaning against the entryway. "I take it you two talked?"

Mallory yelped, dropping her purse to the ground. Her keys, phone, and a set of lipsticks scattered around them. "Good Lord, Alice. You scared the crap out of me."

"I did?" she asked, squatting down to retrieve a rogue pack of gum. "Lady, I've been trying to get a hold of you for days. I'm literally here for a proof of life call."

Mallory held out her bag for Alice to dump everything in. "That seems a bit dramatic." She pushed past her bestie into her apartment.

Alice raised an eyebrow. Mallory was so busted. "Oh? I'm dramatic. I'll remember that the next time you swing by my place at ten o'clock at night."

Once inside, Mallory tossed her bag onto the coffee table and flopped down on the couch. "I have five minutes before I need to get to work. Please, do your worst."

Alice dutifully took her perch on the other end of the sofa and chuckled. "Start by answering my initial question."

"I'm still recovering from my heart attack to remember what that was." Mallory winked.

"Yeah, nice try. I asked if you guys talked."

"Among other things," Mallory retorted, unable to hide her satisfied grin.

Alice tossed a throw pillow at Mallory's head and squealed. "Start. Talking. Now. I have to be at the library in ten minutes, and I need as much gossip as possible. Or at least enough to compete with the busy bodies of Buckeye Falls."

Mallory paused, her post-Beckett flush fading to a green pallor. "What do you mean, the busy bodies?"

Alice scoffed. "Mal, need I remind you about my own dating history in this town? There are no secrets."

"Beckett and I are friends," she started, hating the lie on her tongue.

"No, honey. You and I are friends. You two are clearly more." Alice toyed with the edge of a throw pillow before continuing. "At the library last night, Lynn mentioned that Mrs. Sanders saw you leaving his place in the"—she held up her hands to do air quotes—"wee hours of the morning."

Mallory groaned, covering her face to hide from the news. "What are the odds the gossip doesn't make it to the diner?" Not only was the diner the best restaurant in town, but it was also the hub of the town's gossip mill. The only competition might be Alice's sister-in-law's house, but she wasn't going to bring Natalie into this. While the nicest woman, she loved to delve into the gossip—as long as she wasn't the focus.

"Do you really want me to answer that?" Alice asked, a frown marring her lovely face. Mallory loved her friend, truly.

"How is Evan and CeCe's wedding not the talk of the town?"

"Pfft." Alice flapped a hand, her trademark smirk in place. "Everyone is excited, but that's not news. They've been in love for a while, and unless one of them runs off to Elm River with someone else, no one will bat an eye. Now you know what is hot gossip? The maid of honor and the best man shacking up."

"We are not shacking up." Mallory countered, the flush back in her cheeks. Why was she such a bad liar?

"Um, do I need to pick up a dictionary at the library for you? You're literally doing a walk of shame." Her friend gestured to her crumpled clothes from the night before, and Mallory conceded the point.

"I'm going to need to tell Evan, aren't I?"

Alice cocked her head and examined Mallory's pinched expression. "The engagement party is this weekend, right?"

"Yeah."

"I think you need to tell him, both of you, after that. The guy is in love, let him have his moment with his lady, but then you need to fess up."

"Remember the good old days?" Mallory asked, head tossed back and staring at the ceiling.

Alice shook her head. "What good old days?"

"When you'd barge into the hospital ranting and raving about your love life." That statement earned Mallory another pillow toss to the head. "Hey." She batted away the offending cushion and laughed. "I should have saved the security footage. Then I could remind you that you're not always right."

Alice pulled herself to her feet, holding out a hand for Mallory. "C'mon, honey. You need to get ready for work, and I'm running late. Just remember, for once I'm right, and you need to talk to Beckett. Buckeye Falls is about to burst your bubble."

Mallory walked Alice to the door and gave her a hug. Just a year ago, this woman was a stranger, and now she couldn't imagine her life without her. "I miss you, Alice. Once this is settled, I'd love for you and James to double date with us."

"I'd love nothing more." Alice pulled back and sighed. "But first, work and real life. Then the four of us will do something fabulous."

"It's a date."

Once Alice was ushered back outside, Mallory ran into the bathroom for quite possibly the fastest shower in recorded history. She was in the middle of braiding her hair when her phone rang. Using her elbow, she answered the call and put it on speaker.

"Hey, Em. I'm getting ready for work. Is everything okay?"

Through the line, she heard her sister snort. "Oh yeah, peachy. I was just calling about a few odds and ends for the engagement party."

At the sound of another voice, Fernando sauntered into the bathroom to investigate. He jumped up onto the sink and tiptoed around her phone, makeup bag, and collection of hairbrushes. With her hands occupied with her hair, Mallory didn't have a chance to pet the beast before he grew agitated.

"Don't even think about it." Mallory warned as Fernando's paw went in the air to strike. Only a week ago, she was fishing some of her favorite lipsticks out of the toilet when he went on a spree. Using her foot, she flipped down the toilet seat.

"Huh?" Emily asked, completely unaware of her sister's predicament.

"Sorry, it's Fernando. We're having a battle of wills, and I think he's winning."

Her sister laughed. "I don't know why you keep that animal in your house. He's a menace."

"He's a sweetheart, and if I wouldn't have taken him they were going to put him down."

Emily muttered, "Still could," before changing the subject. "Anyway, back to this weekend and the engagement party."

Mallory tied off her braid and dusted her face with

powder while Emily droned on with logistics of how certain relatives were getting to the party. By the time she was walking to her car, she had a mug of coffee in one hand, her purse in the other, and her phone wedged between her ear and shoulder. She'd probably require another visit to the chiropractor, but that was a problem that would have to wait.

When the car turned on, Mallory set up Bluetooth and pulled into traffic. "What else do you need for the weekend? I'll be at work soon." Deftly avoiding a cyclist, Mallory groaned when she saw she was running late.

"I'll be quick. My first question, have you told Evan about Nana's ring?"

The question caused Mallory's foot to slip on the pedal and the car lurched forward. After spewing her favorite profanities into the world, Mallory rallied. "Are you trying to cause an accident? God, Em. No, I haven't. The ring is a non-issue. It's on CeCe's finger, end of story."

"Pfft, hardly. Evan needs to know how you feel."

Mallory rolled her eyes, delighting that her sister couldn't flick her for her rudeness. "Oh yeah, great idea. Let me just upset him right before his engagement dinner."

Not skipping a beat, Emily soldiered on. "Speaking of upsetting Evan, I heard you're bringing Beckett as your date."

This time Mallory narrowly avoided hitting a pickup truck as she merged onto the highway. The other driver slowed down long enough to flip her the bird before speeding away. She couldn't blame him. "Yeah, I'm not going there now. We're going as friends."

Emily was incredulous, her tone dripping with sarcasm. "Really? Then I'll also drop my fifteen pounds of baby weight by Saturday. Easy peasy."

"You look lovely, let's not start that conversation again." Emily had the body of a super model, and since giving birth to Tyson she'd filled out and looked like one of the Amazonian women from *Wonder Woman*. Somehow those

209

genes completely skipped over Mallory, stupid heredity.

Finally, Mallory arrived at the hospital and parked close to the entrance. "I'm at work and really have to go. I'll be sure to text Aunt Lucy the directions to the diner, don't worry about that."

"You're the best," Emily quipped. "And I'll make sure to remind you to tell Evan the truth. Love you." And with that, her very unhelpful sister hung up on her.

Mallory threw her head back and blinked back frustrated tears. Perhaps if she just centered herself, she wouldn't explode in the middle of the hospital parking garage?

Her musings were interrupted by a knock on the door that caused her to jump and hit the horn. Janis sprang backward, covering her chest with her hand. "Sorry, Mallory. I didn't mean to frighten you."

Mallory grabbed her bags and joined her coworker on the way inside. "No worries, Jan. Sorry to scare you. I'm in my own head this morning."

This was what she needed, a neutral party who didn't know a damn thing about her family, Beckett, or the ring. Yet no sooner were they inside when Janis burst her bubble. "No worries, Hun. I heard from Harold Meyer that the engagement party is this weekend. He mentioned you're bringing that cute redhead from the ladder accident?"

Mallory's feet skittered on the tiled floor, and she almost knocked over a patient's IV pole. "What?"

Janis frowned. "I might have misunderstood."

Mallory led the way to the break room where they stashed their purses and washed their hands. "No, you heard correctly. I just didn't realize the party's host's father-in-law would be giving a play-by-play of my dating life."

Janis held the door open with her elbow and scoffed. "Oh, come on, we all saw how Mr. Fox looked at you. He's smitten."

The earth tilted under Mallory, and she had to focus on breathing. If a random acquaintance knew of her and Beckett, then what hope did they have of keeping it a secret any longer? She needed to find Beckett and change their plan. They couldn't wait until after the party. It was too risky.

But all her plans of making this right evaporated at the first code red of the shift. Fourteen hours later Mallory pulled out of the parking garage weighed down with fatigue. When she arrived at home and found Beckett inside playing with Fernando and a pair of French bread pizzas in the oven, she didn't have the energy to plan. All Mallory wanted was a night of peace with the man she loved. Was that too much to ask?

CHAPTER 21

The engagement party was as lovely and perfect as Mallory imagined. Max had shut down the diner, offering guests the run of the whole restaurant. CeCe's parents had flown in separately, and despite her nerves over them getting along, it seemed they were. Mallory didn't know them well, but they weren't yelling or glaring, so she considered that a win.

Of course, her parents were there, her mother flitting about like she was the one in charge. Mallory thought it was cute that CeCe let her think that. Nothing could be more annoying than Pamela Lawson if she didn't get her way. Although, Mallory was certain, her father Dale could give them all a run for their money. Sophie, Emily, their husbands, and kids represented the rest of the Lawson clan.

Not for the first time, Mallory wished she had her own plus one to keep an eye on her. Their secret dating was nebulous at best, and she yearned for a true partner like her siblings had. As if being summoned from her daydreams, Beckett appeared at her side with a glass of wine and a plate stacked with snacks. He looked handsome in a light gray suit that made his eyes pop. His glasses were in place, but a small blob of cocktail sauce clung to the corner of one lens.

Placing a hand at the small of her back, he steered Mallory toward the corner of the counter where there were two vacant stools. "Thought we could both use a break," he said as he arranged the plates and glasses. Mallory missed the contact, but she appreciated the refreshments.

"Where's the cheesy bites?" she asked, peering under a napkin.

"This ain't my first rodeo." Beckett winked, sliding a plate overflowing with the little delicacies. Mallory greedily popped two in her mouth before Beckett had a chance to sit down. "Hey now, save some for me. I took my life into my own hands when I went searching for these. I'm pretty sure the mayor's wife tried to stab me with a shrimp fork."

Mallory snorted, mostly because she knew Natalie could totally take Beckett down if she wanted to…utensils not required. "Thank you for your service." She held up a cheesy bite between her fingers, and much to her delight, Beckett leaned in with his mouth open. Deciding it was best not to overthink this public display, she inched closed and placed the morsel on his tongue. It was an intimate gesture, one they'd shared countless times. But now, sitting at her brother's engagement party surrounded by everyone she loved, it felt monumental. More importantly, it felt right.

Beckett made a guttural sound that brought a flush to Mallory's cheeks. "What the hell does CeCe do to these things? I swear, there's got to be crack in there or something." He wiped his mouth with the back of his hand before grabbing one of the wine glasses. "I hope you didn't mind white. I took the first thing I found."

Sipping from her glass, Mallory savored the crisp fruitiness of the wine for a moment. She nodded her approval and watched Beckett munch on a tiny puff pastry ladened with shrimp. His eyes flashed when the spicy sauce hit his tongue, but he recovered quickly with a cough.

Beckett looked as delectable as the appetizers they were currently devouring. His red hair was slicked back, giving the perfect opportunity to stare at his five o'clock shadow and tortoise shell glasses. Yet again, they were slightly askew, but he didn't seem to notice.

Mallory yanked at the hem of her dress, which was the same blue as Beckett's shirt. When she arrived and saw they coordinated without planning, it brought a lump to her throat that she was still trying to ignore. Yet again, without even trying to, they were in sync.

As if reading her mind, Beckett leaned closer to whisper in her ear. "You look gorgeous tonight."

Mallory shivered at the sensation of his breath on her neck. "Thanks, so do you." Idly, she reached out to smooth his tie back into place. She felt the warmth of his skin through the cotton of his shirt, and reminded herself they weren't supposed to be doing this. They weren't supposed to look like a couple. This was Evan and CeCe's time, and she needed to remember that.

"Are you coming over to my place later?" Beckett asked, his eyes locked on hers.

Attempting to hide her growing blush, Mallory sipped from her glass and looked around the room. No one seemed to be paying them any attention, but still she worried. "I want to, but I'll have to see what my sisters are up to."

Beckett nodded, toying with the charm bracelet on Mallory's wrist. The metal charms clattered together like a miniature windchime. "Your sisters like me," Beckett said, a smile tugging at the corner of his lips. "I could always just tag along like when we were kids."

Mallory returned his grin, because he wasn't wrong. Sophie and Emily adored him, but that wasn't the issue. The issue was that she wanted Beckett with her as her boyfriend, as her plus-one. Not to mention, Emily was on to them and wouldn't make it easy on him.

Just as she was about to say something, Evan and CeCe approached. They were arm in arm, both wearing matching smiles and heart-eyes. CeCe was in a very un-CeCe ensemble of a midi dress the color of whipped cream paired with ballet flats. Her blond hair was pulled up into a

215

chignon, and she even wore a touch of makeup. She practically radiated next to Evan. Her brother wore a white Oxford and tie with wedges of cheese on it. He was adorably Evan, and her heart swelled.

"There you two are." CeCe pulled Mallory in for a quick hug and swatted Beckett on the arm. "How's the food?"

Beckett gestured toward their empty plates, not a crumb left on them. "Freaking amazing. I can't believe you cooked for your own party."

Mallory and Evan said in unison, "I can."

CeCe rolled her eyes but laughed with the group. "Sue me. I am a bit of a control freak in the kitchen."

"If these are the results, you won't get an argument from me."

For a few moments, the foursome chatted about the food and the party. The atmosphere was relaxed, and Mallory leaned into Beckett's side. Her feet were killing her in these heels, which she promised herself she'd destroy as soon as the evening was over. Whether intentional or not, Beckett leaned back, providing a solid support. This close, she could smell the warm cedar of his cologne.

"Foxy, I almost forgot." Evan theatrically slapped his forehead, his tell that whatever he was about to say was in no way a surprise. Apparently none of the Lawsons could lie worth a damn. "I've got someone for you to meet."

Beckett's glass froze mid-way to his lips as his eyes quickly darted to Mallory. "Oh, yeah?" His tone was casual, but he tensed beside her.

Evan nudged CeCe in the side before continuing. "Yeah, she's a friend of CeCe's."

Mallory looked around the diner, eager to see which single women roamed among them. She'd met a few of CeCe's friends, but most of them lived in Buckeye Falls. Obviously Alice, Ginny, and Natalie weren't going to be competition. Suddenly a pop of purple appeared in the crowd and a lithe woman in her late twenties joined them. She looked vaguely familiar, and Mallory wracked her brain

216

to remember where she'd met this woman.

"Julia!" CeCe exclaimed, breaking away from Evan's side to hug her friend. "We were just talking about you."

Evan took Beckett's hand and yanked him a step closer to the other woman. "Julia, you need to meet my best man, Beckett Fox. Foxy and I go way back." He clapped his friend on the back and continued, "This is Julia. She used to work with CeCe up in Chicago."

The appreciative stare Julia sent Beckett's way made Mallory's toes curl—which was pretty painful in these shoes. "Very nice to meet you, Beckett." Her voice was deep and velvety, like she was speaking through her own personal sound system.

Dutifully, Beckett took her hand and shook it, dropping it like it was on fire. "Nice to meet you, too."

For a moment, no one said anything, and Mallory couldn't handle the silence. "And I'm Mallory, Evan's sister. I think we met at the food truck competition last year."

Finally, Julia looked away from Beckett and nodded at Mallory. "Oh yeah, hey."

"Hey," Mallory replied lamely, hating the entire interlude. It was obvious from the looks everyone was sharing that she was the odd person out—yet again. If they had been honest with Evan, they could have avoided this awkward attempt at matchmaking.

CeCe clapped her hands, grabbing everyone's attention. "I need to grab a few more things for the cupcakes, and Evan needs a few minutes with the Lawsons." Turning to Mallory, she asked, "Do you mind helping me in the back for a few minutes?"

Evan nodded like it was the greatest idea he'd ever heard in his entire life. "That's a great idea! Then Julia and Beckett can get to know each other."

Mallory faced Beckett, waiting for him to say something, anything to show he wasn't interested in getting to know Julia. But he didn't do anything other than nod and smile at the other woman. Mallory had had enough. "Show me where the cupcakes are," she said to CeCe as she stomped off. Her feet howled in pain, but she couldn't slow her pace. She needed to get away from everyone.

From behind her, she heard CeCe greet new guests on their way to the back. As soon as she reached the kitchen, Mallory kicked off her shoes and hurled them to the corner. CeCe's footfalls faltered when she joined her future sister-in-law. "What's wrong?"

"These freaking shoes. I don't know why I thought they were a good idea. I should stick with what I know, which are crocs and sneakers."

CeCe stepped over to the far wall where a bank of lockers stood. She opened one of them and tossed a pair of Converse to Mallory. "They're probably a size too small, but leave them unlaced and you'll be fine."

"Thanks," Mallory said, doing just that. She could hardly wiggle her toes, but it was better than standing barefoot in the diner's kitchen.

CeCe went to work pulling out trays of cupcakes from the chiller drawer before gathering jars of sprinkles. "We just need to put a few shakes of each on each cupcake. I'm not getting that technical today."

"You got it." Mallory quickly washed her hands and got to work on the decorations. She slid a completed tray closer to CeCe who nodded her approval.

"You're a natural. If you ever get tired of saving lives, I can always use a hand."

Mallory chuckled, but kept her focus on the task at hand. If she focused on sprinkles, she wouldn't think of the love connection happening just beyond the kitchen's doors.

"I'm sorry, you know."

"For what?" Mallory asked, keeping her attention on a finicky cupcake that was falling out of its wrapper.

"For Evan's matchmaking with Beckett and Julia. Evan didn't share his plans until we were walking over to greet you guys."

Mallory froze at CeCe's statement. She carefully put the

cupcake down and met her gaze. "It's fine. It's not like we're official or anything." She shook the sprinkle cannister too hard, covering one of the cakes with a half cup of edible confetti. Muttering to herself, she shook off the excess before shoving the treat in her mouth. She chewed and fought off a wave of tears. She would not break down at the engagement party.

CeCe handed her a paper towel and glass of water. "Take a moment. I didn't mean to upset you."

Mallory dabbed at her lips with the towel and focused on slowing her breathing. "I'm fine. It's fine. Beckett and I aren't—"

"Completely in love with each other? Yeah, I'm not buying that."

Mallory spluttered, trying to think of the perfect excuse. Crumbs fell from her mouth, a sad version of confetti. "We're just friends."

"Uh-huh. I don't buy that for a heartbeat. You already forgot our conversation from last week? I don't think friends feed each other cheese and fix each other's hair." She thrust her hands on her hips and sighed. "I saw the looks you two were giving each other back there. Beckett looked like he'd rather tame a pack of wild lions that talk with Julia. And you, miss grumpy pants, look like someone punted Fernando across the diner. You two are clearly made for each other." CeCe trailed her finger through the pile of sprinkles and added, "You need to tell Evan the truth."

"I know." Mallory's pulse hammered in her temples. She idly rubbed the tender skin, willing herself out of a headache. If CeCe had figured it out, how hadn't Evan?

Reading her mind, CeCe soldiered on. "And I'm guessing my sweet fiancé is clueless about you two, right? God, I love that man with all my heart, but he certainly can't see the forest for the trees."

"We...we..." Mallory felt like a broken record, repeating nonsense while CeCe raised an eyebrow.

Evan burst through the kitchen door, an even bigger

219

smile on his face than the last time she saw him. "Guess what," he declared, striding to CeCe and picking her up. He twirled her in a circle before placing her back on the ground and kissing her senseless. "We're going out after the engagement party. Mom and Dad will watch the kids, so all us couples can have a night out. Alice suggested the pub in Elm River, what do you say?"

"The couples?" Mallory asked, already hating where this was going.

Flinging an arm around CeCe's shoulder, her brother grinned. "Yeah, and you of course. Julia and Beckett seem to be hitting it off, so I thought we'd see where that goes."

In that instant, Mallory truly hated her brother and his blind optimism toward love. She wished he'd wear a pair of rose-colored glasses for her and Beckett, but apparently not. "Hard pass," she spat, plodding toward the rear exit.

"Mal?" Evan chased after her, snagging her elbow before she could make her escape. She couldn't look at him because she was moments away from a total, nuclear meltdown. This wasn't happening, it couldn't. She would not make a scene at her brother's engagement party.

"I've got a headache. You guys have fun." She shrugged off her brother's hand and pushed outside. Behind her, she heard CeCe shouting for her to come back, but she couldn't.

Mallory hated being a drama queen, but right now she couldn't fathom spending time with a bunch of couples pretending she wasn't in one, pretending she hadn't been in love with Beckett for fifteen stupid years. This wasn't a new dynamic, unfortunately, being tacked on as the single person; the one who couldn't find their other half. It made the whole moment more frustrating because she had found her other half. But Beckett chose to stay quiet, to literally take another woman out for the night. Yet again, she'd gotten it all wrong. Their stolen kisses and secret nights together weren't the beginning of something permanent. They were a continuation of the same pattern they'd been in forever.

Maybe it was finally time to break the pattern?

It took her the drive home to realize she was still in CeCe's old sneakers, the fabric too tight on her toes. Mallory kept the shoes on because they felt as awkward and useless as she did at that moment.

CHAPTER 22

Beckett was in hell. He hadn't had a chance to find Mallory before she left, and now he had a very drunk Julia on his hands—literally. "You look so cute in your glasses," Julia slurred, her third cocktail of the evening dangling from her fingers. Her other hand tugged on his collar, and Beckett didn't know how to pull free without hurting the poor woman.

"Julia," he gasped as she spilled her appletini on the leg of his slacks. The neon-green liquid made it appear like an alien vomited all over him, which would be preferable to his current situation. "I really need to get up for a moment." Beckett was so far down in the booth, he was practically horizontal.

At the behest of Alice, Mallory's bestie who clearly wanted her here instead of Julia, all the couples had caravanned over to Elm River to continue the party. The pub had a huge circular booth that sat a dozen people, and right now, he and Julia were stuck in the middle. From his perch in hell, Beckett saw Evan and CeCe slow dancing on the tiny dancefloor, her head resting on Evan's shoulder. He wished he could have enjoyed his friend's happiness a little longer, but Julia decided to be helpful.

223

"Oh noooo," she cooed when she spied her spilled drink. "I got you all wet." She hiccupped before grabbing a paper napkin and blotting at his leg.

Beckett lurched as far away as he could, cupping her hand and stopping her efforts. "Please, Julia. It's fine."

Across the booth, he heard the very distinct snicker of Alice Snyder. Turning to face her he asked, "A little help here?"

Alice shook her head, draining the last of her wine. "C'mon, James," she said to her boyfriend. "I think I feel like dancing." She glared as she slid from the booth and out into the din of the rest of the party.

He couldn't blame Alice, as she was aware of his and Mallory's muddled status. Actually, that wasn't fair. The status wasn't muddled, he knew exactly what he wanted. And what he wanted wasn't sitting here with a drunk stranger in a bar he didn't know without the woman of his dreams.

When Evan and CeCe introduced Julia, he assumed they would small talk for a moment while Mallory helped CeCe. Simple enough. He could handle inane chatter for five minutes. When Alice suggested everyone go to Elm River to continue the party, he was all for it. But when Mallory wasn't there and Julia was shoved into his car, Beckett wanted to puke. This wasn't how it was supposed to go, and he couldn't get Mallory to answer her phone.

"I fink ve should dance too," Julia slurred into Beckett's ear, the scent of sour apples hitting his nostrils. Turning his head, he scanned the pub for any sign of help and trying not to gag at the smell of stale booze.

Sophie and Emily were currently dancing circles around Evan to one of his favorite K-Pop tunes, while Alice and James spoke animatedly with Natalie and Anthony. He couldn't find CeCe, but he hoped she'd make an appearance soon to save him from her friend. "I don't know if dancing sounds good right now," he said mostly to himself since Julia was currently fascinated with the state of the sugar packet caddy on the table.

"Look at these little envelopes." Giggling, Julia pulled out all the packets and stacked them in front of her. Balling up her fist, she smashed it down until the packets crumbled and sugar substitute puffed into the air. "Now it's snowing," she exclaimed, trailing her fingers through the mess.

Yeah, Beckett needed to get out of there. Now that they were the only pair in the booth, he slid his way to freedom. "I'll be right back," he promised, knowing full well he wasn't coming back if he could help it.

Plodding out to the dance floor, he waved to get Evan's attention. "Where's CeCe?" he yelled into his friend's ear, hoping he could be heard over the sound system.

Evan lifted his shoulders, seeming completely unphased by Beckett's situation. "Dunno, but she promised to find us some food." Judging from the dark smudges under Evan's blue eyes and the slouch in his frame, he wasn't the only one who over imbibed.

"Got it." Beckett flashed a smile before turning and searching for the bride-to-be. He needed to figure out how to get Julia back to her hotel, and he wasn't about to volunteer for the task. At the entrance to the pub a young hostess piled up menus and looked ready to head out herself. "Excuse me," he said, hoping he didn't look as disheveled as he felt.

The expression the hostess gave him confirmed he looked like a wrung-out sponge. "Yeah?"

"Have you seen a petite blonde in a white dress around?"

With a snort, the hostess nodded. "You mean the scary lady?"

Beckett bit back a laugh, because he personally wouldn't consider CeCe scary—unless food was involved. "Was she asking about food?"

"Pfft, you can say that. I told her the fries were frozen from our vendor, and she had a fit. Asked to see the chef and stormed off toward the kitchen. We never let customers back there, but I don't get paid enough for that level of fierce." She put away the last menu and strode out the door.

Beckett glanced over his shoulder, finding Julia asleep at the table. A sugar packet was stuck to her cheek, but she seemed unharmed. Good, at least she wouldn't run away before he found help. Heading to the rear of the restaurant, he heard CeCe before he stepped into the kitchen.

"Look man," she said, hands on her hips. Even standing in a stranger's kitchen in her engagement finery, she was a force. "I know your poutine is the best in Ohio, that's not what I'm saying."

The chef, a man in his thirties wearing a bandana and expression of utter shock, mirrored her posture. "Look lady, I don't know who you think you are. You can't just barge into my kitchen and critique the food. It's a pub for crying out loud, not a Michelin-star restaurant."

CeCe huffed out a sigh, but she did not back down. "I'm just saying that if you cut your potatoes from fresh, you'd have a better product overall."

"And I'm saying that I'm not made of money and don't have the time and staff to peel and cut for every order. Now if you'll let me get back to it, I'll feed you and your friends."

Clasping her hands in prayer, CeCe soldiered on. "But can I at least show you the difference?"

The chef was incredulous. "You want to make your own food? In my kitchen?" Pausing a moment to scan her outfit he added, "In that get up?"

She nodded once, her chin tipped up. "Yes."

"Lady, you're nuts. I can't decide if I should laugh or call the cops."

Beckett made his presence known, stepping up to CeCe and resting his hand on her shoulder. Her skin vibrated with frustration and tension. "I don't know if you know who you're talking to. This is CeCe LaRue. Her food truck won the—" but his explanation died on his tongue when the chef barked out a laugh.

"No freaking way, I thought you looked familiar." He stepped back and gestured to the prep counter. "Ms. LaRue, make yourself at home."

CeCe shot Beckett an approving look before striding to the sink and washing her hands. "Watch and learn, buddy," she teased.

Having never seen CeCe in her element, Beckett pointed to a stool in the corner of the cramped space. "You mind if I set up shop and watch the master?" Evan had talked his ear off about CeCe's culinary prowess, and he wanted a free show.

"The more the merrier," the other chef deadpanned. Turning to CeCe he said, "I'm Shane, by the way."

"Shane, hand me that chef's knife and a cutting board."

Twenty minutes later, the most gorgeous plate of fries was presented to Shane and Beckett. "Watch out, they're going to be scalding." CeCe quickly added a pinch of parsley with a flourish before handing each man a fork. Beckett took his life into his own hands and stabbed a fry, shoving it into his mouth before he could think better of it.

The fry was hot, but perfectly seasoned with a fluffy interior and crunchy exterior. It was, quite simply, the best potato he'd eaten in his entire life. "Holy crap," he said, covering his mouth while he chewed. "CeCe, if Evan wasn't marrying you, I would."

Shane nodded his agreement, snagging a handful before anyone could stop him. "You might have convinced me."

CeCe looked smug, and rightfully so. "Thank you, gentlemen." Facing Shane she added, "Do you mind getting these out to my friends? I'll clean up my mess."

The other chef shot her a thumbs-up before loading plates with food and going out to the dining room. Beckett rolled up his shirt sleeves. "Let me help with that."

For a few minutes, they worked in silence, the clattering of dishes drowning out the canned popped music coming from the overhead speakers. CeCe handed Beckett a spatula and pointed to a drawer to his left. "I'm guessing this goes in there."

The sparkle of her engagement ring caught his attention,

227

and for a moment, all he could think about was Mallory. The ring was still stunning, catching the dim light and shooting red and white flares against the wall. Yet it didn't feel right, seeing it on someone else's hand—even though he knew the owner and her betrothed would truly live happily ever after.

How can I mourn an object, Beckett? How can I be this sad over something that was never really mine?

Mallory's words echoed through his head, rattling around until all Beckett heard was the clattering of the dishwasher lid closing. He hated seeing her so upset, and he wished he had a solution.

"Damnit," CeCe muttered behind him.

Fearing she was hurt, Beckett spun around to investigate. CeCe clutched her left hand to her chest and grimaced. "Crap, are you okay?" He scanned her for injuries, but she seemed fine.

CeCe blew a lock of hair off her forehead and leaned against the counter. "Nothing, I'm fine."

Beckett handed her a towel, hoping it would help whatever hurt. CeCe took the towel and twisted it in her hands. She frowned down at her left hand, the ring twinkling in response. "You don't look fine. Is there anything I can do?"

CeCe sighed, tossing the towel onto the counter. "I keep catching my hand when I'm working. It's this darned thing." She held up her hand and groaned. "I guess I could take the ring off to cook, but I hate not wearing it."

Beckett felt bile tickle the back of his throat. He needed to play this cool. "You, erm, don't like the ring?"

A faint smile tugged at her lips and CeCe gave a tiny bob of her head. "It's a stunning Lawson family heirloom. What's not to love?"

Anyone with eyes could read between the lines on that statement. Not for the first time, he wondered how much thought Evan really put into the ring selection. He loved Evan like a brother, but that didn't mean he wasn't a man about things. He could see his buddy going with the family heirloom for tradition's sake, but also out of ease. It was a hell of a lot easier to have a ring on hand than to find the perfect one—the one meant for his woman.

"Sometimes," Beckett started on a sigh, "it's hard to find the perfect engagement ring. It's okay if the first one isn't a success."

CeCe flexed her hand in front of her, studying the ring like it held the answers to the universe. "Evan loves this ring."

He stepped closer, keeping his tone light. "Evan loves *you*. I'm sure if you told him how you felt about the ring, he'd make it right."

And I'd make it right by putting it on Mallory's finger.

"I don't know, Beckett. I think that—" but she never got a chance to finish her thoughts, as the man himself strode into the kitchen.

"I should have known you'd be here," Evan said. His blond hair was matted to his temples, sweat dotting his upper lip. "Sophie, Em, and I are all danced out. When I went in search of my girl, I was told you were schooling the chef on how to fry potatoes."

CeCe flashed a look at Beckett before closing the distance to Evan. That look spoke volumes, and Beckett was not about to break that trust. "You know me." She laughed as she pecked her fiancé on the cheek. "Beckett was helping me clean up."

"And now Beckett needs to ask a favor," he said, chuckling at Evan's expression. "Your attempts at matchmaking failed, man. I'd like someone to get Julia home."

CeCe gave Beckett another look he couldn't decipher before offering a solution. "Why don't you head out and bring poor Mallory her shoes?"

Evan wrinkled his brow. "Why doesn't Mal have shoes?"

Beckett felt his stomach sink, a sense of dread creeping down his spine. "Is she okay?"

"She said she had a headache and wanted to get out of

229

those shoes. I'm sure she's fine." CeCe patted around her dress until she reached into a hidden pocket. "Let me walk you out and get the shoes." Over her shoulder she said to Evan, "Bring Julia out front. I'll meet you both there." Evan shot them a thumbs-up and ducked back into the dining room.

CeCe sprinted ahead, occasionally glancing around them as if they were being followed. When they reached her truck, she whipped around and whispered, "We have about sixty seconds for me to tell you a lot of information."

Beckett blinked, suddenly feeling like he was back in school at the principal's office. "Okay?"

"Don't say a thing about the ring to Evan. Please? I overreacted and everything is fine." She took a deep breath before she continued, "And you need to check on Mallory. I don't know what is happening with you two, but she was clearly upset when she left the diner."

Running a hand down his face, Beckett swore under his breath. "I need to find her."

CeCe opened her trunk and tossed him a pair of heels. "You do, and the sooner the better. I'm sorry we tried setting you and Julia up." She hesitated only a moment before adding, "But you two need to come clean to Evan."

"I know," Beckett groaned. "What a mess."

CeCe opened the driver's door. "Only if you let it be. Go get her."

Clutching Mallory's shoes, Beckett stepped back and watched CeCe pull up to the front of the pub. He stalked over to his car and carefully laid the heels on the passenger's seat. Mallory must have been pretty upset to leave without her shoes. A knot formed in his stomach at all that had transpired that night, and Beckett wasn't sure he didn't need an antacid.

Getting behind the wheel, he thanked his lucky stars he hadn't drank at the pub. He needed a clear head for what he was about to do. He just hoped Cinderella was ready to see her Prince Charming.

CHAPTER 23

"Mallory, please let me in." Beckett rested his head against her closed front door, willing her to at least pretend he had been knocking for five minutes. Never had he been so glad for Buckeye Falls and their low crime rate, as not even one neighbor came out to investigate his late-night visit.

From inside, he heard footfalls and a thud. Knocking again, he finally tried the knob and found it locked. Raking a hand through his hair, Beckett struggled to come up with a plan. He wouldn't literally break her door down, but he also couldn't stand here and listen to her—potentially—suffering.

Suddenly, he remembered the Lawson family home and their habit of keeping keys in loose bricks by the door. Feeling around the bricks of the door frame, Beckett found a loose block and pulled it free. Just as he'd hoped, a single key was nestled in the void. "I'm coming in," he announced as he opened the door to her apartment.

He found Mallory instantly, slumped on the sofa with an arm over her face. Her dress from the night was rumpled, and he could smell the alcohol on her breath from five feet away. Fernando sat on her torso, kneading his paws into

Mallory's belly.

"Jesus, Mal. Are you okay? Talk to me."

He closed the distance in two long strides, easing down on his knees. Beckett carefully pulled her arm from her face and swiped a rogue lock of chestnut hair off her forehead. Her eyes were closed, but her lips were moving in silent conversation. "What did you do, Mal?" Beckett stood and went to the kitchen in search of water and some ibuprofen. In a matter of hours, she was going to have the worst hangover.

With a careful hand, he helped Mallory sit up and propped pillows behind her. Fernando was not a fan of losing his spot and hissed before darting under the couch. Mallory's head lolled forward, but he was there to steady her. "I'm not a baby," she muttered, more to herself than Beckett. He was certain she didn't know he was there.

"I know you're not, sweetheart." Beckett's heart shuddered in his chest. He hated to see Mallory like this, especially knowing he was the reason. He cursed himself for not saying something at the diner, for letting Evan's matchmaking get the better of him—yet again.

"I vant to sleeeeeeeep," Mallory droned, her mouth continuing to move after she was done speaking. Her slurred speech sounded like the Count from Sesame Street, but Beckett wasn't about to alert her to that. He'd share that little gem for later, when everyone was sober and speaking to each other again. *God, hopefully that will be sooner rather than later...*

Beckett pressed two pills into her hand and held out the glass of water. "You can sleep soon, but first, I need you to drink this and take these."

Mallory blinked awake long enough to take the glass from him. Her movements were jerky, and some of the water splashed down the front of her dress. "Oops." She giggled as she popped the ibuprofen into her mouth and downed them in one swallow. "I'm a mmmmmeeeessssss," she said the last word as a long slur, thumping back onto the

232

couch cushion. "I vant it to stop hurting," she said, her blue gaze downcast.

Beckett squeezed her hand and sighed. This was killing him. "I know, but the headache will go away soon."

Mallory shook her head so forcefully, her braid pulsed on her shoulders. "No, no, no," she argued, waving her free hand through the air. When she was done making random gestures, she balled her fist and thwacked it on her chest. "I want *this* to stop hurting," she corrected him. "It hurts all the time." Her eyes fluttered closed and Beckett's knees gave out.

Allowing gravity to take over, he crouched on the floor and cupped her face in his hands. *This* was going to kill him, watching Mallory suffer under another misunderstanding. "Mal, I know you won't remember this," Beckett said, his throat closing around his confession, his eyes burning with fresh tears. "But I love you. I'm so sorry about tonight, and I'm always going to be sorry for what happened before. I will make this right, I promise."

Blowing raspberries with her tongue, Mallory gave a stilted laugh. "Words are cheap, mister. And besides." She huffed and tried to situate herself better on the couch. "I want to hear them from Beckett. I'm sure you're a nice man, but you're not the one I want…" Her drunken admission left him stunned.

"It's me, sweetheart. Beckett."

Mallory rolled onto her back and covered her face with her arm again. "No, you're not. He's out with Juuuuuulllllllliiiiaaaa. Yet again, I'm not good enough."

It would have been less painful if the roof had caved in and crushed him right then and there. Beckett rubbed over his sternum; the aching so acute he was surprised he was still breathing. "Mallory, you've always been good enough." Letting out a humorless laugh, he continued. "You're the gold standard to every woman I've dated. I'm so sorry you never knew that, and as soon as you're sober, I'm going to show you how much you mean to me."

At first, Mallory didn't respond. Her lifeless form sprawled on the couch, legs straight and arms at odd angles. Beckett cleared his throat, anxious to see if Mallory had indeed heard him. "You seem like a nice guy," she muttered into a cushion. "But I'm in love with someone else."

Shoving his glasses up his nose, Beckett frowned. He was certain he was the someone else, but badgering a half comatose Mallory was a fool's errand. "Oh, yeah?" he asked casually.

Mallory rolled around, curling up into a little ball. "Yeah. He's my friend, but he doesn't see me. I'm just his friend's sister." She wiggled her bottom and curled more into herself; her next words nearly inaudible from her drunken cocoon. "I'm not worth the risk."

Beckett yanked off his glasses and rubbed his temples. Despite his own sober state, his head pounded with the need to fix this situation. He couldn't believe they were back here again, and moreover, he couldn't believe that Mallory didn't already know how he felt.

It was frankly embarrassing how often they'd been down this road, the path worn and familiar. What was that old adage? The definition of insanity was doing the same thing over again and expecting different results? Look up Beckett Fox in the dictionary, and there would be a full spread of his freckled face under "I".

"His Gram," Mallory mumbled, the mention of his grandmother shaking him back to the present. "She used to say we belonged together. Isn't that nice?" She rolled over, tucking her knees up to her torso, her braid falling over her cheek and obscuring his view of her face.

"Oh, yeah?" he asked, knowing exactly the situation that Mallory spoke of. He rested his arm on the sofa, his fingers smoothing over Mallory's cheek so he could see her eyes.

When they were kids, and when she was scared, Mallory loved to hide around the farm, curled up into a ball. By the time he or Evan found her, one of them would have to coax her from her cocoon. Back when they were teenagers,

234

Mallory had come to the farm to help Gram with canning preserves. Looking back at that time, Beckett knew his grandmother missed having more family around. Every time the Lawson kids came over, she found a variety of activities to keep everyone engaged and happy.

On this day, Mallory had been dumped by a boy she met in the high school orchestra. They had only gone on a couple of dates, but Mallory seemed smitten. During the entirety of that brief courtship, Beckett found anything he could do to keep busy. The last thing he needed were more reminders that, yet again, he'd missed his opportunity with Mallory. His World of Warcraft characters were doing really well, not to mention his curve ball was looking fierce. He'd also managed to harvest a row's worth of apples on his own before the foreman scolded him for taking his team's job.

Evan hadn't joined his sister that day, so Beckett was in the den with Gramps watching football highlights. He'd gone to the kitchen in search of something to drink when he'd heard hushed voices and his grandmother's comforting tone. "Now dear," she'd said while carefully spooning hot jam into waiting jars. "Sometimes people are brought into our lives to show us what we're missing. They fill a gap you didn't know you had, complementing your life, and in some cases, making it better."

Mallory had snorted, covering her mouth and apologizing. "Sorry, Gram, but Colin was not that guy."

His grandmother had winked and chuckled. "I know, dear, that's why I'm telling you to wait for the man who is. Who knows, he may be closer than you think."

Beckett had held his breath, willing his feet to move and bring him to Mallory's side. Instead, he stood in the shadows like a weirdo and eavesdropped on their private conversation. Just as he was crippled with guilt over his covert listening, Mallory knocked the wind out of his sails.

"There is someone," Mallory said carefully. "But he's not interested in me at all. I might as well be invisible."

Gram sealed a jar and handed it to Mallory. "Have you

told this boy how you feel?"

Mallory sighed, her body deflating with the effort. "If he doesn't see it now, he never will."

Turning her head to hide her smile, Gram soldiered on. "I'm going to let you in on a little secret, Mallory. Men are not that bright." Mallory tittered but didn't interrupt the life lesson. "I will love Richard and Beckett until my dying breath, but those two cannot find their way out of a paper bag. Sometimes with men, you need to spell it out."

Mallory stacked the last of the jars and wiped her hands on a tea towel. She padded to the fridge and took a pitcher of iced tea and filled two glasses. "I think if I spell it out, that will be the end of our friendship."

Gram took her tea from Mallory and they clinked glasses. "Then it doesn't sound like a friendship worth keeping."

Beckett shook himself back to the present, adjusting one of the pillows on the couch to support Mallory's neck. So much time had been wasted on not telling each other how they felt. It weighed him down, hunching his shoulders with the weight of all the what-ifs.

"We're going to figure this out, Mal."

Mallory let out a little snore, nestling closer to the pillows. Beckett rested his head on the edge of the couch, staying close in case she needed anything. He wasn't going anywhere, and when the light of day hit, he would make it clear that he was done hiding from their feelings. Yes, it was a risk to dive into a relationship. He had no idea how Evan would react, but it didn't matter. He wouldn't put Mallory through another moment of secrets and lies. Evan would understand. Frankly, he had to.

He didn't think their hearts could handle any more.

*

Mallory woke with a crick in her neck and the walls spinning around her. Squeezing her eyes shut, she willed her brain to put the pieces together. Why was she sleeping on the couch? Why was she still in last night's dress? And more importantly, who was the person snoring on the floor?

As she bolted upright, two cushions landed beside her with a soft thud. Mallory rubbed the sleep from her eyes and peered over her perch to find Beckett. He was passed out, his glasses crooked and lips parted in sleep. Ginger waves fell over his forehead, and she had to ball her fist to keep from reaching out.

This didn't make any sense. Beckett had left with CeCe's friend. Yet again, he'd chosen to please Evan and leave her alone to deal with the emotional damage. Twisting free from her couch fort, Mallory tiptoed into the bathroom. The sight that greeted her in the mirror was worse than she could have imagined. Her mascara was smudged all over her cheeks, her breath reeked of vodka and regrets. Glancing at the time on her phone, she realized it was already nine thirty.

She thanked her forethought to take the day off work, as she wouldn't be saving any lives in this state. After quickly brushing her teeth and splashing water on her face, she emerged to find a still-sleeping Beckett.

He looked incredibly uncomfortable sprawled out like that, but she wasn't about to wake him. If anything, she was about to pad outside and drive out of town until she ran out of gas. How ridiculous were they? Dancing around their feelings for damn near their whole lives. The time had clearly come to break the cycle, and Mallory was the one to do it. Yes, last night had hurt. Watching him walk away broke what was left of her heart, and she couldn't keep doing this. If for no other reason than her stomach couldn't handle the binge drinking.

Finally, Beckett stirred, wiggling around until he finally opened his eyes. "Hey," he said through the dwindling moments of sleep.

"Hey yourself," she replied on a sigh. Her mother, and her sisters, had mastered the Lawson Ladies' Look years ago, and she'd recently become very astute as well. Brow knitted, she crossed her arms and pursed her lips. "What are you doing here?"

Beckett eased himself to a more vertical position, although the grimace on his face proved he might be too old to crash on random couches—or in this case, floors. "I came to return your shoes, and to check on you. We didn't get a chance to talk before you left."

Mallory was incredulous. "Before I left? You make it sound like I had better plans than watching my secret boyfriend leave with another woman."

Beckett frowned. "I'm also here to clear that whole thing up. You know I'm not into Julia, right? Christ, Mal. You really think I wanted to go out with another woman?"

"How could I think otherwise when you keep repeating this pattern?" Mallory flapped her hands between them, her charm bracelet tinkling in the quiet space.

White-hot rage bubbled up inside her, and Mallory relished the heat of anger. It felt good; she felt justified in her response. Who the hell was Beckett Fox anyway to play with her emotions like this? She was done, and it was time for him to know it.

"Repeating the pattern?"

Mallory nodded, holding up her hand as she counted down the damning evidence. "Yes, a pattern. Beckett, no one has dumped me more than you. I have a list if you're interested." She didn't bother waiting for an answer before she started tallying his offenses. "First, how could we forget the homecoming dance in high school?'

"That was..." But his argument was silenced by a couch cushion to the face, Mallory wasn't playing around.

"First, high school homecoming. No matter how many years ago that was," she added, a smirk of satisfaction curling her lips. "And then we have every summer break of college. Each and every time we started something, you would end it." He opened his mouth to interrupt, but the look on her face silenced him. "And how could we forget Gram's funeral? I show up to give you support, to have you lean on me while you grieve, and you leave with Evan for a night on the town with who the hell knows. If that wasn't painful enough, we finally come to a truce, to a way to be together. And at the first test of Evan's meddling, you're off like a shot with another woman. I cannot keep this going, Beckett. It's exhausting being your second choice. I must have enough pride to stop this." A tear fell down her cheek, and Mallory angrily swiped it away. "I think I deserve better than this. It's killing me."

"I've got nothing of value to say to that argument. You make some good points, Mal, but that isn't the whole story."

She threw her arms wide in invitation. "Then enlighten me, Beckett. Tell me why I'm not worth the risk."

"Don't you get it? Don't you see?" Beckett's voice cracked on the question, his bottom lip quivering despite his best efforts. His pale skin was blotchy with red patches sweeping up to meet the frame of his glasses.

Mallory exhaled, striving to keep herself calm. She had an encyclopedia's worth of facts to spew, but now wasn't the time. Now was the time for Beckett's truth. "What is it? What don't I see?"

Beckett paced around her, his hands alternating between balling to fists and running through his hair. The red curls were a mess, and she yearned to reach out and smooth them back; yearned to smooth his rough edges so he didn't carry this pain anymore. This shared pain was tearing them apart.

"You're all I have left," he finally said, voice low and worn with emotion. "You, Evan, hell, even the Lawson family. That's all I've got now."

"Don't you see? You've already had us."

"No." He laughed, but there wasn't an ounce of humor in it. "I don't, Mal. Because either way, I'm losing someone. I'm either telling my best friend I broke the bro code two decades ago and love his sister, or I'm telling you that I can't be with you for fear of losing my buddy. How freaking sad is that?" He threw his arms up, the air between them charged as if lightning were about to strike. "I've been beating myself up over this for years. I always thought I'd figure it out. Keep my friendship with Ev, but have you in my life."

Mallory held her breath, unsure of how to comfort Beckett when he was wild with emotions. Her normally stoic friend was crumbling before her eyes, and she had no words of comfort, nothing to reassure him that it would all work out in the end. "No matter what happens, you'll have me in your life."

Beckett's head fell back and he stared at the ceiling for a moment. His throat bobbed as he swallowed, the flush still bright and angry on his skin. "I want all of you, Mal. I want it all." His head dipped back and he snagged her gaze. His gray eyes were electric behind his smudged glasses, and Mallory didn't know if she should be afraid or turned on. "You know what I realized last night at the engagement party? Having you on my arm, walking through the evening together? This freaking sucks."

Misunderstanding his words, Mallory flinched. "Oh," she said lamely, hating that she didn't have the words to make this situation better; didn't have the words to show Beckett they were worth all the potential heart ache.

Finally, if only for an instant, Beckett's demeanor cracked and he chuckled. "It didn't suck because I was with you, Mal. It sucked because I wanted to be *with* you. I didn't want your parents making jabs about us not finding dates, your sisters saying we settled for each other." He banged his hand on his chest. "I wanted to have you on my arm, hands linked, stolen kisses in front of the whole damn world. I want you, all of you. And I want everyone in our lives to know it and understand it. To see how much we make sense, because from where I'm standing, there won't be anyone else."

Mallory's feet itched to run to him, to close the distance and promise nothing but perfection moving forward. But the image of him leaving with Julia, the lack of explanation when Evan pushed, that still echoed in her mind. "But you didn't say anything to Evan. Beckett, you left with another woman without a backward glance."

Beckett ran a hand down his face, his glasses catching at the bridge of his nose. Shoulders sagging, he fell back onto the couch, long limbs akimbo. "Mallory." The sound of her full name brought her up short. "I could not keep far away enough from that poor woman. No matter where I went, she was there. And all I could think was that I wanted to be anywhere with you. Hell, even in a spaceship headed toward the sun would have been a welcome alternative."

"Then why did you let me come home alone? Why did you make me out to be the fool, again?"

"Because I don't have anyone else." His argument was barely a whisper. At first, Mallory didn't know what to say, she hated that they were back here again. She'd made a promise to herself never to wait around for Beckett Fox to make the right decision, to choose her.

"I don't know how else to tell you that—"

"My dad didn't even come to Gramps's funeral." Beckett's admission rang throughout Mallory's apartment, and she felt her knees give out.

Easing herself onto the far end of the couch, she pivoted to face him. Beckett didn't move, his head resting on a cushion, gaze locked at a spot in the distance known only to him. "What?"

He licked his lips and sighed. "My dad *texted*," he emphasized the word, his mouth curled in disgust. "He texted to say he didn't want to make the trip from California. He heard from the attorney that Gramps left the farm to me, and he didn't see a reason to come back."

Abandoning her own emotions, Mallory reached out and took Beckett's hand. She squeezed it with all her might, hoping he could feel her support through their twined fingers. "Your father isn't a good person," she started, hating that she didn't have more than platitudes to offer. "I'm sorry he didn't come back."

Beckett didn't move, his hand as limp as a dead fish in

her own, but he didn't pull away. "I stood there, at the entrance to the orchard where Gram and Gramps are buried, waiting for Dad to show. I'd called, nearly begged him to join me. I needed the support after losing the most important person in my life. The son of a bitch never even returned my calls."

"I'm so sorry." Mallory's apology was a whisper lost to the moment. They were just words, words that held nothing of value.

"As I stood there," Beckett continued, his eyes locked in place, "I thought to myself, this is it. I don't have anyone else who cares about me. Then I thought of you and Evan, and I knew I needed to be closer to you both." Slowly, he turned his head to face her, and Mallory's heart cracked in half at his hopeless expression. "I can't explain it, Mal, but the thought of not having you both in my life guts me. If I'm not Foxy, I'm no one."

"That's not true," Mallory tried to argue, but Beckett wasn't having it.

"I have my online friends, strangers who share my love of video games and fantasy worlds, but I don't have connections with anyone else. I don't want to be alone anymore, but I don't know how to fix this."

Suddenly, he pulled himself to standing and strode toward the door. "I want to be with you, but I can't lose my only friend too. I don't know how to be everything to everyone, but I promise I'll try." His hand on the door knob, Beckett turned and added, "I don't want to lose you, Mal."

Cemented to the couch, Mallory watched helplessly as Beckett closed the door behind him with a quiet snick. He was still grieving, he was still raw... and he was still hers.

Mallory didn't know how, but they had to figure this out. Since getting Beckett back in her life, everything burst with color and warmth. She couldn't fathom a future without his crooked glasses and red hair in her life. He wasn't alone in this world, and she needed to find a way to prove it.

And the sooner, the better.

CHAPTER 24

"What has gotten into you, man?" Evan asked, hands thrust onto his hips in frustration. "You've been acting weird all day, and all I'm trying to do is get our tuxedos."

Beckett knew what was bothering him—or at least part of it—but he was not going to dissect his feelings now. Not when his best friend was standing in front of a three-way mirror while a tailor worked on his wedding day tux, the smile on his lips so infectious it could make the world's biggest skeptic believe in love.

And that was the thing, Beckett did believe in love. He had for years, decades even. He believed as soon as he put that ring on Mallory's finger in his grandparent's farm. He believed the first time they kissed, all bumbling and awkward. He believed it when he took Mallory to the prom, felt her pulse racing as he held her hand and spun her around the dance floor. He believed at the beginning of the summer when she dropped her gossip magazines in the parking lot, her defense of the rags written all over her lovely face. He believed when she helped him clean up the farm house, her patient gaze never leaving his while he cried and cried for the parents that felt like strangers, for the life he wasn't sure he wanted.

243

"I'm fine," he said, not quite meeting Evan's eye. "I just think that—"

"Think what?" Evan turned to snag his gaze, the tailor tsking as he stabbed Evan with a straight pin. "Ow."

The tailor gave a long-suffering sigh and harrumphed. "Please try not to be so animated, sir."

Beckett thought back to last night, watching CeCe fiddle with the ring, her admission that it wasn't really her style but meant so much to Evan. He knew in his heart of hearts that if Evan suspected CeCe wasn't in love with that ring he'd tear it from her finger and buy her the Hope Diamond. But he promised CeCe he wouldn't betray her confidence, even though Mallory could benefit from the honesty.

"Foxy, you're scaring me. What happened last night?"

Beckett toyed with the hem of his own jacket, suddenly very interested in the mother-of-pearl buttons. If only Evan knew how *everything* happened last night. Yet again, he'd hurt Mallory in his attempts to please his best friend, and he was sick to death of this merry-go-round. He wanted off the ride, he was tired of the games.

"Nothing but good food and friends happened last night."

Evan didn't look satisfied, but he did as the tailor asked and faced forward. Beckett thought he was out of the woods until Evan shimmied out of the tuxedo and handed it to the attendant, hands trembling slightly. As he pulled his T-shirt back on, he hesitated and gasped. Spinning on his heel, he stalked forward and shoved Beckett on the shoulder.

"What the hell, Lawless?" Beckett accused, shocked by the outburst. In their decades of friendship, Evan had never shown anything but a grin and easy-going nature.

Evan frowned, his blue eyes turning dark. "You don't like CeCe." The statement knocked Beckett back on his heels.

"What?"

"I saw you speaking in the pub, man. She looked a little upset, but later said it was just all the chaos of the day."

Beckett's head spun with a myriad of excuses, but he came up blank. "She was tired. There were like a million people there, and she showed up that other chef."

Evan scoffed. "There were twenty people there, and she shows up other chefs all the time. You're the only one she was upset with. What did you say?"

Beckett had to hand it to Evan. He'd never seen a man get this angry while still not wearing pants. Throw in the fact that Evan stalked the dressing room in his Spider-Man boxers and the scene was almost too much. He made a mental note to tell Mallory about it.

Mallory. Just thinking about her gave him the resolve to end the madness. True, it wasn't his story to tell, but there were two distressed women in this situation, and he'd be damned if he didn't say something.

"I don't hate your fiancée, you idiot."

Evan ran a hand through his hair, the blond waves landing haphazard across his forehead. Even on the sunny side of thirty, his buddy looked as young and vulnerable as their first day of school. "Then what the hell is going on?"

Beckett took a deep breath and readied himself for the wrath of Evan. "CeCe hates her engagement ring. Okay? I found her upset because it kept getting snagged on her dress." The color drained from Evan's face, leaving him as white as his undershirt. "I'm sorry, I didn't want to say anything, because it's between the two of you." And him and Mallory if Beckett were being honest. He would do anything to see that ring on her finger, but first needed to be a good friend and clean up this mess.

Evan eased himself down on the nearest chair, his knees shaking. "She hates the ring?"

Beckett grimaced. "*Hate* is a strong word. I just think it isn't her style, and she didn't want to hurt your feelings."

"She said she loved it," Evan said to no one in particular. His sightless gaze roamed the dressing room until Beckett couldn't stand it. He strode over to the stack of Evan's clothes and handed him his jeans and sneakers.

245

"Get dressed. This conversation is best served over beer and greasy pizza. My place is only two blocks away."

One hour, a six pack, and a pizza later, the two men were sprawled out on the couch, an old kung-fu movie playing on the TV. Evan hadn't said much since they arrived, and Beckett couldn't blame him. He tried his best to lighten the mood, asking stupid questions about the movie to get a rise out of Evan.

"Isn't that Bruce Lee?" he asked, gesturing to the TV with his empty beer bottle. Not only was it clearly not the martial artist, but it wasn't even a man. A woman in a yellow dress ran across the screen to hide from the bad guys, who were also clearly not the legend.

"Yeah," Evan sighed, tossing a pizza crust onto the coffee table and missing the box completely.

Beckett groaned and turned off the TV, shoving the remote next to the pizza box. He'd clean up this mess later, but first he needed to get his buddy back. "Okay, listen up, Lawless." He nudged him with his elbow. "We're going to do what I absolutely hate."

"Talk about feelings?"

Beckett brandished his empty beer bottle and rolled his eyes. "Correct. We're going to talk about feelings. When CeCe gets off work, just go over and talk to her."

Evan frowned. "She probably wants to call off the wedding." Evan couldn't have said something more outlandish if he tried. *Hey, when I'm done dumping the woman I love, how about I take up chainsaw juggling?*

"What?" Beckett was incredulous.

Evan jumped to his feet and paced into the kitchen, pulling out a beer and popping the top without offering one to Beckett. Taking a long pull, he downed half the bottle before he made it back to the couch.

"You know it's rude to drink your friend's last beer without even offering it to him."

Evan flipped him the bird. "Yeah, I think I'm allowed to drown my sorrows because the woman I love hates me."

246

"Okay." Beckett made a show of checking his watch. "This pity party can last for another sixty seconds, and then I'm calling it. CeCe doesn't hate you; she is just not a fan of your nana's ring. Don't you want her to be happy about the ring she's supposed to wear for the rest of her life?"

Finally, Evan seemed to listen. He bobbed his head a couple of times before finishing the beer and letting out a belch that was better served for a college dorm room. "I'm so freaking confused."

"You know how you can fix that?" Beckett teased, standing to collect their trash. He sensed a shift in his friend's demeanor and hoped that meant he'd have his apartment to himself again. Evan was great, but his social battery was waning fast. "Go over and see CeCe. Doesn't she get off work soon?"

Evan burped again, this time covering his mouth and grunting an apology. "I'm too drunk to drive," he mused.

Beckett tossed the box in the trash and clattered the beer bottles into the recycling bin. The echo of broken glass echoed in his tiny apartment. During times like this, he missed the farm house with its cavernous rooms and homey vibes. He could have roamed the rows of apple trees for hours clearing his head. Instead, he might as well have been back in college cleaning up after frat brothers.

Jingling his keys, he tossed Evan his shoes and chuckled. "I'll drive you over to CeCe's, but you need to not be a big baby about this. I feel terrible that I blabbed, but you need to hear her out."

Evan stumbled as he put his shoes back on, but he quickly corrected and ran his hands through his hair. "How do I look?"

Beckett took in his friend's rumbled appearance, from the T-shirt with a pizza stain to the dark smudges under his startlingly blue eyes. Those were the same eyes he'd stared into for most of his life, always reflecting back acceptance and warmth. He owed Evan the truth, owed him the full story of him and Mallory. It was time.

247

Whether it was years of friendship or just dumb luck, Evan seemed to read his mind. "You know," he said as he buckled into Beckett's passenger seat. When the car turned on, he silenced the radio and faced Beckett. "You didn't seem to hit it off with Julia. What happened?"

Beckett squeezed the steering wheel so tightly, he was surprised it didn't crack in half. "She's not my type."

Evan snorted. "How come no girl I find you is your type? No matter who I bring around, she's never good enough."

That wasn't true at all. If anything, Evan had brought perfection to his door and couldn't match the excellence of Mallory. "I don't know, Lawless. I'm just not as good with the ladies as you are."

"Yeah, right." Evan punched his arm and leaned back in his seat. "I want you to be as happy with someone as I am with CeCe."

Beckett's throat tightened at his friend's admission, his grip loosening to make a turn onto CeCe's street. "I want that, too." He let the truth out on an exhale, hoping Evan wouldn't pick up on how tortured he sounded.

Just as Beckett put the car in park, Evan spun to face him, his gaze stern yet serious. "I want you to know something, Beckett." The lack of his nickname brought his pulse skyrocketing.

"Um, yeah?" A bead of sweat rolled down his temple, and he regretted turning off the car. Not only was it stifling, but he felt he was about to make a quick exit.

"If you're..." Evan's words faltered as he flapped his hands between them. "What I mean is, if you're..." Evan's head fell back and he groaned. "Dammit, I'm really bad at this."

"Uh, considering I don't know what's going on, I'd agree." Beckett strived to keep his tone light, but he was petrified.

Muttering to himself, Evan finally caught Beckett's eye and blurted, "It's cool if you're gay. I'll stop throwing women at you. I just wish you would have told me, man."

Beckett couldn't help it. He burst out laughing. It could have been the stress of the last few days or the general absurdity of Evan's assumptions, but he couldn't hold back his reaction if he tried. "What?" He coughed as his laughter subsided.

For his part, Evan was mortified and looked like he wanted to melt into the car's upholstery. "That's not the reaction I expected." He rubbed the back of his neck.

Removing his glasses, Beckett dabbed at his eyes with the back of his hand. "I'm sorry, Lawless, it's really nice of you to support me coming out. The only problem is, I'm not gay."

Evan's expression shifted to shock, his eyebrows reaching his hairline. "You're not?"

"Not even a little bit."

"Then why won't you go out with any of these women?" Evan threw his arms in the air. "It's almost like you're trying to die alone."

This is it, Beckett told himself. The moment he'd been waiting for. He needed to tell Evan the truth. "I don't want to die alone," he said, his voice steady despite his racing heart.

"Then why don't you date more?"

Beckett slumped forward, his head resting on the steering wheel. He couldn't look Evan in the eye with his confession, didn't want to see the look of hurt and anger mare his affable face. "I'm in love with someone, and it hasn't worked out."

"Oh," Evan said on a sigh. "Damn, Foxy, I'm sorry. Is it anyone I know?"

Just rip off the Band-Aid, Beckett!

Squeezing his eyes shut, Beckett savored the last moment of having Evan on his side, the last moment of being Foxy to his Lawless. "Yeah, you know her."

"Who is it?" Evan leaned forward, and Beckett regretted spilling the beans in close quarters. All Evan had to do was reach out and he'd have Beckett in a head lock before he could blink.

"It's Mallory."

For a moment, Beckett didn't think he'd said her name. The silence was overwhelming, threatening to choke him to death. Unable to bear it, he slowly turned his head until he could see Evan. His mouth was moving like he was speaking, but no words came.

"Can you please say something?" Beckett begged, hating the reaction and not knowing what it meant.

Evan licked his lips, his gaze still not reaching the other side of the car. "Mallory." He said her name like it was a foreign word on this tongue. "Mallory."

"Yes, it's Mal."

The use of her nickname woke Evan up, and he reached out and flicked Beckett square in the forehead. "You're into my sister?"

"Well, yeah. But it's more than that."

Evan was incredulous. "More than that? What, is it because she helped after your accident? Dude, it'll pass."

"No, you're not hearing me. It's been years, this isn't a new infatuation."

His blue eyes turned to gray storm clouds at this. "Years? You've kept this secret from me for years?"

Beckett wanted the ground to open up and eat him whole. The look of disappointment, of devastation, was almost too much. "Yes, and I've hated lying about it."

Evan fumbled for the door knob, bursting through the door and tripping on the curb. He corrected in the nick of time and whirled around, stomping toward Beckett. "You've been into my sister and lied to me for years?"

In record time, Evan rounded the car and had Beckett by the shoulders, shaking him like he wanted him to crumble apart. Little did he know it was already happening; little pieces of Beckett chipped away at the devastation in Evan's gaze. "I didn't know how to tell you," Beckett said lamely, loathing that his explanation fell flat.

"I can't believe you." Evan shoved Beckett against the car and paced back and forth, his hands flexing at his side.

Beckett took his glasses off, folded them and placed them in his shirt pocket. He knew what was coming and really didn't want to get new glasses. Closing his eyes, he waited for the punch. It didn't take long.

Evan clocked him with a right hook to the face. The wind was out of Beckett before he hit the ground. Wheezing, he stayed on all-fours until he filled his lungs with air. "Get up," Evan barked, looking like a feral stranger instead of his childhood best friend.

Footsteps grew loud around them, and CeCe appeared. "What the hell is going on?" she asked, a look of horror on her face. "Beckett, oh my God." She rushed over to help him on his feet before turning to Evan. "Care to fill me in on this caveman routine?"

Evan thrust his finger in the air, pointing at Beckett and nearly foaming at the mouth. "He's into Mallory."

CeCe rolled her eyes. She muttered something under her breath before rallying. "Are you serious?"

Misunderstanding her reaction, Evan puffed out his chest in victory. "Yeah, and I'm going to kick his ass."

CeCe stifled a laugh and stepped between the two men. "First of all, no one is kicking anything. Second, it's about damn time."

"Huh?"

Now it was CeCe's turn, striding up to Evan and flicking him square in the forehead. "Babe, are you blind?"

"Ow." Evan covered his forehead and bobbed to avoid another flick. "What are you talking about?"

"Um, the worst-kept secret in Buckeye Falls?" CeCe asked, her voice tinged with laughter. "I love you, but you're blind as a bat if you haven't seen it before."

Evan shot a hurt look at Beckett, who felt it as acutely as the punch to the face. "Seen what?"

"They're obviously into each other. My God, Ev. You didn't see it at Beckett's? Or at the engagement party?"

Evan's gaze sharpened. "Have you kissed my sister?"

The telltale blush of guilt swirled up Beckett's neck in record time, turning him into Burning Man. If Evan only knew what all they had done together, he'd be part of the pavement by now. "Um, yes?"

CeCe snickered and tugged on Evan's arm when he stepped forward. "Whoa there, cowboy. Let's all take a deep breath." She sniffed the air. "Are you drunk?" She whirled around to face Beckett. "Why is my fiancé drunk in the middle of the day?"

Beckett held up his hands, he wasn't getting punched twice today. "And this is my cue to exit."

Evan leaned around CeCe, who had quickly become a human shield. "This isn't over, man."

CeCe huffed. "I think it is. Thanks for bringing him home."

Beckett flashed a look he hoped conveyed *sorry for spilling the beans on the engagement ring. Feel free to stop by and pummel me after dinner.*

Beckett got behind the wheel and headed toward home—real home. His brain on auto-pilot, Beckett was back in the farm house in record time. He let himself inside and found an old bag of peas in the freezer. Shoving them over his swelling eye, he strode out to the orchards.

While still in their orderly rows, the trees were weighed down with fruit that needed harvesting. The air was heavy with the scent of apples, a bitter sweetness that stung his nostrils. Birds flitted overhead, a few of their nests nestled between clusters of branches. Last season, the fruit had rotted on the trees, but maybe it was time for some changes. Beckett didn't want to lose this place, especially since he likely lost his best friend today.

This place was home, and no matter what happened with the Lawsons, Beckett knew in his bones he couldn't sell it. No one else would love the land, the house, and the general splendor like he did. *Like Mallory did...*

But he shook that thought away. He couldn't think

about Mallory right now; it was almost as painful as the growing welt on his face. As his legs took him further into the trees, the wind picked up as the sun dipped lower in the horizon.

Go get your girl...

He would, he just didn't know how. Everything he'd strived to keep perfect and together had crumbled at his feet. For all his efforts, Beckett now stood alone, the apple trees, a black eye, and a thawing bag of peas his only company.

Maybe this whole situation was headed for disaster all along. And maybe Gramps was an old romantic who couldn't see it coming. When Beckett reached the top of the hill, the familiar view brought him the comfort he craved. The house sat below, nestled in the rolling hills, a beacon calling him back.

No matter what happened with Evan and Mallory, Beckett knew he wasn't going anywhere. He couldn't fathom living anywhere else. He might be alone, but at least Beckett had found his home again.

CHAPTER 25

Mallory scrubbed her face, hoping that her cleanser would do more than erase blackheads. She needed the image of Beckett obliterated from her mind. The haunted look in his eyes as he left, the defeated slump in his shoulders; it gutted her. She'd known the man for most of her life, and it was clear he was still trudging his way through grief. It wasn't her place to fault him his own process, but it hurt that he wouldn't lean on her more, wouldn't trust that they would be okay in the end.

When she was as fresh-faced as anyone nearing thirty with a monster hangover could be, she padded out to the kitchen in search of fattening foods. Alcohol wasn't appealing, but she needed something comforting to soften the edges of the last twenty-four hours.

After she pulled out a loaf of bread and block of cheese, her culinary efforts were interrupted by the jangling of keys in her front door. Mallory spun around in time to see Evan bound into the apartment, his jaw tense and eyes wild. "Ev?" she asked, wiping her hands on a tea towel.

At first he didn't say anything, simply stared at her like she was the one acting crazy. Then he turned and stalked back to the living room. He ate up the floor with his long

255

strides, and she hoped her neighbors couldn't hear him stomping. It sounded like a pair of elephants in tap shoes. Fernando came out long enough to investigate before hissing and dashing into the bathroom.

Mallory joined her brother, only then noticing the bandage around his hand. "What happened to your hand?" She stepped forward, already frowning at the subpar bandage work. "Let me see."

Evan held his arms up, their own version of keep-away. "No, Mal. I'm fine."

"What happened? Did you hurt yourself at the diner?" It wouldn't be the first time Evan showed up with a minor burn or a nick from a chef's knife.

Evan shook his head.

"Let me see." She urged, jumping and waving her arms. "I'm guessing you haven't seen a professional, so stop being a big baby."

Side-stepping her, Evan sighed. "Leave it, I'm fine."

"You're obviously not, so let me—"

"I punched Beckett." Evan's admission echoed throughout the room, his words shocking them both. Behind her, Fernando meowed, seemingly just as appalled by the news.

"I'm sorry, what?" Mallory stumbled back as if she was the one being struck. "Why did you do that?"

"I don't understand," Evan said, pacing back and forth, acting as if she didn't just ask an important—and valid—question. Her apartment had never felt overly spacious, but right now she was surprised her brother could fit inside with all his barely contained rage. "Why didn't you just tell me?"

Mallory took a deep breath, readying herself for a fight with Evan. They were siblings, so this was hardly her first rodeo with bickering and arguments. But she knew this was different. She'd done the one thing Evan couldn't stand— treating him like a kid. They were barely eighteen months apart, and she knew he felt the sting of her betrayal acutely, like a jellyfish sneak attack.

"Ev," she started, only to be silenced by Evan grunting.

"Has he hurt you? Ever done anything you didn't want?" His questions were so outlandish, Mallory pursed her lips to keep from laughing.

"Beckett's never willingly hurt me, but our relationship hasn't always been easy."

"Oh, geez," Evan sighed. "Your relationship. I don't know if I can hear this." He covered his ears with his hands and turned his back, his shoulders tense. "Ugh, this is too much."

Mallory had so many questions, least of which was the state of Beckett's face. Did he break his glasses? Did he fight back? Was he hurt right now? She grew dizzy with the myriad of questions and sat on the arm of the couch for support. "Evan, I need you to tell me what happened."

Evan whirled around but kept his distance. "Why? I feel like I'm the only person in Buckeye Falls that doesn't know the full story."

Mallory raised an eyebrow. "The story of me and Beckett?"

"Gah! I'm still not ready for this."

If she was being honest, neither was Mallory. Her brother had a knack for theatrics when he was in a mood, but this seemed like too much. What had Beckett said to get a punch to the face?

"How's Beckett?"

"How the hell should I know? He left when CeCe came outside. Frankly, I don't know if I want to see him again."

"Oh, boy." Mallory groaned. "You're not serious. You've been friends for your whole lives. You're going to throw that away because we're dating?" *Or whatever we're doing...*

Evan scoffed. "Yeah, it's because of *that*. But it's also the whole ring thing."

Mallory froze, unsure what Evan meant by that. "The ring thing?"

Evan finally stopped his tap routine and flopped onto

257

the couch, kicking his legs out and resting them on the coffee table. His nervous energy couldn't be contained, and he continued wiggling his legs. The movement shook a stack of gossip magazines to the floor, but Mallory didn't have the energy to care.

"You're telling me you don't know?" With his head thrown back, she could only see his profile, the vein in his temple throbbing an alarming tempo. He looked like their father every time the Browns lost a game, but she kept that tidbit to herself.

"I'm serious, Ev. Calm down and tell me the whole story. I'm clueless here."

Evan swallowed hard, taking a moment to collect himself. "CeCe hates Nana Lawson's ring. She told Beckett at the engagement party. Then he let it slip right after telling me he's been sneaking around with you. Some best man he turned out to be."

Mallory's hand flew up to her mouth, barely containing her gasp. "CeCe doesn't like Nana's ring? What are you going to do?"

With a snort, Evan sprang back to his feet and stomped into the kitchen. "Please tell me there's beer here." He didn't wait for a response, rattling the contents of her fridge around until he found what he was looking for. Stalking back into the living room, he didn't bother offering Mallory a drink.

"I'm good, thanks." She deadpanned, her mind still whirling with the fact that CeCe didn't want the ring.

"You want to hear something hilarious?" He spat, eyes brimming with frustrated tears.

Mallory snorted. "It'd be a nice change of topic."

"Emily called on my way out here. I unloaded all the Beckett and Nana's ring drama, only for her to add another cherry on this crap sundae."

Mallory paled, collapsing onto the couch by her brother. Fernando, for once, sensed she needed him. He sauntered out from the hallway and climbed into her lap, tail looping around her forearm. "What did Em say?" she asked, voice strained.

"You'll love this," he groaned. He took a long pull from the beer before slamming it on the coffee table. He raked his hands through his hair and muttered to himself. By the time he was done, half of his blond locks were tousled to almost vertical heights. "Em said you always wanted Nana's ring. That it was *your* dream to inherit it. I have been in the dark on every aspect of my engagement since the beginning. My best man is in love with my sister, my sister didn't want me to use the ring, and my fiancée hates the ring. How does everyone know everything except me? Why do I always feel like the idiot kid of the family?"

Knowing it was bad form to point out how he *was* acting childish, Mallory tried another tactic. Holding up her hands, she slowly scooted toward her brother, trying not to corner him like a trapped animal. "Ev, can I just have one minute to explain?" Her voice was thick, as if she'd downed a gallon of honey. "Please."

Sensing her turmoil, he put his sister out of her misery by dropping his arms to his sides and letting out a sigh. "I'll give you two minutes."

The corner of her lip quirked, but she wasn't about to waste her opportunity to explain herself. "I didn't know how to tell you." She started, licking her lips and willing her heart rate to slow. "Nana used to let me play with the ring, remember?"

"Yeah, kind of. You two were always the closest."

Mallory allowed herself a moment to smile at that, because Nana was one of her favorite people, along with Gram. "Thanks for saying that, but I don't want to get off topic."

"Then why not just say something, Mal? I felt like such a fool. Do you know how that made me look? I thought we were close."

His words had their desired effect, rocking Mallory back into the cushions like she'd been slapped. "Ev." She reached

259

out, Fernando darting back down the hallway, but her brother wasn't finished.

"And you know the worst part? I looked like some stupid kid who got carried away with a fanciful idea. God, I'm always the young, dumb one." He leaned forward and dropped his head into his hands. Now Mallory was done keeping her distance.

She scooted over, taking his hands in hers and pulling them free until he finally met her matching blue gaze. "Evan, you need to listen to me. No one thinks you're a kid, or a fool, or anything else you're worried about. If anything, they think I'm the old spinster sister who can't let go of a childish fantasy."

Evan wrinkled his nose in confusion. "What are you talking about? No one thinks you're any of those things. Especially Beckett."

Mallory's heart expanded—no exploded—in her ribcage. "What do you mean?"

"Yeah, pretty sure I'm going to have to kick his ass if he doesn't get back together with you. But then I'll have to kick his ass if he does." He shook his head, clearing his head. "I literally have no idea what's going on anymore."

"Brother, you'll have to get in line. Ever since Beckett came to town, I don't know which end is up."

Finally, Evan's trademark grin made an appearance, damn near lighting up the room. "Aren't we a pair?"

Mallory reached and pinched his arm. "Certainly are."

Evan drained the last of his beer and sighed. "I promise I'll be an adult and take CeCe out to find her perfect ring."

Mallory shot him a thumbs-up. "And Beckett?"

"I'll try not to murder him at the rehearsal dinner. At least I have a few weeks to get used to this."

Mallory huffed out a laugh. "Progress."

For a moment, his megawatt smile melted as he asked, "You're really into Beckett? Like this is more than a passing crush?"

He was giving her an out, a way to avoid the trickiness

and messiness of the situation. But Mallory was tired of the easy way out, and she was tired of lying about how she felt about Beckett, about how he made her feel. Mallory hugged a cushion to her chest and sighed. "I'm in love with him." If this surprised Evan, he didn't show it. "And in case you're wondering, I have been for, like, my whole life."

That got a reaction. "Say what?" He blinked a few times, his left eye twitching like his brain had short-circuited. "You've been in love with Foxy this whole time?"

Mallory lifted a shoulder and grimaced. "Basically. Do you hate me?"

Evan ran a hand down his face and sighed. "I don't hate you, Mal. But I will have to kill my best friend if you tell me he did something to hurt you. I've seen you guys lately, and it's like there's an electric forcefield between you."

Mallory was incredulous. "You've seen electricity? Ev, come on."

Rolling his eyes he sighed. "Fine. CeCe saw it, and gave me a ludicrously long description of my blindness and ignorance."

"I love her," Mallory said, unable to hold back her grin.

Evan's lips tipped up. "So do I. Now get back to the forcefield part." He winced as he said it, but she was proud of him for asking.

Unsure how much to divulge, Mallory decided the full truth was best. She didn't know where she stood with Beckett, and she wasn't about to lose the goodwill with her brother. Her world only made sense if Evan was in her life. "I said some things I shouldn't have after the engagement party. He came over after he left with Julia, and I just—" Even saying the other woman's name now left a bitter taste in her mouth. She knew in her heart that nothing happened and Beckett felt cornered, but that didn't stop the hurt from being left behind. Again.

"Good Lord," Evan said on a groan. "I need to stop fixing him up with random women."

Mallory leaned forward and flicked him on the forehead.

"Could you, please? It's kind of annoying."

Evan pushed himself to standing and held out a hand for Mallory to join him. Pulling her to his chest, he squeezed her firmly before stepping back and letting his arms fall. "I love you, Mal. But I'm going to go home and beg CeCe's forgiveness for giving her the wrong ring."

"That woman loves you more than a good loaf of sourdough bread. You could put a rubber band on her finger and she'd love you."

"Yeah, but she deserves more than that." Evan's smile returned at the mention of CeCe, and Mallory's heart swelled with love and pride. He'd gone through life with his heart on his sleeve, and finally the right woman had snagged it. She couldn't think of a better partner for her brother.

Now that things were out in the open with Evan, she hoped she and Beckett could find their own happily ever after. They'd certainly taken an eternity to get here, and she thought they deserved one more fighting chance at forever.

CHAPTER 26

It had been forty-eight hours since his best friend punched him in the face, and Beckett wasn't sure what to do. He'd promised himself he'd give both Lawson siblings space, which didn't sit right with him. He wasn't used to being back without any contact from either of them, yet here he was.

Beckett took some time in the orchards though, the trees bringing him a sense of purpose he didn't know he was missing. He'd reached out to the former foreman about getting the crew back for the next season. This farm, these trees, were his grandparent's legacy; he wasn't going to squander that a moment longer. If he was coming out of mourning, then the land was too.

Unwilling to go back to his apartment, he'd stayed at the farm house and busied himself with pottering around. Since the orchards got some much-needed attention, the house deserved the same treatment. He'd fixed the last shutter without falling to his death, a huge bonus, and now he was working on a loose floorboard on the porch. With his ear buds in, he hadn't heard Evan's car as it drove down the gravel driveway, and only his shadow blocking his work caused him to pause.

Popping his ear buds out, he lifted his head to Evan, shielding his eyes with his free hand. "If you came here for a rematch, can I at least finish this plank? I'd hate to leave this project unfinished."

Evan held out a hand to help Beckett to his feet, his expression unreadable. "Thanks," Beckett said, letting the hammer drop to his feet with a thud. He dusted his hands on his pant legs before building up the courage to meet his friend's eye.

"I'm sorry I punched you." Evan's blue gaze was not on Beckett's face, but somewhere off his shoulder. It was hardly the best apology he'd ever received, but he wasn't about to complain either. Evan was here, and he wasn't currently beating the snot out of him. That counted for something, right?

"Apology accepted. I can't say I wouldn't do the same if the shoe were on the other foot."

Evan shook his head. "It doesn't matter, it wasn't the right thing to do. CeCe and Mal both read me the riot act about it." A huff escaped him as his shoulders slumped. He looked truly dejected. "I'm sorry for hitting you. It doesn't sit right with me, Foxy."

Beckett deflated at the sound of his nickname, a kernel of hope popping in his chest. Maybe all wasn't lost with Evan after all. "Seriously, Lawless. Don't worry about."

Evan smirked at the sound of his own nickname and toed the hammer on the porch floor. "Need a little help with this?"

"I wouldn't say no." Beckett thrust his hands on his hips. "You mind a little woodworking?"

Without another word, Evan got down on all-fours, the hammer already prying up the warped board. "Hand me the new board and some of the longer nails." Beckett did as he was told and the pair worked in companionable silence until the new boards were installed. While it wasn't a difficult task, having his buddy's help saved Beckett at least an hour.

"Thanks, man. This really saved me some time."

Evan helped Beckett collect their tools and followed him inside the house and into the kitchen. Beckett poured two glasses of water and kicked out a chair for Evan to sit. "You thinking of selling this place?" Evan spun the glass in his hands, swirling a pattern in the condensation.

Beckett took a drink and eased back into his chair. "Honestly, I don't think I can. I know it's a little isolated out here, but this is my home. I like my apartment in Buckeye Falls, but I couldn't handle someone else living here." He traced a line on the table with his finger, feeling himself relax at the truth. "I reached out to our old foreman, and he's going to have a crew ready for next season. It's time for this place to feel like home again."

This *was* his home, no matter what happened with Mallory. His grandparents left the house to him, and it was his responsibility to make it a home for the next generation of Foxes. He just hoped they had startling blue eyes and thick, chocolaty hair...or at least better vision than their father. The thought made Beckett adjust his glasses, leaving a spot of water on the frame.

"I'm glad, seriously. There's a lot of good memories in this old place." Evan's expression took on a wistful quality.

It was impossible not to go down Memory Lane with Evan here. Thinking about the old times, from mud fights outside to helping Gramps with the fencing in the spring, to apple picking in the fall with Gram, the pair had so many good times on this property. "There certainly are." Beckett agreed, letting out a sigh. He was about to change the subject when Evan cleared his throat.

"See, here's the thing."

"Yeah?" His friend's tone had changed just enough to make Beckett nervous. He didn't think he'd get another slug to the face, but these days, who the hell knew?

"If you hurt her, I'm going to have to kill you."

Beckett stilled, unsure how to react. The very last thing he wanted to do was hurt Mallory again. He'd sooner take a bullet. Yet to have Evan address the elephant in the room, it took his breath away. "Totally understandable," he replied.

Evan rubbed the back of his neck, his lips turning down in the corners. "I know we don't like"—he hesitated, flapping his hands between them—"talk about the women in our lives in detail."

Beckett nodded, biting back a laugh. Not only had Evan bored him to death with CeCe chatter over the last year, but he'd texted Beckett at all hours when they had temporarily broken up. If he hadn't been on the road for work, he would have been with Mallory knocking some sense into his friend. Yet he knew what Evan was getting at.

With Beckett's previous girlfriends, who were admittedly few and far between, he wasn't big on spilling the beans. Practically, he understood it was because the girls were place holders, keeping him distracted until Mallory was back in his orbit. Of course, they were nice girls, women he still considered friends, but they weren't end game.

They weren't Mallory Lawson.

"You're right, we don't really go into details, huh?"

Evan drained the last of his water, the grimace on his face proving he needed something stronger. "I, uh, don't need to know how things are…" he groaned and shook his head. "Like, I just need to know that things are like, good with you two."

Beckett bit his bottom lip, which shook with the need to laugh. "Totally understandable."

"And like," Evan continued, although he started to turn a worrisome shade of green. "If you're going to ask Mal out again, you'll have to be serious about this. No messing around."

"I won't, mess around I mean. When I ask her again, that is it for me."

Evan exhaled, yet the muscles in his jaw were as tight as a drum. "So that means, you'll have to marry her." Evan finally caught his gaze, his lips quirking up in the corner. "I'm assuming you've already thought about this?"

266

Beckett adjusted his glasses and blinked a few times, debating how honest to be with his best friend. But he was done keeping secrets, done lying about how he felt about Mallory.

"Let me put it to you this way, Lawless. Do you still have that ring?"

Evan threw his head back and barked out a laugh. "Thank God." He chuckled as he fished in his pocket. Sliding a small black box across the kitchen table, he let out a long breath. "I can't say I'm used to the idea of you and Mal together, but CeCe reminded me she could do a hell of a lot worse." Waiting a moment, he added, "And so could you."

Beckett was not an emotional guy, but his eyes burned with tears. After years of worrying how Evan would react, he'd just been given his blessing to not only date Mallory, but marry her.

"Thank you." Beckett's throat tightened, and he drank the rest of his water, willing the tears to stay at bay. "I promise I'll do right by Mallory, and I'm sorry I wasn't honest with you before. To be honest, I didn't want to jeopardize our friendship. Especially after Gramps died, you guys are all I have left."

Evan clapped a hand on Beckett's shoulder and squeezed. "That's not true, Foxy. You've got a whole town who loves you. You're a Buckeye now, like it or not."

Beckett liked it, a whole hell of a lot.

After he opened the ring box, the ruby glinted in the waning sunlight. He'd waited his whole life to touch this ring again, to slide it onto Mallory's hand one last time. "You know what's crazy?" he asked, an unmistakable tremor in his voice.

Evan shook his head, not interrupting the moment.

"I've been waiting for this moment, having the ring back. The last time I had it, we were playing up in the orchards."

"Holy crap," Evan breathed, his eyes doubling in size.

"You mean that time I pretended to marry you and Mallory?"

Beckett nodded, his grin unmistakable. "Yeah, that was it for me. I know we were kids, but there was something about it all. A rightness that settled over me on that hill."

Evan rubbed at his eyes with his sleeve and muttered something to himself before he finally met Beckett's gaze again. "I'm sorry I got in the way of you two."

Scoffing, Beckett shook his head. "No, Lawless, we got in our own way."

"She's crazy about you. You know that, right?"

"Let's hope she'll give me one more chance."

Evan pushed back his chair and got to his feet. The sun hung low in the sky, and he had places to be. "She has to, Foxy. Now that the cat's out of the bag, you two need to get together."

When they reached the front door, Evan pulled Beckett in for a quick bro hug.

"Thanks for the ring, Evan." He stilled at the sound of his given name, but he didn't flinch. "I'm sorry I wasn't honest with you."

"I'm sorry I didn't give you the chance." Evan smiled, his face morphing into its usual happy default. His golden retriever best friend was back, thank the Lord. "Now enough of this love talk. I'm going to go home to my fiancée, who finally has the ring she wants. You need to call Mal, and if she isn't your date to the rehearsal dinner, I'll have to uninvite you both." He winked and opened the door.

Both men stopped dead in their tracks when they found Mallory on the porch, her hand raised like she was about to knock. "Oh," she exhaled, and Beckett nearly pushed Evan out of the way to get to her. "Please tell me there weren't any more fisticuffs." Her voice dripped with fatigue.

Evan lightly punched her in the arm and rolled his eyes. "Get over yourself, Mal." Turning to Beckett he added, "Later, Foxy." After bounding down the porch steps, he slid behind the wheel and disappeared in a cloud of dust and K-Pop.

Beckett pivoted, facing Mallory and studying her lovely face. Her eyes were still wide, sizing him up as well. Her hair was up, looped around her head in a crown of braids. She looked like she could be on the box of hot cocoa mix. "Can I come in?" she asked, eyebrow raised.

"Yeah," he said, stepping back and waving her inside. He caught a whiff of her familiar blackberry scent as she stepped over the threshold into the house. Since he hadn't turned on many lights, the house felt dark yet cozy. "Let me get some lights and—" He took a step back, but Mallory's arm shot out to stop his escape.

She didn't say a word but tugged him back to her. Tentatively, she reached up and touched the delicate skin around his swollen eye. "Does it hurt?" Her question wasn't clinical, yet he didn't have an answer.

He didn't have any words as her fingers grazed down his face and rested on his shoulders. Beckett dipped his head, resting it on her forehead as they simply enjoyed the moment of closeness. He hadn't held Mallory in his arms for an eternity, and he planned to savor the opportunity. They had so much to discuss, but words seemed useless right now. Now wasn't the time for planning, now was the time for holding her.

Enveloping her in a hug, he cradled Mallory like the delicate treasure she was. "It doesn't hurt anymore," he said, only referring to his eye slightly. The gaping chasm in his ribcage closed, leaving Beckett feeling almost whole again. Sure, he'd always grieve the loss of his grandparents, but at least Evan wasn't going anywhere. And judging by how tightly Mallory held on to him, she wasn't either.

"I want to show you something," he said, pressing a tender kiss to her forehead before reluctantly stepping back. "Go for a walk with me?"

If she was surprised by his request, she didn't show it. "Sure."

Beckett smiled down at Mallory, clad in leggings and sneakers. She was dressed perfectly for what he had planned. "Meet me on the porch in one minute." He kissed her temple before stepping back and jogging into the kitchen.

Grateful that Mallory hadn't followed him, Beckett scooped up the ring box and tucked it into his jeans' pocket. On his way out the door, he grabbed his hoodie and met Mallory on the porch. She stood with her back to him, hugging herself against the cooling September air. "Here," he said as he flung the unzipped hoodie over her shoulders. "Follow me."

Linking their hands together, Beckett stepped off the porch and into his future. Regardless of what was about to happen, he knew it would all work out for the best. Mallory was here, and he was more than ready for them to start the next chapter.

CHAPTER 27

Mallory wasn't sure what she expected when she arrived at Beckett's house. When she pulled up and saw Evan's car, she feared her brother had gone all macho man again and was pummeling Beckett into steak tartar. Never mind the fact that Beckett was able to hold his own, she knew he'd lay down and take whatever punishment Evan doled out. Fortunately, that wasn't the case. Both men appeared to be intact—Mallory could only hope that sentiment continued with her heart when she and Beckett were done talking.

And talking was what they should be doing, not hiking through the orchards as the sun set. Granted, she wasn't really upset. This was one of her favorite places, and being out here with Beckett felt right. Her left hand clung to his as he led the way through rows of trees. It was harvest time, so the scent of ripe apples permeated the air around them. The song of a few insects kept tempo with her racing heart as Beckett finally got to a familiar clearing.

"This is my favorite place to watch the sun set," Beckett announced when they reached the top of the trail. He spun her around to face the sun, wrapping his arms around her and pulling her against his frame. Resting his chin on top of her head, he let out a contented sigh. "This is my favorite

271

place for other reasons," he said, his arms tightening slightly around her waist.

"Oh, yeah?" she asked, breathless. Was it possible Beckett still thought about that sunny afternoon nearly fifteen years ago? Did he still think about the magic of the moment, of the wind in the trees and their adolescent racing hearts?

"Yeah." Beckett nuzzled closer, peppering her neck with kisses. Her skin pebbled with goosebumps as he trailed kisses into the neckline of his hoodie. "I'm regretting bundling you up," he teased, nipping at the skin of her earlobe.

Mallory was about to strip down to her skivvies if this continued, but she didn't want to ruin the moment with her own lust. Instead, she asked, "Why is this your favorite place?"

For a second, Beckett was contemplative. She felt his slow inhales and exhales while they watched the sun disappear behind a row of trees. The sky was streaked with pinks and purples, the color scheme of her childhood. "This is my favorite place because it holds all my favorite memories."

Mallory's breath hitched, but she didn't interrupt. "Gram used to take me up here to pick apples before the crew got harvesting. We'd fill as many bushels as we could carry and bring them back to the house. She'd bake pies, cupcakes, and fry up those little apple fritters. Gosh, I miss those."

Mallory's stomach growled at the memory of the crispy, sweet dough balls. Beckett's Gram could bake better than anyone she'd ever met—except for maybe CeCe. "I remember the apple sauce she'd can and send home with me and Ev."

"That was good, too." Beckett hummed, his arms still holding Mallory close.

"What other memories do you have up here?" she asked, unwilling to drop this line of conversation.

"I remember Gramps taking me up here too, and we'd walk the grounds and track the trees for harvest. Sometimes we'd bring the goats and sheep up here and they'd run around like absolute idiots." He chuckled at the private memory, and her heart ached for him. His grandfather was the most important role model and ally Beckett had, and she hated that the sweet old man was gone. Although she did pull comfort from knowing he was reunited with his beloved wife.

Leaning back into Beckett's embrace, Mallory reveled in his nearness. Despite Evan knowing the truth, a small part of her feared Beckett would disappear if she didn't hold tight. He sometimes felt as ethereal as the morning fog.

"My favorite memory here," Beckett continued, oblivious to her inner turmoil, "was almost fifteen years ago."

Mallory's heart thundered in her chest, begging him to confirm her own favorite memories on this hill. "Oh, yeah?"

Beckett spun her around until they faced each other. Even in the fading twilight, she could make out his expression. His gray eyes gleamed behind his crooked glasses, and his smile was certain and bright. "Yeah," he confirmed, drawing his hands up to cup her face. He kissed her, too quickly for Mallory's taste, before stepping back.

"I know we were only kids," he started, shoving his hands in his pockets, "but marrying you up on this hill was one of the best days of my life."

Mallory felt foolish parroting his own statements back to him, but she couldn't find her own words. "Best days of your life?"

"Of course. I shared my first kiss with my favorite person." He shrugged, like the admission didn't cost a lot, like it wasn't costing her the same high price. If Beckett didn't realize what he was doing with his words, he threatened to hurt her worse than ever before. "I replay that day in my head on repeat, Mallory. Especially on my darker days, as it's the only thing that makes me smile." His thumb swept over her cheek, catching a tear she didn't realize was falling. "I made some pretty bold promises for a preteen." He chuckled. "And I know my vows have been broken over the years." A flush crept up his neck at the admission, but he soldiered on. "But I'm ready to commit again if you are. This time forever."

Knees wobbling, Mallory clutched Beckett's shoulders for support. "Beckett, what are you saying?"

Deep in her heart, she knew what he said was genuine, knew he wouldn't break her heart again. But suddenly it seemed too good to be true. Her brother knew the truth, and Beckett was done hiding his feelings. Could it really be that simple?

Stepping back, Beckett shoved his hand back into his jeans before retrieving a very familiar black box. Slowly, he lowered himself down on one knee and opened the box. The ruby glinted up at her, winking the promise of a happily ever after. "Mallory Lawson, you are an amazing woman, my best friend." He shook his head and quietly added, "Don't tell Evan."

Unable to hold back, Mallory snorted and rolled her eyes. "Get back to the Mallory portion of the Lawson lovefest, please." She squeezed his hand, and Beckett laughed.

"Yes, ma'am." Beckett took the ring out of the box and slid it onto her ring finger. The band fit like it was made for her, sliding into place perfectly. "Mallory, I've been in love with you for decades, and I'd love to spend the rest of my life proving that love to you. I want to make you French bread pizzas every day, I want to build pillow forts in the farm house with you, I want to raise our kids here, and I want to grow old with you here. I want our future to be bright and filled with love." His gray eyes found hers, and she could have drowned in the moody pools. "Will you marry me?"

Mallory's knees finally gave out and she fell to the ground in front of him. This was the most perfect proposal a girl could ask for and from the perfect man. "Yes," she said, unable to stop the smile from engulfing her face. "Yes, Beckett." Just as she was about to pull him in for a kiss, she looked down at Nana's ring on her finger. "How did you get this?"

Beckett shook his head and tilted her face up toward his. "I'll explain everything later, but I kind of want to kiss you. A lot."

"Fair enough." Mallory tugged Beckett closer by his collar, and their lips collided.

The pair had shared countless kisses over the years, but none like this one. This one felt shiny and new, filled with hope and the promise of forever.

CHAPTER 28

"Are you sure I should wear the ring?" Mallory asked Beckett for the fiftieth time in as many minutes.

Beckett fidgeted as she pulled him closer, holding him in place with her one hand while the other rummaged in her makeup bag. "I don't think this is necessary," he muttered, angling his face away from her foundation sponge. "And I told you yes, wear it please. I'm not going out with my fiancée without the engagement ring."

Mallory swiped a blob of foundation under his eye before Beckett could wiggle free. "Hold still," she ordered, wiping the excess off and attempting to blend. "I won't have you looking like a hooligan who gets into bar fights at their rehearsal dinner."

"Pfft, I'd probably get a little more respect from your father if I did," Beckett grumbled, but it was half-hearted. They both knew her father, while not a fan of most humans, loved Beckett.

"Uh-huh, I'm sure you want to look like that when we tell my family."

Mallory had been uncertain about when to tell her family about their engagement. Her parents didn't really know their full history, and her sisters would likely bombard her with a

277

million asinine questions. More importantly, she didn't want to steal CeCe and Evan's thunder. This was their weekend, after all.

Beckett finally stopped fidgeting and sat still while Mallory smoothed out the foundation. While still obvious to her, it was harder to see the bruise. "At least your face isn't swollen anymore." She slid his glasses back into place and nodded. "That's actually not too bad."

"Just what every man wants to hear from the woman he loves," he droned, but winked to soften the blow. "Can I kiss you now?"

"Nope," Mallory said with a smirk. "I just put on my own makeup. You'll have to wait until tonight."

"Wow, tonight is going to be torture." Beckett pouted, but she knew there was no heat in his words. He was just as excited to celebrate Evan and CeCe as she was. Plus, they were about to go public with their own news.

When they'd gone over to CeCe and Evan's place the night before, they both agreed that Mallory and Beckett needed to share their engagement while everyone was together. Yet again, Mallory was touched by CeCe's willingness to share her happiness with others. She was no bridezilla, and if anything, she appreciated slightly less attention on her.

"Shoot, we need to go." Mallory checked her smart watch and grimaced. She forgot they had an extra thirty minutes to drive now that they were at the farm house.

Beckett had canceled his lease and already had most of his stuff back at the house. Mallory reached out to her landlord and got a deal on breaking her lease. Fortunately, Janis knew a former patient that needed a place ASAP. Within a week, Mallory—and Fernando—would be living with Beckett full time at the farm.

No more secrets.

No more hiding.

Just a future with the man she loved.

How on earth did she get that lucky?

278

Beckett snagged her purse and held the front door open. "Your chariot awaits, Ms. Lawson."

Mallory checked her hair in the mirror by the door, pausing to tuck a rogue lock back into place. She'd spent nearly an hour braiding and curling her hair for the evening. "You know what I'm looking forward to?"

"When I get to call you Mrs. Foxy?" Beckett smirked, leaning in to kiss her cheek.

"Um, maybe we'll work on the married nicknames. Evan gave his blessing for us to live happily ever after. Let's not take the poor guy's nickname, too."

Beckett chuckled. "Fair enough. C'mon, the future Mrs. Fox." He looped his arm in hers and strode to the car.

By the time they made it to the diner, the place was bursting at the seams. Max had shut down for the night, and Ginny and Natalie had decorated. When they entered the space, it smelled like garlic and cheese, yet the lighting was low and the tables had votives and tasteful flower arrangements. Mallory couldn't wait to see what the ladies had in store for the wedding day, because this was already stunning.

"Mal, over here!" Emily waved from across the diner. Tyson toddled around her, talking to himself while Zach tried to catch him. Their eldest sister, Sophie, emerged from the kitchen with an armful of wine bottles.

Beckett took Mallory's jacket and hung it by the door. "I'll go help Sophie before she drops one of those." He stepped forward before Mallory could say a word. Damn this thoughtful man. It was nearly impossible not to kiss him when he acted this way.

"Hey, Em." Mallory greeted her sister with a quick hug before squatting down to grab Tyson. "Got you," she teased as she held her nephew, his legs kicking for purchase.

"Hey, Mallory," Zach said, handing his wife a glass of wine before offering one to Mallory. "I'll take this goober. You ladies enjoy."

Mallory raised her hand to wave at Tyson, but Emily

snatched her forearm. "Ouch," she huffed as her sister tilted her hand and squinted.

"What. The. Hell. Is. This?" Emily's question was slow and deliberate, and Mallory had to fight from squirming free. Her voice even lower, she hissed, "Did you just steal the bride's ring? Ev's going to freak out."

Sophie, never one to miss sisterly drama, quickly joined them. "What's going on?" Her focus was solely on Mallory, even though she was the one with a hand pulled against her back. *Ah, the joys of sisterly dynamics.*

"Um, can I please point out the fact that Emily's the instigator?"

Sophie reached out and flicked Mallory on the forehead. "Ow!" She broke free of Emily's hold and rubbed the spot with her left hand.

Finally, Sophie saw the ring and gasped. "Holy crap," she exhaled, her eyes growing ten sizes. "What the hell is going on?"

Emily was triumphant. "That's what I want to know."

Mallory balled her hands at her sides and lifted her chin. "I have news, but I don't want you two making a scene."

"Fat chance of that happening," Beckett said, joining the trio and handing Sophie her own wine glass. "Pretty much everyone in here is watching the Lawson sisters."

Emily raised an eyebrow at Beckett. "You seem pretty happy."

Rocking back on his heels, Beckett merely grinned. "Yep."

"Why?" Emily asked, peering over her wine glass at him and Mallory. "In fact, you're both too happy."

Sophie snorted. "Can we please get to the issue of Mallory wearing…" Her words died on her tongue as realization dawned. "Holy shit," she spluttered. "Holy shit!" She now exclaimed, drawing the attention of everyone in the diner.

Mallory grimaced, hating herself for forgetting her sisters and their flair for the dramatic. Before she could say anything, Emily burst into tears. "It's happened, it's finally freaking happened."

"Girls." Their mother arrived at the perfect moment to watch Emily's mascara run down her face. "You're making a scene, and I…" Flattening a hand over her heart, she stammered, "Emily, what's the matter?"

Mallory opened her mouth to respond, but Emily beat her to the punch. "Beckett and Mallory are engaged."

Sophie finished the announcement with, "And it's about damn time."

Their mother spun in a circle, unable to hold her gaze on more than one daughter at a time. Evan joined them, clapping his hand on Beckett's back. "I guess this proves that literally everyone knew about you two except for me, huh?"

Beckett shrugged. "Looks like it?"

"Pamela?" Their father joined the fray and grasped his wife's elbow. "You're white as a ghost, what is going on?"

Reaching out, she snatched her youngest daughter's hand and studied the ruby shining on her ring finger. Glancing up at Beckett, she quickly confirmed what she already knew. "Mallory and Beckett are engaged. Isn't it wonderful?"

Her father recovered his shock quickly and reached out to shake Beckett's hand. "Nice work, son. Welcome to the family."

Mallory watched with pride as her family welcomed Beckett into theirs, officially. Despite her knowing they would love Beckett as one of their own, she knew Beckett needed to see—and experience—it for himself. He was far from alone in the world, and it was high time he understood that.

After ten minutes of applause and well wishes, the party got back to the focus that mattered—Evan and CeCe. Everyone took their seats and the happy couple celebrated their impending nuptials the only way they knew how, with copious amounts of food.

When the desserts were cleared, Mallory took Beckett's hand and pulled him outside for a moment of peace. "That went surprisingly well." She yanked him down by his tie and planted a kiss on his lips.

Beckett moaned his approval before pulling back and asking, "So I can mess up your makeup now?"

Mallory snorted. "Yes, you can, but maybe don't grope me in front of my entire family?" She gestured toward the diner, where a row of Lawsons had their noses pressed to the windows. A chorus of cheers erupted when Beckett closed the distance and kissed her again.

"I love you, Mal," Beckett said between kisses.

"I love you, too." Mallory pulled back and sighed. "Now take me home and away from all these prying eyes."

"With pleasure." Beckett draped his arm around his shoulder and walked them toward the car.

Mallory couldn't believe they'd made it here, but she was eternally grateful that they had. Her life only made sense when Beckett was a part of it. "I meant to ask you," she said as she climbed into the car. Beckett hovered in the open doorway, the lights of the diner's sign reflected in his glasses.

"What?"

"Your toast back there, what did that mean?"

Beckett flushed but didn't break eye contact. "It was something Gramps had made me promise. He wanted me to go get my girl, and I was just telling Evan I was happy he found his as well."

"That's very sweet," Mallory said, her heart swelling at the thought of sweet old Gramps. "Now take your girl home."

"With pleasure." Beckett leaned in and kissed her, short and chaste on the lips. She watched him round the car and slide behind the wheel, his free hand resting on her knee for the whole drive back to the farm.

As they drove down the gravel drive to the familiar house in the distance, Mallory felt something click into place. She was happy, really and truly content in the moment. All her fears had melted away when her family congratulated them that night. She and Beckett were about to start their lives together. Throughout it all, they'd found each other. They'd found their forever.

EPILOGUE

One Year Later

"I now pronounce you husband and wife," Evan said, an infectious grin plastered on his face. The sunlight caused his blond hair to appear as white as the bride's dress.

It took them over sixteen years, but the trio was back under the old oak tree. It felt so familiar, yet so new.

"You were my first kiss, Mallory. And I'm happy to say you'll be the last." Beckett's hands raised to cup Mallory's cheeks, although he was careful of her veil. The antique lace was another part of Nana Lawson that was here for the day. Just like before, the ruby ring sparkled from her left hand—although now the fit was perfect. And even more perfect, it was officially hers. Beckett looked forward to decades of watching that ring sparkle on his wife's hand.

Mallory closed the remaining distance, her lips eagerly finding her husband's. Beckett felt the tug of his tie as Mallory yanked him closer. "Careful, Mal," he whispered between kisses. "These old ties aren't as durable as you think." He winked when she flushed and dropped the fabric.

285

To go with the theme of honoring their grandparents, he'd worn Gramps's favorite tie. The fabric was black, and from a distance, it looked like it was peppered with little red spots, but they were apples. It was a nod to the man who built the land they stood on from nothing. It was a nod to love.

"Time for pizza?" Beckett asked, his dimples popping as he held back a laugh.

"I'd say I'd race you, but you know." She held up the hem of her dress, wiggling her foot and the kitten heels that weren't made for running through orchards.

Beckett looped his arm around her waist and tugged her close. Despite the photographer in their faces, he whispered, "I'll save you a slice."

Mallory had insisted on keeping everything casual, everything just like they were in their everyday lives. That meant that most of Buckeye Falls had come out to support Mallory and Beckett. Alice and James were in charge of decorations, and Mallory was pleased to see her bestie's husband delivered on the artful floral arrangements. Max and CeCe were in charge of food, naturally, and Mallory could hardly wait to get her first piece of French bread pizza.

Since everyone wanted to be a bridesmaid, Mallory and Beckett decided not to have attendants. Instead, they wanted all their favorite people in the front row watching them make it official; make a commitment to last a lifetime. That didn't mean her sisters and Alice didn't gripe about a missed opportunity, but Mallory didn't mind. What mattered was having everyone she loved here.

CeCe leaned over and whispered in Alice's ear, "I can't believe we're about to serve pizza at this wedding. I feel like I'm back in grade school."

Alice patted her hand and shook with suppressed laughter. "Relax, you know that's just the appetizer. Calm her jets, Madam Chef."

Mallory clasped Beckett's hand in hers, unwilling to step

away from the moment—although she could smell the pizza from where they stood. "I love you," she whispered, leaning close enough to catch a whiff of his cologne.

"I love you more," her husband replied, closing the distance for a very un-family friendly kiss. Finally breaking apart, he added, "C'mon, let's party so we can go home."

Her gaze swung back to the house, their house, waiting for them to start their new life together. It may have taken them two decades, but Mallory and Beckett were finally home. Forever started right now.

The End

ACKNOWLEDGEMENTS

I'd like to start by thanking the Inkspell Publishing team, especially Melissa and Audrey, for their help with this book. Writing the last novel in a series is no small feat, and I appreciate your dedication to getting Mallory and Beckett's HEA just right.

To the other Inkspell Publishing authors who champion my writing and the Buckeye Falls series—thank you for your support and positivity as we navigate our writing journeys.

To the fearless—and fabulous—Liz Donatelli. Thank you for creating Romance RoundUp and giving us a platform to discuss romance books and have way too much fun. You inspire me every day with your passion for the romance industry.

To Thelma, Ernie, and the Jets. You ladies have listened to me vent, rant, and rave about writing more often than you probably wanted to. But I love you all and could not fathom a world without your support, memes, and laughs.

To my parents and sister, who continue to brag about my writing journey and share in the stumbles and triumphs. Love you all to pieces!

To the readers that found this series and love the residents of Buckeye Falls as much as I do. Your support and enthusiasm make this wild writing journey worthwhile.

Last, and certainly never least, to my husband. I literally could not do this without you, your support, your smile, and your sense of humor. I love you Curly, and I cherish that you share in my writing dream.

DON'T MISS ANOTHER BUCKEYE FALLS STORY

Falling Home

Welcome to Buckeye Falls, Ohio!
'Tis the Season for Second Chances...And this couple is going to need a Christmas Miracle!

When New York transplant Ginny Meyer returns to her small hometown to help her father recover from surgery, she isn't looking for any complications. No Christmas caroling, no cookie decorating, and certainly no time spent with her ex-husband, Max. The trouble is, she's looped into helping with the Christmas Jubilee—and a certain ex is her planning partner. Now all her plans to avoid Max disappear in a puff of tinsel. But she can resist his charms, right?

Max Sanchez has three great loves in his life—his diner, Christmas, and his ex-wife. He's spent two years missing the woman who broke his heart and left town, and he'll use any excuse to spend time with her. Max hopes some holiday cheer, and his famous cheese enchiladas, can help them find their way back together. Buckeye Falls hasn't felt the same since Ginny left, and Max can tell she's warming to the idea of staying in town. Now if only he could get her to stay with him…

With a little help from the residents of Buckeye Falls, this Christmas is bringing more than presents under the tree.

Author Libby Kay's books are perfect for fans of Kristan Higgins' second chance romances or Sharon Sala's smalltown romances. Readers will fall in love with Buckeye Falls, Ohio and the townspeople as they embrace the holiday season. Slip in to this enchanting smalltown and stay awhile! You might just fall in love…

EXCERPT:

Blinking, Ginny begged her eyes to see someone else standing before her. It was as if her memories willed themselves back to life. Beside her, her father perked up and lifted his free hand. "Max, over here." Max turned around, and Ginny felt the air leave her lungs. This was no trick of her mind. It was the real deal. *Well, hell …*

Time had been good to Max; there was no denying it. His dark hair was longer now, curling at the base of his neck. A few flecks of gray threatened to take over his temples, but he managed to look mature rather than haggard. Instead of the clean-shaven face she remembered, his chiseled jawline was now peppered with a few days of stubble. Suddenly, Ginny understood all the fuss with lumbersexuals.

Max's brown eyes darkened when he saw her, but his steps didn't falter. "Harold, good to see you." He moved one of his shopping bags to his other arm and shook her father's hand. When he turned to her, Ginny felt her breath hitch as he reached out his hand for a shake. *Really? They were in the hand-shaking phase of their relationship?*

Ginny reached out and took his hand, a shot of awareness coursing through her body as his fingers wrapped around hers. "Max," she said his name in greeting, hoping her tone was light, carefree.

"Gin." Max swallowed and squeezed her hand before

letting it go. He didn't say anything at first, just studied her. She was glad she had listened to her father about makeup. Bumping into her ex-husband with bedhead and sans mascara would have been mortifying.

Ginny was helpless for a moment, staring at Max like a fool. Perhaps she'd fallen into an alternate universe when she left the turnpike? Maybe her rental car was a time machine where she felt pulled to a man who bruised her heart? A man whose heart was certainly broken by her.

Either oblivious or uncaring of her current slack-jawed state, Max surprised her by stepping closer and giving her a genuine smile. "I'm glad you're back," he said. "It's really good to see you."

In that moment, staring into his warm gaze, Ginny couldn't disagree. Being so close to Max, so close to the worn paths of their past, she felt comfortable. This didn't feel like a foreign place; it felt like home.

Falling For You

Welcome to Buckeye Falls, Ohio!
Sparks fly in this small town as everyone's favorite gruff pastry chef finally gives the sweetest guy in town a chance.

CeCe LaRue knows what she wants in life, and in the kitchen, and that's control. She doesn't have time for distractions—from her past or present. But that doesn't mean a certain bright-eyed coworker hasn't captured her heart.

Evan Lawson is a chronic optimist, and he brings his sunny disposition to everything he does, especially his job at the diner. It's obvious why he loves his job so much, and it has everything to do with CeCe. He's been crushing on her for a while, but he's biding his time. Much like the perfect recipe, love cannot be rushed.

When a major food competition comes to town, Evan is thrilled at the prospect of competing. Despite her stellar culinary skills, CeCe is hesitant to participate. The celebrity chef host is more than a pretty face; he's the painful past she's been outrunning for years.

Can CeCe open herself up to the prospect of love and give Evan a chance? Can Evan's optimism keep them both afloat?

Falling For You is part of the Buckeye Falls series and can be enjoyed as a stand-alone read. Author Libby Kay's books are perfect for fans of Penny Reid and Sharon Sala's smalltown romances. These sweet romances will have readers falling in love with Buckeye Falls, Ohio. Slip in to this enchanting smalltown and stay awhile! You might just fall in love...

EXCERPT:

They were friends, friends with a whole lot of potential. Surely this magnetic pull wasn't one-sided?

"I think I could be serious about you," CeCe finally said, the words shaking Evan back to the moment. "And I don't know what to do about that."

Evan felt his heart explode in his chest. "You do?"

CeCe slowly raised her hand and cupped his cheek, having to stand on tiptoe to make up for their height difference. How easily he forgot her height when they were together. She was such a force, she filled up every space she was in. Her energy, her passion for what she did, radiated around her.

Even now, standing outside with only the din of the pub surrounding them, CeCe was all he could see, feel, and touch. Her thumb swiped around his lips, making him shiver. "I do."

Words escaping him, Evan closed the distance to kiss her. It was slow, tender. They were feeling each other out, finding the angles where they fit best. Cradling her face in his hands, the world around them evaporated. CeCe moaned, and Evan swallowed it, wanting to savor every little thing she gave him. Kissing CeCe felt crucial, like he'd die without her touch, die without having the privilege of her.

Falling Again

Welcome back to Buckeye Falls, Ohio!
Does this small town mayor have the political savvy to negotiate his way back into his wife's heart?

From the outside, Mayor Anthony Snyder and his wife Natalie have it all. Adorable children, a lovely home, and a

295

never-ending supply of free food from the local diner. But behind closed doors, this duo struggles to stay connected. The sparkle they show Buckeye Falls has turned a little dull on the home front.

Over the last decade, things became hectic in the Snyder household. Anthony was elected to office, following in his father's footsteps. Unfortunately, he's reminded regularly that these are big shoes to fill. Being the best mayor takes a lot of time—time he's not spending with his family.

Natalie prides herself on being everything to everyone, but the job of a wife hasn't been smooth sailing. Wrapped up in her own growing business and their kids' activities, her time with Anthony has dwindled faster than her secret stash of Halloween candy. Natalie longs for quality time with the man she loves, but it never seems to be in the cards.

A chance to visit their family lake house promises a week away from it all, but can these two reconnect when there's no distractions? Or is it time for these high achievers to admit that love might be the one thing they can't master?

With a little help from the residents of Buckeye Falls, this power couple will find their way back to happily ever after.

***Falling Again* is the third book in the Buckeye Falls series, but it can be enjoyed as a standalone read. Featuring similar marriage conflicts as in Lyssa Kay Adams' *The Bromance Book Club* and the small-town romance of Susan Mallery's *Fool's Gold* series, fans will love this second chance love story. After all, who doesn't deserve to fall in love again?**

EXCERPT:

"Anthony saw me topless, and vice versa, for the first time in ages yesterday."

Ginny raised an eyebrow. "Isn't that a good thing?"

"It would be if we'd done anything about it. Both times we were cleaning up after the kids and didn't even acknowledge it happened. Or I guess that it didn't happen."

Ginny paused, clearly unsure how to continue. "Has it been a while since you two—" she swirled her mug in the air, gesturing for Natalie to finish the sentence. Apparently, her friend wasn't going easy on her this morning.

"Had sex? Yes. It's been a while. It's been so long that I don't even remember the basic mechanics of the deed. And don't even ask me when it was. Sometime between Otis's conception and last Thursday." Natalie sank back in her chair and groaned. "This is bad."

*

Placing her hand over his mouth to shut him up, Natalie shook her head. "Stop that. You are a wonderful husband and father. Just because we hit a rough patch doesn't mean all the ways you love us don't shine through." Beneath her hand, Anthony sighed. He sounded so defeated; she wanted to wrap him in a blanket and hide him from the world. "I've made some mistakes too. You're not allowed to play the blame game alone. It's a two-player game."

Faking the Fall

Sparks fly when a reclusive artist meets his muse in

this new installment of the Buckeye Falls series.

Alice Snyder knows her reputation—and if she didn't, Buckeye Falls loves to remind her. She may come from the town's First Family, but that doesn't mean she plays by the rules. After a decade of traveling and going to school, she's back home and ready to settle down, or at least relax for a while. The trouble is, her neighbors are determined to find her a husband. She needs a way to get them off her back...

When James Gibson, a divorced artist, flees New York for the peace of small-town Ohio, he's excited to get painting again. The only trouble is, he's completely blocked. Despite his best efforts, his collection of canvases are blank and he's at a career crossroads. A chance meeting with the mayor's sister throws James's routine off balance, and he's eager to spend more time with this quirky spitfire.

And Alice might have the solution to both their problems...

Fake Date.

She gets the Nosey Nellies off her back, and James gets time with a woman who inspires him both *inside and outside* the studio.

Just a few weeks of pretending, and they'll move on. Simple, right? The trouble is the more time they spend together, the realer their relationship feels. The laughter, the stolen kisses—it all starts to feel like more.

Can these two be honest with each other and find their happily-ever-after, or are they doomed for a *real* breakup?

Libby Kay's FAKING THE FALL redeems Buckeye Falls's spinster troublemaker with a fake relationship romance filled with sweet small town vibes. FAKING THE FALL will bring to mind amazing books like Practice Makes Perfect by Sarah Adams and Fix Her Up by Tessa Bailey. But best of all, it returns readers to the small Ohio town and the familiar characters from the previous Buckeye Falls books. All the zany, overbearing, and well-meaning ones! So sit back and grab FAKING THE FALL for the latest roller-coaster romance by Libby Kay.

EXCERPT:

A lock of chocolatey hair had fallen from her ponytail. James lifted his hand and tucked the silky strands behind her ear. Her skin was as soft as rose petals, and he suddenly forgot this wasn't real. That this sweet woman standing in front of him wasn't his. James dipped his head and saw the moment Alice registered his intent. Her green eyes grew dark and her tongue poked out to moisten her bottom lip. There was no going back now.

"Alice." James croaked her name through the lump in his throat. He had to taste her, just once.

"Kiss me," she whispered.

She tasted like ginger—warm, spicy and inviting. James couldn't believe his luck that he was actually kissing Alice. His hands slid up to cup her cheek, cradling her against him. Their lips nipped at each other, curious yet hungry. He hadn't shared a kiss like that in far too long. The world around him burst into color—bold reds and sharp oranges.

Just when James was ready to deepen the kiss, Alice pulled back. Resting her hands on his chest, she sighed. "I think that worked," she said, her breathing labored.

"What?" James asked, struggling to clear his head.

Alice gestured over his shoulder. "Roxie and Jennie followed us out. I just wanted to make sure they—" But her explanation died on her tongue. James stepped back, his arms falling limp at his sides.

It was all for show. That moment of color and passion meant nothing to Alice. "I'll get you home," he said, keeping his gaze focused anywhere but on her.

Now Available In Ebook And Print Where Books Are Sold

ABOUT THE AUTHOR

Libby Kay lives in the city in the heart of the Midwest with her husband. When she's not writing, Libby loves reading romance novels of any kind. Stories of people falling in love nourish her soul. Contemporary or Regency, sweet or hot, as long as there is a happily ever after—she's in love!

When not surrounded by books, Libby can be found baking in her kitchen, binging true crime shows, or on the road with her husband, traveling as far as their bank account will allow.

Libby cohosts the Romance Roundup podcast with Liz Donatelli on the Reader Seeks Romance Channel where they recommend romance books and interview authors, influencers, and publishers. Check it out for your weekly dose of romance!

Website: https://www.libbykayauthor.com/

Instagram and Facebook: @LibbyKayAuthor
Goodreads: @LibbyKay